THE
SEVENTH
TERRACE

THE
SEVENTH
TERRACE

SIXTUS BECKMESSER

Copyright © 2024 Sixtus Beckmesser

The moral right of the author has been asserted.

Apart from any fair dealing for the purposes of research or private study, or criticism or review, as permitted under the Copyright, Designs and Patents Act 1988, this publication may only be reproduced, stored or transmitted, in any form or by any means, with the prior permission in writing of the publishers, or in the case of reprographic reproduction in accordance with the terms of licences issued by the Copyright Licensing Agency. Enquiries concerning reproduction outside those terms should be sent to the publishers.

This is a work of fiction. Names, characters, businesses, places, events and incidents are either the products of the author's imagination or used in a fictitious manner. Any resemblance to actual persons, living or dead, or actual events is purely coincidental.

Troubador Publishing Ltd
Unit E2 Airfield Business Park,
Harrison Road, Market Harborough,
Leicestershire LE16 7UL
Tel: 0116 279 2299
Email: books@troubador.co.uk
Web: www.troubador.co.uk

ISBN 9781805144441

British Library Cataloguing in Publication Data.
A catalogue record for this book is available from the British Library.

Printed and bound in Great Britain by 4edge Limited
Typeset in 12pt Adobe Garamond Pro by Troubador Publishing Ltd, Leicester, UK

Matador is an imprint of Troubador Publishing

*To all my musical friends particularly Alan Ridgewell ad others in
The Wagner Society of London*

> *ed io faceacon l'ombra più rovente*
> *parer la fiamma; e pure a tanto indizio*
> *vid'io molt'ombre. Andando, poner mente.*
>
> DANTE: *PURGATORIO* XXVI vv7-9[1]

---

1   My shadow made the flames deeper red
    and even in this slight evidence, I saw.
    Which caused many souls to wonder as they passed

CONTENTS

1	London	3
2	Vienna	11
3	Politics	22
4	Disaster	40
5	The Match	49
6	Muddle	59
7	Progress	69
8	The Phoenix	79
9	The Precipice	84
10	Der Wonne Saal	91
11	Jan	108
12	Sieglinde and Siegmund	117
13	The Children of Lir	138
14	Winterreise	156
15	The Ball	166
16	After the Ball	180
17	The Rhein Journey	191
18	Das Wissende Weib	203
	Acknowledgements	216

LIVONIA

PART FIVE

1
LONDON

Diana ist kundig, die Nacht zu erhellen,

WEBER: DER FREISCHÜTZ ACT 3 SC 4[1]

Helge von Grunstrand stared musingly into the fine stone grate with its blazing log fire in the great hall of Schloss Krenek. Usually he found the fire soothing – massively comforting after the turbulent times that they had lived through, but this evening there was a shred of doubt and he felt uncomfortable. Detty would be up from the Lodge in a minute and he would find that reassuring. Then he realised with a pang that she wouldn't be coming. She was in London singing *Agathe* in *Der Freischütz* at Covent Garden. He shouldn't be selfish. This was an important career step for Bernadette. Anyway, supposedly gay, he didn't know why he relied so massively on his feisty, undeniably straight, devotedly married dramatic soprano colleague.

She had caused a sensation with her impromptu *Brünnhilde* at Bayreuth and also made the world's press, and gossip columns, with her *Leonore* at Königshof. She had returned in triumph to Bayreuth to sing

---

1   Diana knows how to light up the night

the *Tannhäuser Elisabeth*. But for all that, this was only her second major role in a metropolitan opera house – one of the world's big six and it had to be important. He felt that he shouldn't rely on her as a prop. He thought that was feeble but they had faced so much together and her resilience had been tested many times and never found wanting. Unlike many, he didn't lust after her. He had his own partner, the first clarinet in an Italian orchestra, a nice enough guy although they met relatively seldom, being separated by half Europe. His only feminine company was his adored bitch, *die Soufleuse*, the prompter, who was his constant companion. He wondered if he really was gay. The distant relationship with Carlo was convenient but was it anything more? He was fond of him but couldn't say in truth that he loved him. On the other hand, he had never felt more than mildly interested in a woman and as a leading conductor many opportunities had presented themselves. Perhaps music was too important to him really to care about anything else? His little country, fairly big amongst its Baltic neighbours but pathetically vulnerable when faced with a voracious giant on its eastern borders was, he was sure, under threat. Russia, which had been sympathetic, if never quite an ally, during the civil war was now in the grip of an ambitious authoritarian who did little to disguise his ambition of restoring the Soviet and Tsarist Empire.

'Get on with the music and let the politics look after themselves' he told himself sternly and went back to studying the rough but original score by the most talented of his composition students.

*

She was going to sing Strauss songs at the Wigmore Hall on her way home. How dare she? The former student teacher from Kildare had to pinch herself to realise that she was now one of the most sought-after sopranos in Europe, which meant the world. Before the last performance of *Der Freischütz,* at Covent Garden she had been taken to lunch at Rules by her impossible agent Julian. She cursed it as another complication and didn't want to go out to lunch before singing. It seemed a shame to go to a good restaurant and lunch on salad and mineral water but it was the only date they both could make. At least it was a nice atmosphere and convenient. Just round the corner from the opera house, it represented the best and the worst of Britain – the elegant but almost rural taste which raised the despised English food to an unexpected radiance but that was combined with the overbearing snobbishness which made the English think that they still ruled a third of the world. However, the food was good. At least Julian had done a lot to get her a major Covent Garden role. I must be nice to him – at least over lunch – she said to herself.

'You really ought to come home, Bernadette, you know.' Forgetting her resolution.

'Really?' she muttered.

'Well, it's not safe. The Russians are on the war path.'

'Are you telling me?' she said.

He looked embarrassed. His Radley and Keble shield suddenly fell. For a moment he looked contrite:

'I'm sorry, I know your CV better than most people.'

'You wrote most of the English version,' she said with a friendly grin. For a moment, he grinned back rather attractively. Why couldn't he always be like this – she thought? He was a good agent; it would be great if he was also a friend. Perhaps she had been unfair to him for all this time. She thought – am I being the archetypical primitive Irish girl – hating and afraid of the Saxons? There was certainly no danger that Julian was going to rape her during the lunch session at Rules. Anyway, she thought with a mental grin, he wouldn't be a match for her. Be nice to him, he deserves it, she said to herself.

She thanked him warmly for lunch and headed round to the opera house and the last performance of a hugely enjoyable '*Der Freischütz*'. There was no final performance party, probably because the dress rehearsal of '*Siegfried*' was to take place on the morrow in the afternoon. This was part of the new Covent Garden *Ring* being done in stages, with a new American soprano as *Brünnhilde* who was highly regarded, but who also had a reputation for cancelling. Although she was known to suffer from jet lag, she always scheduled her trans-Atlantic flights close to the final rehearsals. Annaliese Seiling, the still young doyenne of current dramatic sopranos, and now a firm friend of Detty's had sent her an encrypted email from Berlin, which read, 'Don't hit the bar too soon, Bernadette – you might be needed again. Anyway, you could, how do you say in English? Knock the spots off her!'

Detty giggled and replied 'Any time, I'm ready, please tell the ROH top brass. You did me the greatest favour ever injuring yourself at Bayreuth but I'm sorry that it hurt.'

Annaliese had fallen fracturing several ribs the day before a performance which had catapulted Detty into the leading role of the *'Siegfried' Brünnhilde* with less than a day's notice. This was one of the two events which had served to establish her reputation.

'No problem, Detti, but I suppose it was frustrating at the time. How's your *Isolde* with Hank going?'

She was still grinning over the girly exchange of emails with the great diva when she arrived in her dressing room. After the show, she chatted for a few minutes with the knot of enthusiasts outside the stage door in Floral Street. She then walked down Wellington Street deep in thought. Why, oh why, did we have to fall apart and start fighting or threatening to fight again? The overweening ambition of a power-hungry dictator was now threatening her dear adopted country from over their vulnerable border, as never before. She had talked to Malinov, the defence minister, only a day or two before coming to London. He was ageing and grim. Unspoken she had the impression that he had given his all for Livonia's freedom and simply couldn't face the threat all over again. 'Even Marc, Detty, couldn't roll back the Russians if they made a concerted attempt. And as a German, could he even try? The last time was different. The support was needed and the whole world knew it was a just cause and Russia was more liberal in those days. This is much messier. They are rabble rousing the Russian speaking folk just as Hitler did the Germans in the Sudetenland in 1938'.

She reached the Savoy and went up to her suite. She came down to earth with a bump. Liese Isolde von Ritter was giving her an accusing evil eye, it said clearly. 'You may be a Prima Donna but you're my mum and I'm hungry and I've been waiting far too long.' The demanding grizzle impetuously began.

'She's been as good as gold until you came in' said Gianna, defensively.

'*È sempre così*' replied Detty, the Italian coming naturally to her even after singing German all the evening. Once the three-month-old Leading Lady was firmly fixed on Detty's breast everybody relaxed a bit. Detty reflected how lucky she was to have the Italian girl. When Detty's third pregnancy had declared itself Gianna had decided that University could be put off indefinitely. A long drawn out *laurea* in Italy seemed a poor alternative to staying with her laid-back Irish boss with her blossoming career. Being with Detty and sharing her exciting international life was much more fun.

'Anything happened this evening?' Detty asked.

'Nothing at all, Signora.'

Despite every effort Detty had made to become on mutual first name terms with Gianna and give each other the *Tu/Du* in their usual languages she had stayed at 'Signora' although she supposed that was a step forward from 'Frau Gräfin'.

After satisfying her voracious daughter, Detty turned her attention to the mushroom omelette provided by Room Service. She wondered, not for the first time, why she had ordered it. It seemed a simple straightforward thing after a show and the distant but light Rules lunch, but on reflection she wondered again why English mushrooms could be so boring. For a moment she fantasised away to the wonders of *die Steinpilzen* and *die Pfifferlinge* that she enjoyed in late summer when at home in Oberdorf for the Bayreuth season. She smiled at the thought of the loaded wicker basket provided at the Schloss postern door by old Jonas from the Wald, because he still had a soft spot for Hildegard. His excuse was that he knew that *Die Junge Gräfin* adored them. After she had learnt that he, in his turn, loved his Schnapps, Detty had taken a bottle of Jameson to his house at Christmas time. His reaction had been that he had received the Holy Grail. The bottle remained on his *Anrichte* – far too sacred to actually be drunk.

The other three performances had all gone well. Her tenor and stage lover as *Max* was, a native German from Cologne who, knowing her Hanseatic affinity, had reminded her that, far down the Rhein as it was, Cologne also had once been a *Hansestadt*. She had giggled at this proud statement and instead of taking offence, he laughed too.

'You have to remember Klaus that I am only an adopted Livonian and that my birth roots lie in the bogs of Ireland.'

After that it was fun to sing together. The other men were Welsh basses and baritones and Detty's enduring admiration for Welsh singers shone through. She remembered the fixes that Haydn Roberts had helped her to resolve over the years and her immense and sincere debt to him. Her *Ännchen* was an Australian soubrette with a lively sense of humour. It was a happy cast and Detty was grateful for it.

'Not like next week' commented David, the head of music staff. Detty had cocked an eye at him questioningly:

'Next week, as well as working on the new *Ring* we have Carbonara and a soubrette from California who he insisted on bringing with him for the Donizetti. We know nothing about her and if she can't sing the media will roast us. I said that we were a big enough house to resist that sort of blackmail but I was overruled. Anyway, if we had cancelled Carbonara, he would have sued us for a fortune and the media would still have roasted us. You can't win.'

Detty could do nothing but look sympathetic. She knew a bit about Maestro Carbonara from the spine-chilling story of Walter Liebig at the Königshof *Die Meistersinger* two years before[2]. The trouble was that he, Carbonara, was the most famous living conductor and his dark side was hidden by the glitter of his public adulation.

That night the horrors returned. The Armourer was changed into the bewhiskered Carbonara and leered over her preparing to torture her. She awoke in a fearful panic. Gradually she came to, sweating profusely with irrational fear. She looked anxiously at Liese sleeping peacefully in the carry cot beside the bed and, reassured, tried to get back to sleep. Why did it always happen after a great night singing, she wondered? She then had a modest breakfast at The Savoy and put her feet up for an hour before heading to Oxford Circus and Wigmore Street in time to warm up.

The Strauss recital at the Wigmore Hall had made her more anxious than *Agathe* at Covent Garden. Partly this was because the recitalist is

---

2   See *Ruhe*

always so exposed, with no team, no orchestra, just the support of an accompanist and concentrated music on her or his own. She had a new accompanist. Much as she would have loved Gertrude Meyer, her close friend and usual accompanist, to come over, this proved impossible due to Trudi's other commitments in an increasingly crowded engagement diary. The long-suffering Julian had found her an extremely talented young Irish pianist. She got on well with her fellow countryman but he was new and different from Trudi. Added to this was the prestige of the famous small hall. There were so many ghosts sitting on her young shoulders. She also felt a smidge of insecurity. She loved lieder singing and passionately wanted to succeed in this part of her career. She had had some successes but she was also haunted by her performance in a previous charity recital in Nuremberg which had had 'mixed' reviews. Over the time since, it had come, possibly unjustifiably, to lodge in her memory as a major failure.

It was an all-Strauss programme. They had worked hard to make it interesting and had taken a few risks early in the programme, without hazarding too much. She started with a first group of four of the lesser-known Brentano songs. She then went on to von Gilm's *Die Nacht, Die Georgine* and *Allerseelen* finishing with Goethe's *Gefunde,* which both the poet and composer had dedicated to their wives. In the second half she stuck to the well-known songs including the Opus 27 pieces *Ruhe, meine Seele, Cäcilie, Hemliche Afforderung* and *Morgan.* She then lightened the tone with *Schlechtes Wetter* before finishing with Dehmel's *Wiegenlied* and an awe inspiring *Befreit.* They were greeted by prolonged and very warm applause and she felt happy to signal to Michael, her accompanist, for the encore which she explained to the audience was, although a very well-known piece, particularly special for her. She had kept back *Zueignung* deliberately for an encore and she now sang it triumphantly and with great pleasure. There was more very warm applause and she felt pleased. The ghost of Nuremberg had been removed by a very satisfactory performance in the presence of a famously expert and critical audience.

On the flight back to Berlin she cuddled her daughter and thought hard and oddly about Massimo Carbonara who had featured so unpleasantly and prominently in her nightmare of the previous evening. She had never even met the man although, of course, his appearance was familiar to her from a thousand CD covers and posters. And yet, and yet... Walter Liebig's spine-chilling story stuck in her mind.

2
VIENNA

Dort seh'ich Grane,
mein selig Ross

WAGNER: *SIEGFRIED* ACT3 SC3[3]

The *Schloss* suffused a warm feeling of contentment not least because Marc had come from Ingolstadt that morning to take them back to Bavaria for a short break. They drove back and after two very long days on the road, settled in at Oberdorf. Marc stared thoughtfully into his *Krug* of *1464 Landbier -EXPORT- Bärentrunk Dunkel*. Detty watched him expectantly. She had just received from her agent, Julian, in London an invitation to sing the name role in Strauss's *Salome* at the *Wiener Staatsoper*. She was bubbling with excitement and expected Marc to be enthusiastic. She felt let down. What was the problem? The pause continued as Marc went on to staring at his beer, as if inspiration would come from the dark brew under its creamy head.

'You see,' he said eventually, 'I don't like the idea of you stripping off in front of the ogling eyes of two thousand lecherous Viennese.'

---

3   There is Grane my sacred horse

'Two thousand two hundred and twenty-seven, if you count the standing – I looked it up – anyway they won't all be ogling, at lease fifty per cent will be women.'

Surprised as she was, she made light of a side of her husband that she hadn't seen before. Marc had tolerated, albeit reluctantly, Detty risking her life and worse for the Livonian cause, now he was worried about her exposing herself to the lecherous gaze of a well-heeled Viennese opera audience. She waited while the *Krug* of Dunkel revolved again slowly. Marc's next comment when the *Krug* came to rest, really startled her, then made her burst out laughing.

'Anyway, you can't assume the women won't ogle you. Knowing Vienna, a good proportion of them are probably Lesbians.'

'Yes and a good proportion of the men, as is usual in opera audiences. I will be gay too.'

'Who's conducting?' 'Carbonara' said Detty casually and held her breath 'he should provide an adequate chaperone.'

'Chaperone!' Marc exploded 'Knowing his reputation he's probably only asked you to watch you strip off and see if you're suitable for the dressing room afterwards.'

'That's unkind and unfair,'

Detty remembered Marc's words as she prepared for the *Sitzprobe* in Vienna. She felt uncomfortable. Munich was proper, Bayreuth stiff until you were accepted, London, for all its faults friendly, Florence in its troubles charming, as long as you didn't want to get paid quickly, but this was intimidating. It wasn't just the formidable history of the *Staatsoper* or the critical public. After all, she had dealt with that or worse running the gauntlet earlier that year as *Amelia* in Milan. No, it was just an uncomfortable threatening feeling which took her back to her first days at the Sacred Heart Convent in Moltravia.

The great conductor had been almost obsequiously courteous to her but she still felt a shudder run down her spine. She usually looked forward to performances. The tingle of stage fright added excitement. She was hooked on adrenaline and it helped her give her best but this time the thrill of each performance was surrounded by a penumbra of anxiety. It had gone OK. Her voice she reckoned was better than it had ever been. The critical audience was enthusiastic and the first notices condescendingly positive. The best that she could expect in Vienna she thought, but she was glad when it was over. She surprised herself by feeling relieved. Carbonara sought her out after the penultimate performance first quizzing her again on Livonia then at the end saying that he was organising a dinner at the Vestibül restaurant at the Burg Theatre and would she come. He obviously noted her dubious expression and added quickly, 'It's for the whole cast but of course you will be the guest of honour.' He then went back to quizzing her about Livonia. The dinner had' been good. The food was delicious. Carbonara was the courteous host and indeed the principals of the cast, the director and some members of the orchestra were all present. It must have cost Carbonara a load of money but he didn't seem to mind. She had been able to get a taxi back to the Bristol without any improper suggestions. Nonetheless she had felt uncomfortable and as she boarded the Berlin flight the morning after, it was as if a weight had been lifted off her shoulders. The relief increased as she had connected to Königshof.

Exhausted, she had driven through the gates of Krenek, said 'Hi' to Gianna and Niki at the Lodge and then after a word of explanation, went straight to the *Schloss* hoping to find something to eat and a drink. Helge had been there sitting alone in the great hall with a pile of hand copied scores beside his cup of coffee. He seemed relieved that he could take a break from the students' composition exercises. As they embraced after his warm '*Wilkommen zu Hause!*' Detty had been aware that somebody had come into the hall behind her. Suddenly facing Helge, she was grabbed from behind by two large strong hands and lifted into the air. She squealed like a surprised schoolchild.

'*Meine Retterin!*' exclaimed a familiar musical baritone voice and Detty turned to see Walter Liebig grinning from ear to ear. Typical of him, she smiled, to refer to her triumphant role in *Fidelio* at the same time as the part that she had played in his own recovery.

'My heroine – you have saved my career. I did *Sachs* in San Francisco and Frankfurt over the last three months and I am doing *Barak* in Hamburg in two weeks. There are bookings for Paris, Berlin and La Scala in the pipeline. I need hardly say that Carbonara is not conducting any of them. I owe it all to you lot and I thought that would come down here for a few days to do some master classes and say thank you properly.'

'I am so delighted, Walter. Although you did it all yourself – the FAZ said that here you sang the best *Pogner* that they had ever heard and what a shame that the definitive *Sachs* of our time seemed to have given up the role. That must have helped. The only downside of all this is that I hope that we can still retain you at an affordable fee here.' Walter had been suddenly serious.

'How could I ever forget what you did for me? I love singing and you gave it back to me. You will always come first.'

Then added with a grin, 'Even if you didn't think much of my *Rodolfo*.'

'I thought your *Rodolfo* was fine,' said Detty laughing 'just different.' 'I'll say,' said the still beaming Walter then 'you survived Carbonara with your virginity intact then.'

'I survived Carbonara but he's still not on my Christmas card list. I don't think virginity enters into it as I am an elderly mother of two who has a fierce soldier husband,'

'Is that a warning? Marc once said to me that he had had to get used to everybody in this country being in love with his wife.'

'I think and hope that only goes so far. He also said that in military terms I was equivalent to a fully equipped *Panzer* division. It didn't do a lot for my femininity but it might have put off Carbonara, if it had reached him, but a propos, can I ask you a question?'

'Of course.'

'Can you think of any possible reason why Carbonara has suddenly developed an intense interest in every aspect of Livonia?'

Walter had thought for several minutes while Detty consumed the smoked salmon sandwiches which had suddenly appeared accompanied by a bottle of *Baden Gewurztraminer*. At last, he had said just one word. 'Russia.'

'OK but why is an Austro-Italian associated with Russia?'

'I don't know but I suspect he is. He spent a lot of time there last year ostensibly for musical reasons, but I had heard that he met a lot of the top brass who had nothing to do with music. Only rumour of course.'

*

She had managed to carve out a quick break in Ireland before the *Tristan*. She had to admit to herself that one of the main attractions was seeing her fabulous mare, now a double Champion Hurdle winner, again. She wondered whether she was right to leave Peggy in charge of Niki and Liese. Then she remembered that Gianna was there and that, without in any way offending her mother, she could keep a firm hand on the reins of the children. The thought of reins brought her back to the reason for her trip out. She was heading towards Christy and Deidre's stable at The Curragh. Nothing unusual about that. She had been there many times before and even in the last week she had been down a couple of times to get some riding practice in on Corn Flakes, the genial retired chaser, that Christy kept as part pet, part hack. That day though was different, utterly different, she had got up just after five to be in time for first string. When she had asked Christy whether she could possibly ride out, she hadn't dared hint at which horse she might ride. He had just grinned and said. 'You'll be wanting to ride Firebrand then?'

Her mare Firebrand had landed her second Champion Hurdle at Cheltenham in the spring. It was quite different from the first one. Jess O'Donoghue had settled Firebrand behind the two early leaders. Once they had rounded the bend onto the straight and faced that dreaded hill, Jess had gently pressed the Firebrand throttle and it was all over. At last, the bookies and the public seemed to realise just how good she was and a seasoned pundit remarked that her starting price of four to seven, odds on, looked quite generous after that performance.

Christy's casual question had been almost a statement. Detty had gone pale with her heart pounding. 'I didn't dare ask.'

'She's your mare of course you can ride her.'

'I know but she is very precious and special and you are her trainer.'

There was a short pause then Christie asked. 'You are very tall for a rider, Detty, what do you weigh? Sorry but there's no bashfulness about riders' weights in a racing stable, but you know that anyway.'

For a moment Detty looked anxious. Was her treat going to be snatched away from her?

'Seventy kilos – give or take – 11 stone but I am very happy to be weighed if you want to know exactly.'

Detty held her breath – she wanted to ride so much. 'No that's fine. She will carry 11st10 less the mares' allowance of 7lbs in the Champion Hurdle this year which makes 11st3lbs so you will be riding at just under race weight which is grand. You look to keep yourself very fit – for a singer,'

'That's a bit of a back-handed compliment,' she had grinned 'but I do try and anyway not all singers – even in my range are overweight. Singing depends on the upper body strength so does riding although in a different way, I suppose.

'Detty, you're a good, experienced horsewoman. I know you won't do anything stupid. Ride her and enjoy it.'

She had driven back to Ballyinch on cloud nine only to be scolded by her mother like a wayward schoolgirl. 'We don't see you from one year's end to the next, then when you do come, all you think about is that horse. I think she is more important than the children and certainly more important than your parents.' In the end she had broken into a smile. 'I shall talk to Marc- tell him to try and keep you in order.'

'He's given up trying,'

Smiling at the memory of this exchange, she had turned into the yard and parked. Sam was leading Firebrand already saddled out of her stall. Detty had changed before she left home all she had to do was put on her hat and goggles and take her stick from the back of the car. She walked across the yard and whispered confidentially to Sam. 'I'm terrified. Will I do OK?'

Sam replied with a smile, 'You ride well, I've seen you and anyway she's a perfect lady – enjoy it.'

She had then spent a minute or two talking to Firebrand and stroking her neck as she had done so often before. Somehow Detty found Sam's reassurance coming from this experienced stable girl flattering and comforting as she was given a leg up. With just the tiniest touch with her heels and a whispered command Firebrand moved off to join the assembled string. With the rest, Detty nudged her into a canter and was pleased to keep her position with the others. They turned as they entered the training gallops and she pulled Firebrand up and waited for Christy's instructions. She had looked around. She had known that both of them, horse and rider, were newsworthy and feared that the *paparazzi* might have gathered but the winter Curragh morning was misty still with only the occasional regular scout.

'Detty, go up to the top of the horseshoe with Ian. Bring her down steady, start together, but no need to stay together, then take the three practice hurdles on the inside then let her go for the last three furlongs up the straight. Don't bother about the final schooling hurdles – pull her up slowly before you to get to them – OK? Then do it again –that will be enough- she doesn't need much now.' 'OK, Christy' she had remembered to acknowledge her orders.

Ian riding Kinsale Dawn, the yard's best juvenile, had ranged alongside Firebrand, then he had given her a grin. 'Don't often get to ride out with an owner,' he said laughing but there was nothing obsequious about it, just amusement.

'I'm terrified,' she said.

'You needn't be. You can ride. I guess the boss knew that. He wouldn't let just anybody ride her out – owner or not.'

Then by way of explanation. 'I was behind watching you cantering down. Anyway, she's a perfect lady.'

'That's the second time I've heard her called that this morning.'

'Well, she is.'

Detty had felt ten feet tall after the unaffected praise of Ian then 'OK?' he said. Detty nodded and touched Firebrand with her heels. Detty had ridden a lot since she was a little girl and she had won competitions at gymkhanas and races at point to points, but this was another world. She would never forget the first moment when she had felt the dual Champion Hurdler's surging race power under her. She had never experienced anything like it. The mare's powerful muscles had started working but it was all natural and steady, Detty was just conscious of her mount's controlled strength. Before she knew it they were round the horseshoe and lined up for the first practice hurdle and over with consummate ease. Then they were hurtling towards the second and without any check, stride perfect, they were over. Firebrand worked like the mistress of her craft, that she was. After the third hurdle, Detty dared look round. Ian was several lengths behind. However, it wasn't finished, she had remembered her instructions from Christy, She urged Firebrand forward with hands and heels and the mare duly took off, in another, higher gear, and really accelerated just as she had, thought Detty, up the dreaded hill at Cheltenham. She had flown over the last three furlongs appearing untroubled as her pink breathless rider pulled her up beside Christy's Range Rover.

'How did you find her?' Christy had asked.

'That was unbelievable,' Detty had grinned back.

'OK' he had said 'same again now then that's enough.'

'You'll need to go a long way before you sit on a better,' he had said as she pulled up for the second time 'but you did well and looked good together. You could have ridden a bit shorter. That's my fault- I thought a slightly longer iron might be more comfortable for you but you didn't need it. Anyway, that's not important to-day. She's the best that I have ever had. You had better ride her at Cheltenham.'

'Now you're teasing. It's bad enough watching.' He had grinned.

'I think that she's a smidge better than she was last year. She'll take a lot of beating if we can keep her right. Time for coffee and bacon rolls before the second string.'

She then dismounted took her saddle and spent so long chatting to Firebrand that she nearly missed the coffee and bacon rolls. Detty had realised guiltily that she hadn't thought about her children once. After refreshments she had been given a decent handicap hurdler, Roadside Cowboy, to ride in the second string. As she came back to the yard she determinedly joined the queue to hose down her muddy mount. Previously Sam, the girl who 'did' Firebrand had immediately taken over her charge as soon as Detty had dismounted and Detty hadn't dared to interfere. This time however she was going to make her point. She duly lined up with the other girls and lads to wait for her turn with one of the four hoses.

The girl next to her in the queue was very young and Detty thought that she was new. Detty knew her name from the chat before they rode out. The youngster turned to her and said. 'Miss O'Neill, you don't have to do him, Jo will do him as usual.'

'Do you think that I'm not going to get it right, Sandra?' she teased as her turn came and she reached for her hose and began cleaning the Cowboy's legs.

'No, of course not but ....'

'I was mucking out for Christy as a schoolgirl years ago. I haven't forgotten.'

'But do you really sing in all those grand theatres?'

'I do but, in the end, it must be much the same as getting the 'best turned out' at Leopardstown, as I gather you did last summer. I've never done that but I guess it is the same thrill.'

She had been thoroughly relaxed and had loved riding the Cowboy but realised how different it had felt from having the equine queen of Punchestown and Cheltenham under her. She knew that she had been very privileged.

As she lay in her old bed at Ballyinch, the one she had always had in the school holidays, suddenly her cell phone had rung. She saw Christy's number and froze. Why was he phoning? Was there a problem with Firebrand? Had she done something wrong to her beautiful mare? All the catastrophic thoughts came tumbling out. 'Hi' she had said breathless 'Is there a problem? Is she OK?'

'Calm yourself. She's absolutely fine and she told me this morning that she couldn't wait to get you back on board.'

'Don't tease me. You scared me rigid.'

'I'm really sorry about that. No, I am phoning because we do need to talk – plans –don't you see? Any chance you could come over in the next few days to have a talk?'

'Of course, will tomorrow do? Late morning after the second string.'

'That would be fine – see you then.'

She had still been on cloud nine when her father came in from his patients at lunchtime. She had bounced up to kiss him.

'Detty, what on earth is going on you are bouncing up and down like a twelve-year-old. I haven't seen you like this since you won the Classic Trial at Naas in the Pony Club.'

'Close, Da' she had said 'I rode out on Firebrand this morning and she was wonderful.'

'Ah' he replied.

*

She had turned into the yard and pushed through the boot room, still scented by wet weatherproofs and damp leather. The kitchen had the more welcoming smell of bacon.

'Want one?' Deidre had asked.

'No, I must watch my weight if I want to ride the Champion again.' Deidre had apologised and said it wasn't the season for Barnbrack. Before Detty could answer Christy, dripping wet, had burst in.

'It's a bit raw today. Detty, you did well to make yesterday.'

She had sat patiently drinking her tea. At last, he had come to the point. 'Do you want to go chasing?'

He had looked tense and suddenly Detty had had the impulse to tease. 'I'm better on the Flat – I did win an 800-metre race at Oxford but I think I'll opt out of the big fences.'

Christy then suddenly relaxed and burst out laughing. 'I think you and your mare make a good pair- she's caught your sense of humour.'

'Ah but she's a real lady. Nobody, well perhaps once, has called me that. Have you asked her?'

'Can you try and give me a sensible answer?'

'Come on. What do you think?' She had suddenly looked serious and he had dropped the banter and became the tough professional. 'Well, it's like this. She is good, very good but you know that. After Cheltenham last year I schooled her over fences just to see how she took to it. She jumped them well. Now this is the crunch, I believe that she is good enough to win a Gold Cup as long as she doesn't meet an Arkle but there was only one of them but...'

There had been a long silence. Eventually Detty had broken it. 'I think you are thinking of the immortal Dawn Run who did do the Double but I am a bit superstitious about great hurdlers going chasing.'

There was another long silence. Again, Detty had broken it. 'She's an athlete – incredibly fast and hurdles like no other but I think that she should stay hurdling. I think she would be a formidable chaser but it's against her great talents. I keep thinking of myself singing lyric *bel canto* parts – I can do it – I take pride in doing it but I'm not a natural. I have a dear friend who is and every time I hear her sing, I know the difference, it isn't where my talent or heart really lies – I think Firebrand is the same but perhaps the other way round. She is an incomparable hurdler – let her stay that way perhaps until its time, like me, to think about babies.'

'I am so glad' said Christy, the relief obvious in his face. 'I just didn't want to deprive you both of a Gold Cup which might be in your grasp but in my heart I knew it wasn't right.'

Very solemnly Detty had then said. 'Do you think Dawn Run was ever the same after her Gold Cup? I wasn't born then.' There had been an even longer pause.

'We shall never know,' he had said at last 'No one ever dare ask Paddy Mullins that but for certain she wasn't a Chaser – just so brilliant that she could succeed at a discipline that she didn't really like.'

Detty again had been lost in thought then. 'I don't think I want to take the chance with her – even if it would make her join the immortals.

*

Breathless she settled in her seat after the hassle of getting Niki and Liese into their allotted places and their massive paraphernalia checked in for the hold. 'I think that we've got it all in, Signora.' Gianna demonstrated the Italian skill of being a tower of strength in a crisis. Not for nothing had her grandfather been a captain of *partigiani* in the Appenines. Remarkably he got away with his life, most did not. However, his granddaughter had some of the same strength under fire but not, thank God, like that.

3
POLITICS

Politics has got to be a fun activity.

Alan Clark, UK politician

'Are we going first to Krenek or to Frau Senska?'

'To the Hansehaus, I think, they say they have room for us all.' Detty had a double take. After so long away she was not yet used to Tamara being referred to by her married name – much less correctly by Gianna. Most people in Livonia were happy to call Mara Frau Sensky and Detty wondered how the Italian girl had got the unusual inflection right. Yet another piece of evidence that her companion was extremely bright. She wondered for a moment whether she was being selfish in abetting Gianna in abandoning her laurea which was clearly hers for the taking. Gianna instructed the Taxi in her now almost perfect German. For once the driver hadn't recognised Detty who was, slightly out of character struggling with two small children.

'*Jawohl, meine Frau,*' he replied to Gianna, ignoring the child surrounded Detty which made the latter smile. They were greeted at the Hansehaus by a bouncing smiling Mara. It was the first time they had met after a long gap when Mara had reluctantly left her wedding reception to go on honeymoon.

Even as a peripheral and staid married woman Detty had to admit the wedding evening had been fantastic. The lighted lanterns of the old *Commanderie* flickered casting Byzantine, (or were they Hanseatic?) shadows on the walls. No harm in that thought Detty. There had been an amazing number of young people –Mara's friends from Munich, Saskia's friends from the physio college, the entire FC Königshof squad and most of the staff to say nothing of numerous others. The older generation were well represented too. Sadly, there were some important gaps but those who were there were enjoying themselves.

The two brides sparkled and laughed, looking completely happy and glamorous under the subdued *Commanderie* lighting which displayed their beautiful dresses even better than the austere illumination of the cathedral earlier. Detty felt rather matronly but rejoiced that with a fair amount of subterfuge and planning she had done a good job as stage manager, if not producer of this show. The *Sekt* was carefully and specially labelled with ATDJ forming a monogram over four linked hands. This had been the extra gift from Oberdorf and she knew that Max, who adored Tamara, and was prepared to love the other three, had been to a lot of trouble over it. Saskia was introducing Holly to many of the guests who had heard about her but never seen her. In a very pretty dress the *prima donnina* of the occasion, Holly, was also enjoying the spotlight and the spoonfuls of ice cream which so far miraculously had avoided contact with the dress. After another circle of Holly's royal progress round the guests, Saskia was able to hand her over, for the moment, to her new parents-in-law and seek out Detty.

'Hallo, Frau Holberg.'

For a moment Saskia had looked startled. Then she said. 'It's entirely right that you of all people should be the first to call me by my new name. I've come to thank my fairy godmother again for making my fairy story come true. You are amazing.'

'There have been times when I thought that I was the Wicked Witch of the Woods,' Detty had laughed, not sure whether Saskia's English was up to the alliterative reference. She knew that Saskia was working hard at her English, determined that Holly should continue to develop her first language. She thought that it was quite hard work and she was not sure how Saskia was doing.

*

Once back in Königshof, she had only a few days to prepare for the concert in the Hoftheatre. This was essentially a trial run, giving the young conductor, Martin Holman, who had just been appointed as an assistant to Helge von Grunstrand an opportunity. The programme was Haydn's Clock Symphony, Strauss's Four Last Songs and a trial *Todesverkündigung*.[4] The old theatre wrapped round her like a familiar overcoat. The audience was expectant, respectful like no other. She sang Strauss's Songs after the Haydn. The applause was enthusiastic – arrogantly she expected no less. Then, after the interval.

Siegmund!
Sieh auf mich!
Ich bin's
Der bald du folgst[5]

It was exciting but somehow different. She had never sung the *Die Walküre Brünnhilde* before in front of an audience. She had known parts of it since she was a schoolgirl, over ambitiously attempting to sing *die Bitte an Wotan* with the murmuring of the river Barrow as her only witness. This time she was the senior partner; there was no Hank and no Helge to give her moral support. Her Siegmund was Lev Fortela who had graduated to the role in this concert performance from Jacquino and David. It was a tentative trial beginning to what just might become a Königshof *Ring*. There was a standing ovation and satisfied they then adjourned to Golabki for supper.

Back at the Hansehaus, she had missed the chaos of bedtime which had been expertly managed by Gianna and Mara. 'Married life seems to agree with you, *meine Geliebter.*

---

4   Warning of Death Die Walküre Act2Sc4
5   Siegmund, look upon me
    Soon you must follow me

'It does but I want your advice on a couple of things. But we had better have a glass of Sekt first.'

The children were quietly asleep after the excitement of the arrival back several days before. Gianna had gone to a meeting of the newly formed Italian Cultural Institute. They sat down for a glass of Max's sparkling wine.

'The first problem, Detti, is what we do about accommodation. I really think that we ought to get a place of our own but I don't think I can really leave *Vati* here alone. Particularly, given his position, it would be dreadfully lonely. On the other hand I don't think that it is fair to David to embroil him in the Hansehaus all the time. He has a flat of his own but the lease is nearly up and anyway it's tiny. What do you think?'

'It's strange but I have been thinking about a similar problem. You have been incredibly generous letting us stay here but now with Gianna wanting to stay with us and two children we really must get something for ourselves. Of course, I have the Lodge flat at Krenek but Hank has to share that and anyway being near the road and the drive it's not really suitable for children and there is no garden. Why don't we try for a couple of houses out of town but near a station so we can see something of each other and' she smiled wickedly, 'perhaps share babysitting? If it's convenient enough you can then get back to the Hansehaus to support your father when you need to.'

'Don't you start about babysitting, Frau Komturin. We had hardly finished our honeymoon when my husband became broody – but you are right, I don't think that I can put him off for long.'

'I can recommend it. It's harder work than singing but they are a lot of fun.' They both laughed.' I've got a couple of piano rehearsals for the *Tristan* but apart from that I am free for the next ten days. If you can manage it we could do some house hunting together.'

Mara nodded, 'Then if we find anything we can present the men with a fait accompli.'

Detty grinned, 'You have learnt all about married life. What is the other problem by the way?'

'Ah that's intriguing and frightening. I took a phone call here three days ago from Max Schäfer, the First Minister. I immediately said that

I would put him through to *Vati*. "No, no," he said, "it's you I want to speak to." I was stunned – what did the Minister President want with me? Well to cut a long story short, there is a guy called Konrad Bucher who is a shadow foreign office minister. I gather he is quite a nice chap even though he's on the wrong side. He's a bit old fashioned and obviously right wing. Anyway, he is ill and had been advised by the medics to retire and give up his seat in the *Hansetag*. This will mean a by-election and Herr Schäfer wants me to stand for the government side.' There was a pause. Then Detty said. 'Go on,'

'Well, all sorts of questions flooded into my head. Schäfer went on to say that Bucher only had a small majority at the last election with a big personal following and, with a suitable candidate, he thought we could turn it round. Apparently, by-elections are first past the post, although the general elections are done by proportional representation. Anyway, I said that I would have to think about it and talk to my father. Then Schäfer astounded me again. He said that he already knows. I asked his permission to approach you –he's the President – I had to. He sounded embarrassed when he said that and I think he realised that it was a bit cool asking my father whether I could stand for parliament before he asked me. I asked him what *Vati* had said. He told me that the Herr Präsident didn't really approve but that if I thought it made political sense then he should ask me directly and the Herr Präsident would keep out of it. We left it that I could have a few days to think about it. I need to phone Herr Schäfer the day after to-morrow with a decision.'

'Mara, I think that you would be excellent although I have only just got used to you married and as Frau Ritterin. If you win I shall have to get used to calling you Frau Abgeordneten. What does David say?'

'Oh, he's all for it. He goes around like a cat with a bowl of cream or looking as if he's just scored a hat trick against Real Madrid but hang on,' she laughed, 'I haven't said that I will stand yet, let alone win. But what do you really think?'

'Mara, there are a lot of young people in this country who have had one hell of a time. I think that we need good young minds in the *Hansetag* to represent them and help them. You have a master's degree in psychology and political science therefore you are extremely well qualified to go into politics. You also have a lot of contacts working as your father's hostess. Go for it. What's the constituency by the way?'

'This will really make you laugh – Ziatov.'

'So, you will be representing the Sacred Heart – as you are a former pupil I think that is very appropriate. I have loads more questions and things to discuss but I am thrilled and they can wait until tomorrow.'

*

Two days later, the deed was done and Mara became the official candidate for the Social Democratic party. She worked like a beaver spending all day canvassing and holding meetings, she wanted to prove that she was a serious candidate not just going through the motions as the President's daughter. Officially, as it was only a by-election there should have been little regular TV coverage. However, there were endless interviews covering the 'human' angle which Mara strove hard to bring back to the important issues of the day – the economy, the EU application, health, re-building, and relations with neighbouring states.

It wasn't all plain sailing. At the public meetings she was heckled, sometimes fiercely. 'You are only there because you are the President's little girl. It's all disgraceful privilege. You're just riding on your father's coat tails,' Mara faced the heckler – smiling:

'You seem to have studied my past history, so you will know how privileged I was as the future president's daughter under the previous regime in this country.'

The put down was done with a charming smile which made it even more devastating. The audience all knew how she had almost died under torture by the NAS.

'When it comes to supporting my father in his diplomatic role recently, it has taught me a great deal which, if you do me the honour of electing me, should come in useful.' General applause.

'You are too young for the *Hansetag*. It's not a kindergarten.' She smiled ignoring the insult. 'Yes, I am very young but I have had a lot of experience for my age and I think young adults deserve a say in the country's future. If I am elected, I shall do my best to represent the youth of this country.'

She did have one chance to meet her opponent face to face on early evening TV. He was a pleasant prematurely grey forty something year old who came in a pin stripe suit and sober tie. Mara looked stunning and animated in a black trouser suit. But the real crunch came when they both spoke. The man trotted out the opposition party line, blaming the undoubted acts of terrorism on the government and criticising the European Union for 'not doing enough' to prevent wrongdoers getting into Europe. He was not very articulate and only quoted the official opposition pamphlets. It took Mara only a few minutes to produce arguments that destroyed his case and run rings round his claims, This left him, as *Der Osthanse Kurier*, not normally a strongly pro-government newspaper, put it the following morning, 'dead in the water.'

Detty, keeping strictly officially neutral, rang her friend on a scrambled line to the Hansehaus to congratulate her.' 'It is beginning to look like a one horse, no sorry one mare, race and I know a bit about those.'

Mara laughed 'I know that Caligula was supposed to have made his horse a Consul. Do you think that we ought to make Firebrand a Senator?'

'Can't be here – she's not a citizen, although her owner is an honorary one. We might try the *Seanead Éireann*. She does have an Irish passport. There are those at home who might think she would be an improvement on the current set-up. I couldn't comment. There was once a move to make Arkle President, I believe.'

'Very wise not to comment,' laughed Mara.

Polling day was set for mid-November and to everybody's relief it was fine but very cold. It was a rural constituency and although the constitution made the voting procedure straightforward, the result couldn't be declared until the following morning. At 8 am on a bitter Baltic morning the candidates, their agents, the press and sundry officials gathered outside the small *Rathaus* of Ziatov. Despite the hour there was a reasonable crowd of spectators. Detty had wondered about coming incognito but decided that attending the declaration would not show unseemly party-political bias and after all it was well enough known that she was a close friend of Mara's.

There were several other candidates as well as the two main ones. The *Bürgermeister* read the results in reverse order as was the custom. The green candidate got a reasonable vote but the three others very little. Then came the ones that mattered.

'Anders K.W. Konservative 12,630

Oblova – Senska T.N. Sozial Demokratin 18,972

'I therefore declare that the aforementioned Tamara Nickolaevna Oblova – Senska has been elected to serve as *Abgeordneten* for the *Wahlkreis Ziatov*.'

There was ritual hand shaking and Mara took the microphone and thanked the *Bürgermeister* and the voters of Ziatov for the confidence that they had shown in her. She would try not to let them down. She then thanked her opponent for a fair and courteous contest. She went on to say a few things about the most important issues. She kept it short. Gerhardt Liebermann then shook her hand and congratulated her adding slightly sadly.

'Once I knew who my opponent was I realised that I didn't have much of a chance but I suppose that is politics.'

As soon as Mara got back to be kissed and congratulated by her father, he said to her quietly,

'Mara, I am so proud of you. Yes, you are my little girl and the most precious thing that I have in the world – now.' The 'now' was so sad but he went on quickly.

'But I had to stand back and let you do it by yourself – tackle all the flack, all the horrible things that they would say. But you did it so well. Your mother would have been so proud of you. The broadcast of you dealing with that heckler, it was amazing, you never lost your cool but you slayed him.'

Suddenly there was a phone call. A familiar voice said:

'I would like to take Champagne with the *Abgeordneten* for Ziatov and her husband but I suppose that if I bring it to the Hansehaus I will be besieged by *paparazzi* and anyway it will be considered political bribery. I don't suppose the Honourable Lady can get to Krenek without being followed?'

'Quite simple.' Mara had already adopted unconsciously the

authority of a Congresswoman 'You put the champagne in a backpack – student like – it shouldn't warm up in this weather. You go to the back of the Hansehaus to the Visa entrance then find Pauline. I will warn her. Then you ask for Falk, and Pauline will show you through to the front. Oh, and by the way, as we don't have that many tall Irish red heads applying for Visas, a balaclava and dark glasses should be worn, *schmucke Irin*[6].'

Detty exploded.

'Where did you get that from? You have been conspiring with my husband?'

'Not at all,' said Mara demurely 'It is not all politics you know. I have just been studying my *Tristan und Isolde*. However, I hope they don't have my ex-opponent's concerns about security and arrest you as a terrorist because of the balaclava.'

'Not again!' said Detty with a laugh 'I have been arrested as a terrorist twice already and once more, sort of, by Falk himself but I won't remind him of that. Every time I do he has a seizure and starts stuttering.'

The ruse worked and a few minutes later they were firmly seated in the penthouse salon looking out over the lights of the town as Detty uncorked the *Bollinger*. Nicklaus who seemed to have recovered from the shock of his daughter's precipitate entry into the official world of politics had joined them.

'If you would all switch off your tape recorders,' he said, 'I would like to propose a toast to my lovely daughter who I am so proud to welcome as a congresswoman.'

There was murmured approval and the clinking of glasses.

'I should perhaps add that I had a phone call from Max Schäfer before you got back. He said how delighted he was at the result and how Mara would balance the house and give a voice to the young. He will ring you tomorrow.'

'I am just beginning to realise that it really is a bit of a responsibility' said Mara thoughtfully.

---

6 Elegant Irish woman (Tristan und Isolde Act1)

*

The house hunting went badly. The Baltic weather cut in severely with snow and ice which meant that visiting prospective houses was near impossible. In frustration Detty returned hard to working on *Isolde* and Mara addressed her new duties as an *Abgeordneten*.

Detty met Julia in the Green Room. 'How's *Brangäne* going?'

'It's great – Haydn is amazing.'

'Don't make him even more big headed,' laughed Detty 'but he is good isn't he? How about *Waltraute* next?'

'With you as *Brünnhilde*?'

'Who else do you have in mind?' Detty laughed 'I think Annaliese Seiling is otherwise engaged and although we have become great friends, I would happily scratch her eyes out if she took that part from me here.'

'I hear Frau Seiling is a perfect lady – I am sure that she wouldn't do anything like that.'

'I seem to have a lot of perfect ladies around me.'

Julia looked puzzled. 'Get on with *Brangäne/Waltraute*!'

'*Jawohl,* Frau Komturin!' There was a bit of cheekiness in this response.

*

Next month they were to open the Liese Zahnsdorf Sports Centre. It had risen literally from the ashes. A dreadful piece of battle-scarred waste land had become a fine centre with a state-of-the-art tartan running track, eight tennis courts and a fine indoor sports hall – at least it would have if the struggling contractors could get it ready for the opening in time. They had all done their bit and with luck it should be ready for the great day, The opening was arranged. The music was from the Swans Band celebrating their dead heroine and former Commander and the opening itself after a short address was to be performed by The President. Detty had it in her diary and knew that she was expected to be present but no more.

So far so good but it was the surprise letter which arrived some weeks before the opening that worried her. She held it in her hand, reading the contents. Enclosed was a schedule announcing the order of events for the short gala athletics meeting which was to follow the official opening. She read down the items:

> Invitation 100 metres men
> Invitation 100 metres women
> Invitation 400 metres men
> Invitation 400 metres women
> Invitation 110 metres hurdles men
> Invitation 400 metres hurdles women
> Invitation 1500 metres men

Then she came to it.

> Invitation 1500 metres women

She went on down the list.

> High Jump
> Long Jump
> Triple jump
> Shot, Discus, Javelin etc.

The nation's top athletes and famous guest internationals from friendly neighbouring states had been invited to display their talents before a gala crowd on the opening night. The problem was the second letter which had been enclosed with the schedule. It was very formal – ominous.

> *Dear Frau Komturin,*
> *We, the organising committee for gala opening of the Zahnsdorf Stadium, have been informed of your athletic prowess and we would esteem it a great honour if you would consent to take part in the Invitation 1500 metres for women. I need hardly tell you that your presence in the competition would add a unique gloss to this memorable occasion.*

With heartfelt thanks in anticipation that you might agree,
Dmiti Zahnsdorf
Chair Organising Committee

Who had put him up to this? she thought. She suspected Mara who knew from the old terrible Farm days that she could run pretty fast. Liese had also known and for a moment she thought that this missive would have been typical of her feisty friend, but ghosts don't send letters, do they? Marc – no he wouldn't play this joke – it would be as much as his domestic bliss was worth. Anyway, it was now a fact and she had to deal with it. What was she going to answer?

The plus side; she still ran a great deal and was physically fairly fit. As she daydreamed the years rolled away, she remembered that misty autumn day when she had run the 800 metres of her life on the immortal Iffley Road track at Oxford, where years before Roger Bannister had broken the four-minute mile. She had won and came off the track to hear a plummy Oxford accent in her hearing say;

'You know that Irish girl from The House is not bad'.

Then the minus side caught up with her rapidly. She had done no competitive running since Oxford, she had been tortured, imprisoned and fought in a gruelling civil war, she had had three pregnancies and two children, she had devoted herself to singing. 1500 metres wasn't her best distance (the memorable Iffley Road effort was 800 metres). Now she was being asked to compete against the best middle-distance athletes in the country and some even more prestigious international guests. Livonia was a small country, it's true, with a still relatively undeveloped athletic programme but they all would be professionals, the best around. I'll sleep on it, she thought.

She did sleep after a fashion. Marc had come up from *Ingolstadt* late and slipped into bed beside her. When they woke, at almost the same time, she bounced her dilemma off her husband. To her surprise, he didn't tell her that she needed a mental institution but was quite supportive.

'You're a good athlete, Detty, and you don't have to win. It's your presence they want.'

'I know but I am not – never have been – in that class and I don't like making a fool of myself.'

But she knew that she would have to do it, perhaps it was the ghost of Liese telling her that she had to do it. Being last by half a lap or more was less shameful than chickening out. She turned to Marc and said:

'OK, but you've got a job on hand, Herr Major, you've got to help get your aging, raddled, creaking wife get fit enough to run 1500 metres against this country's top athletes and guests.'

'If you start talking like that, young lady, you will be running with a hot bottom. You are in great shape, pretty fit and you have an athlete's body to die for. I should know it's my favourite thing, – of course you can do it. You may not win but you won't disgrace yourself – go and take a few lessons from Firebrand.'

'There are no hurdles involved – thank God! I was never any good at hurdling – I could never remember which leg was supposed to come first. OK, I had better answer the ever-courteous Dmitri. However, I must practise and you must help me. I have a month fortunately. I am at Krenek for the whole time. I am fairly far forward with *Isolde* and there will still be time to do some work on it. I suppose I could carve out three hours training a day if I re-schedule my teaching and Gianna can manage most of Liese and Niki. I need to get set up though.

Feeling nervous like a pupil at a new school, she approached the leading sports store in Königshof. Yes, she was still doing a fair bit of recreational running but the tow path at Henley or the lake at Krenek only required a T shirt, a pair of Marc's old shorts or some jogging bottoms in winter. This was clearly different. She decided that there should be no subterfuge as she was too well known and, anyway, publicity for the new facility was the point of the exercise. Trying not to blush, she explained her needs to the young shop assistant. He clearly recognised her but managed to keep a professional straight face and addressed her very properly as 'Meine Frau' rather than any of her other titles as she negotiated her way to several pairs of shoes, running shorts, leggings, sports bras and jackets. Money wasn't an issue but she was still surprised by the size of the bill and wondered how impecunious young athletes at school or college managed.

'Would the Frau want a club logo on the kit?' the salesman asked, adding that they supplied suitably monogrammed kit to several of the local colleges and clubs. This hadn't occurred to her and she stammered.

'No, not at present' Her next job was to ring The Sacred Heart Convent where she needed to call in a favour. 'Could I have brief appointment with Reverend Mother – at her convenience, of course?'

She knew the secretary and she had no need to introduce herself. 'Of course, Frau Komturin, she actually has a space at 3.30 this afternoon – a parent has cancelled.'

'Wonderful, put me in.'

She arrived promptly at 3.30 and after a moment's delay was shown in to the Reverent Mother, who greeted her warmly.

'Bernadette, how lovely to see you. Tell me about the new baby.'

Detty filled in Liese's brief biography adding cheekily.

'I've not come to enter her to come here, although from what I've heard perhaps we ought to. I gather that you have quite a waiting list these days.'

'We have but any daughter of yours would be welcome, but I imagine that we have competing institutions in other countries.'

'We haven't really thought about it yet' confessed Detty 'but I am here for a different reason. I wondered if it would be possible to train on your running track?'

Detty was rather taken aback when the Headmistress burst out laughing.

'What has suddenly got into you girls?' Detty noted with some pleasure that from previous warm but slightly stiff formality she had now become one of 'you girls' and she liked it as she waited for an explanation.

'Well, you see, that is the second similar request that I have had today. A certain Frau Kulanova – no, I beg her pardon Frau Holberg, rang me this morning to say she was training for the Gala Stadium opening and as the stadium isn't ready could she use our long jump pit to train for the triple jump. Apparently, she has ten days holiday before the Gala. As she still holds the school record for the triple jump, I would hardly say no but, as with you, I must refer you to Frau Hirvonen, our sports head. She is new since your time but she's lovely and a considerable athlete in her own right. She ran the 5000 metres for Finland. She is also a great coach. The girls love her. I'll ring and see if you can see her now and have chat. She's not got a class until this afternoon's games.

Detty could see why Ilma Hirvonen was popular with the girls. Tall with her Finnish blond looks she had an open smile and an infectious grin. 'Should I be asking for your autograph? I have heard so much about you from the girls and everybody,' she smiled.

Detty laughed. 'No, I just would like you to help me out of a fix. I've made a stupid promise and I am regretting it already.'

'Go on,' said Ilma, instantly becoming more professional.

Detty explained her situation. 'What have you done in the past?' asked Ilma. Detty described her old athletic activities including the Oxford 800 metres. 'It was all a long time ago,' she finished.

'You've not let yourself go to seed – turn round, if you don't mind,' said Ilma looking at her closely, as Detty would have looked at a racehorse. 'We have a month. You won't win but we should be able to get you into some sort of shape so you don't make a fool of yourself.'

'That's all I'm asking.' 'Can you manage the early mornings? There is a bit of light now and we can concentrate better before many of the students are around.' Detty nodded.

'I assume that you would like a bit of coaching and I would be happy to give it to you. Have you got a club by the way? You need one under IAAF rules.'

'No.'

'Neither has Saskia who came this morning. I did some research after she left – apparently there is an old girls' sports club from before the war which is still registered although it hasn't functioned since the war. It has the rather embarrassing name of *Alumnae Cordis*. You and Saskia could use that.'

'I'm not an old girl, although I suppose an ex student teacher is close. If Mother Katerina agrees we will go for it.'

'She will. I have already asked her. I think it might develop and she's rather tickled by the idea.

*

It was sometime later that Saskia received her official invitation to represent her country at the London Olympics. It was later still that she received the invitation to be her country's flag bearer at the opening ceremony.

'To carry the Chalice and Falcon in that vast stadium. I still can't believe it.'

'Make sure that you get some great pictures to give Holly of her famous Mum.' said Detty.

*

The following morning Detty woke in the pale spring sunshine. I must be late for training, she thought, then she realised it was all over and felt slightly sad. A small movement beside her led to a hand with the fingers gently stroking her inner thigh. It happened often and was incredibly sexy. Noises from below confirmed that Gianna was busying herself with the children's breakfast. The owner of the hand stroking her thigh opened his eyes and said in English mimicking her soft Irish accent.

'And how is my raddled, ageing. creaking wife this fine morning, who I believe finished in the middle of an international invitation field of 1500 metres runners yesterday. Did you have a new Zimmer frame?'

'You're horrible,' giggled Detty finding Marc's thigh in turn with her fingers, 'anyway I wasn't in the middle, I was eighth – bottom half.'

'Yes, with the Livonian under 18 champion and a Polish former Olympian behind you. I can't remember who the other two were but everybody was hand-picked. I was so proud of you that I was bursting and it was great that you chose to use your married name – our name – thank you. But wasn't Saskia amazing?'

'My club mate – we might get some new members after that. I couldn't be more delighted for her. After all she's been through, she deserved it.'

4
DISASTER

Quivi la ripa fiamma in fuor balestra,
e la cornice spia fiato in suso,
che la riflette, e via da lei sequestra[7]

DANTE: *PURGATORIO* XXV vv 112-114

She settled to her coffee in her favourite seat in the Cafe Daina with a contented feeling. She always sat slightly behind the display counter where she was not too obvious, but at the same time could see the theatre, watch the passers-by and the comings and goings in the cafe. The rehearsals for *Tristan* were going well. That morning she had had a piano rehearsal of the first and third scenes of Act 1 with Julia and felt that she had got great venom into her narration and curse and that Julia was developing real feeling for *Brangäne*. Next week Hank would be here for the *Sitzprobe* and then they would hand over to the house staff for the technical week before the two dress rehearsals. It

---

7   Here the bank flashes flames and the
    Terrace edge gusts upwards which reflects
    them back making a sheltered path

had been somewhat awkward as they were having to rehearse round the workmen. The government and city council together with some substantial benefactors, had raised enough money to have a second stage constructed behind the theatre and the basement area, currently used for scenery storage, converted into a bar and restaurant.

It was only a wisp of smoke over by the theatre creeping round the corner near the artists' entrance. Detty didn't really notice as she was still thinking about the forthcoming *Tristan*. Then the smoke was a bit more obvious. It was probably coming from one of the cauldrons used to prepare pitch for tanking the basement for waterproofing, she thought. Suddenly there was a loud rumble like a massive thunderclap. The flames leapt right up the side of the building, then higher into the sky with great angry dragons' tongues of flames tinged at the edges with black smoke. There were cries coming from terrified pedestrians and finally the bells of approaching fire appliances. Detty leapt up onto her feet and crossed the square before finally being forced back by the fierce heat and the warning cries of the fire fighters. She stood helplessly watching and feeling that she must help – but how? She had no skills that could help and yet she felt that she must. The feeling of helplessness was somehow familiar and afterwards she realised that it was the same feeling that she had had on the flight back from rescuing the critically ill Mara. She dashed round the theatre trying to assist anyone trying to get out of the burning building. It was useless. There were some familiar faces already. outside. The fire tenders ringed the building pouring massive jets of water into the flames.

Suddenly her *Handy* rang, 'Frau Komturin, we have just the houses that you might want with Frau Tamara.' She didn't hear it and cancelled the call without answering. She raced up and down for hours still thinking that somehow, she must help with the fire. They seemed to be making no progress in stopping the blaze. With a tiny feeling of relief, after several hours, Detty realised that the fire fighters were winning. The flames were dying down. The stench of damp burning was terrible. She sat on one of the stone pillars at the edge of the square and burst into tears. She didn't know how long that she wept for.

Through her tears she realised that somebody was standing over her.

'Oh, Detty' the figure said, 'Come with me.'

'But who is safe? – it was so sudden.' she croaked.

'They haven't found Dr Staufen but everybody else got out.'

'Thank God for that. But our lovely theatre, I once called it a disaster but now I love it so much. How could I have been so cruel?'

'Come with me.' Mara repeated and she led the staggering Detty across the square round to the Hansehaus.

Like a zombie, Detty allowed Mara to drag her into the lift, into the flat and collapsed her into a chair. Mara then busied herself making coffee. The private phone rang and Mara answered.

'Good news, Detty. They have found Dr Staufen. The staircase was an inferno so he came down in the food lift from the Greenroom – not recommended. I haven't a clue how he operated it from inside but it worked.'

She watched Mara spread Niki's trucks over the floor and cuddled Liese but she was on autopilot and her heart was back in the smouldering rubble a short distance away. She roused herself for bedtime and the obligatory story then sat with Mara late into the night. David came in and had to be brought up to date then it was bedtime for them too and exhausted, she slept.

In the morning she woke thinking 'it can't be true' then it hit her first that it was true. She said to herself 'Rouse yourself, woman, there's the hell of a lot to do.' She started on a list: find out the damage assessment? Insurance – check with Helge, – she was pretty sure that none of the orchestra had been trapped but what about their instruments? Again, ask Helge. Then there was the question of whether an alternative venue could be found. She decided that a hot bath was the answer while Gianna, capable as ever, breakfasted the children aided by an increasingly maternal Mara. She was just going to get into the bath when her *Handy* in her bathrobe pocket went off. Shivering she swore quietly then answered the phone – number withheld – what the hell she thought, telesales should all be blocked.

'Hello' she said crossly.

'Frau Komturin, I have the Minister for you.'

'Which minister? She asked puzzled.

'Herr Minister Neumarkt,' then added rather unnecessarily 'Culture, arts, sports and leisure.'

'He doesn't want me to do another charity race, does he?' she was getting her sense of humour back after a dreadful twenty four hours.

'No, Frau Komturin, I think that he wants to talk about the theatre.'

'Ah, please put him on.' she put her robe back on allowing her bath to get cold.

'Frau von Ritter, this is Neumarkt. I have some information for you and we need your help. We have already been able to do a provisional survey of the damage and have found the probable cause.'

'That was very quick work. Was it sabotage?' Detty voiced the doubt that had been filling her mind since the day before.

'At the Ministry we were worried about that too, which is why we ordered this rapid provisional survey. But the answer is that no – it wasn't. It seems that hot debris from a metal cutting operation on the top, the office floor, accidentally entered a riser carrying the services and dropped down into the old scenery store below the stage. Technically, it appears to have been a lack of care on the part of the operator. However, unofficially, there is some sympathy with him as the riser wasn't obvious. There was a lot of equipment on the floor, so he didn't know that it was there. At any event, tragic though it is, it wasn't deliberate. There will be a full enquiry later but that is the present situation. Now I will come to why we need your help. We want to form a working party to oversee the restoration and rebuilding of the theatre. The first thing is to have a tour of the theatre with an expert or experts for a preliminary assessment of the present situation. Can you join us at 11am in the Cafe Daina?'

'Yes, of course' said the bemused Detty 'but why do you need me?'

She wasn't prepared for the gusty laughter from the Minister. 'Do you think that we could do anything to do with music in this city or country – let alone something as important as restoring the National Theatre without involving you, Frau Komturin?'

'OK, but I have been thinking and you may regret it.'

'What do you mean?'

'You'll see, just wait.'

'Sounds ominous, Frau Komturin'
'Could be. See you at 11.'

*

The tour round the theatre was as devastating as Detty feared. The stage and the whole of the backstage space, dressing rooms, green room, offices was a mass of charred, water sodden wreckage. The under-stage storage room where the fire had started was still deemed unsafe by the *Feuerwehrhauptmann* so they could not go down. Somebody had had the bravery and common sense to lower the safety curtain, which had saved the auditorium. It was still a sodden mass with some damage seeping through from the under-stage spaces.

It was a sombre group who assembled at the private room of the Cafe Daina after the tour. The Minister, Dr Staufen, Detty and Helge were joined by the fire captain, the visibly shaken site foreman and the site manager. There was nothing much that they could do without having more information. They agreed to meet again in a week's time at the Ministry when more information would be available.

A week later the meeting took place at the Ministry, which was a converted townhouse behind the central market. Neumarkt opened the proceedings,

'We have got a bit further on. Dr Peyer, here, from the contractors thinks, unofficially for the moment, that their insurers will pay up to the tune of 30 million Euros (they work in Euros) rather than go to Court with an expensive legal case that they would almost certainly lose. Our architect Dr Ivanov and the structural engineer Dr Santini think that the auditorium can be saved and re-structured. This will be quite expensive as there is a lot of water damage and reinforcing will be needed to bring it up to modern safety standards. But this will probably be a bit cheaper than a complete rebuild, to say nothing of the aesthetic and historical factors involved.'

'Once we go to the orchestra pit and behind the proscenium arch, nothing can be saved and we are talking about a complete new build. In rough terms, Dr Ivanov thinks that the insurance money, if it is confirmed, will pay for the structure to be restored. This does not allow for re-equipping the theatre as a working opera house. There will be substantial further expense.'

Detty was half listening – a mad idea was going round in her head. Neumarkt was speaking again.

'There will need to be a lot of discussion and negotiation associated with the theatre restoration. It is a big task. I have discussed it with the Minister Präsident who agrees that the activities of our theatre have made it and the country famous in the world and that its restoration should have high priority. For that reason we have decided to appoint a junior minister in my department charged exclusively with facilitating the restoration. 'Oh my God, thought Detty not a 'suit,' conscious of his political future. That will put a spanner in the works. Aloud she said.

'Did you have anybody in mind, Herr Minister?' 'As a matter of fact, I have, Frau Komturin.' a fleeting smile wickedly flashed over Minister Neumarkt's formal expression. Detty raised a single quizzical eyebrow.

'How does the *Abgeordneten* for *Wahlkreis Ziatov* strike you? I believe you know her? She has demonstrated huge skill and enthusiasm in the short time that she has been with us and the Minister Präsident and I both think that it is time we promoted some young blood to Ministerial rank.'

For once Detty was struck dumb for a moment then said. 'I hope that you realise, Herr Minister, that in view of what I have in mind, you may be about to wreck a long-standing and very precious friendship.'

'That, Frau Komturin, I think, if you will forgive me for saying so, is your problem, – although of course I shall watch closely how things pan out.'

'I understand that. Perhaps now I may be allowed to relieve the Minister-Elect of the care of my children.'

'Naturally, of course, Frau Gräfin, I am sorry we have kept you so long. Perhaps you could find the opportunity to discuss future plans with the Minister Elect over bath time.'

Humour seemed to be returning all round. 'If you think that, Herr Minister, I guess that you haven't bathed a four-year-old and a one year old very recently.'

'*Touché,* Frau Komturin, perhaps over a digestif after dinner?'

'Ah'

*

Mara was telling Niki an improbable story about a Hansa cob which had sailed through the North-West Passage piloted by a Polar bear called Bill. She looked up and grinned as Detty came in.

'He had asked you before today's meeting, hadn't he?'

Mara didn't pretend innocence. She knew that it wouldn't wash. She just said. 'I couldn't possibly comment.'

In fact, Newmark had phoned Mara while Detty was walking back. He had said that I think that I should warn you that Frau von Ritter is on the war path and who knows what will happen when the *Valkyrie* is riding.' He had mixed his metaphors with a chuckle. Detty threw herself onto the Presidential chesterfield.

'You know what the worst part of this problem is, *Frau Ministerin Gewählter?*

Mara shook her head, shaking the fair ringlets cascading round her cheeks, which made her look more like a sophisticated teenager than a Minister Elect.

'It means that we have got to find another babysitter for Gianna's day off. Falk's wife might do it. The other problem is a much more serious one.

'It was Mara's turn to cock an inquisitorial ministerial eyebrow. 'However we manage to rebuild the Hoftheatre, the Green Room canteen must include a respectable *cafetera.*'

'I will minute this from the first meeting of the Steering Committee as a priority request from the *Seniorkomturin* of the Order of Sankt Nicklaus. Now we had better go to bed before I listen to you planning to bankrupt the state with your plans for re-building or, equally serious, we are kept awake all night by a certain *Contessina* trying to emulate her mother in the dramatic soprano *fach.*'

*

Mara threw herself into her new duties with an energy and enthusiasm which had been hinted at during her election campaign. She acquired an office in the Ministry which looked like, and probably had been, a generous sized broom cupboard but it had room for a desk, a computer and a rapidly filling filing cabinet. She shared a secretary, housed in another adjacent cupboard with her fellow junior Minister. It was a small Department but with the rebirth of interest in the arts and in sport, there was a great deal to do.

She tackled Detty a couple of days later.

'As I have achieved Ministerial rank, I am going to lay down some ground rules, Frau Komturin. In order to preserve our friendship and our sanity, the restoration of the theatre will only be discussed in a business setting preferably with my secretary present to take minutes, outside that we will try and behave with each other as normal human beings, as usual – OK? Can we have the first meeting at the Ministry tomorrow and then you can explain your hair brained scheme?'

'*Jawohl*, Frau Ministerin!' Mara couldn't decide for a moment if Detty was taking the micky (that phrase was part of her newly honed English). However she was serious and meant it. It suddenly reminded Detty of something:

'Oh Lord, it had gone completely out of my head, I am so sorry.'

'Would you mind telling me what on earth you are talking about – if it's not the restoration in view of my rule?'

'No, it isn't although the fire is the reason that I forgot about it. A real estate man rang me on my *Handy* just as the theatre caught fire. He said something about having two houses near Ziatov which he thought might suit us both. It went right out of my mind and I haven't told you and I've done nothing about it.'

'Not a great problem. You can ring the Agency now and arrange a time when we both can visit. I am sure that they will understand that we have been preoccupied with the fire.'

'OK, but I am going to break your rule but in a good cause. We need to increase awareness and involve a lot of people in the fund-raising that is going to be needed, particularly if the plan that I will outline at the next meeting is accepted. We need some high-profile charity events both to raise funds and public awareness. I have some ideas – perhaps a charity concert twinned with a rock concert for the young people and likewise a ball for the under twenties or perhaps a glittering affair for the *prominenti*. The main problem is lack of venues – the obvious one – the opera house – is, of course, out of action.'

'We will have to use the *FreiSenderLivonia*'s hall. It's not very glamorous but we can doll it up a bit. I'll ask Masha – she is usually pretty willing but I'd prefer it not to end like my press conference there. However, I have another idea – what about a charity football match? I do have some influence there.'

Mara smiled to herself complacently. Detty knew full well that David was so much in love with his new wife that he would do anything she wanted.

'Fine, as long as you don't want me to play – I did my bit at 1500 metres for the Stadium.'

'No, we will give you a purely ceremonial role, but I could play.' For a moment Mara looked excited. 'How about *Staatsoper Königshof* vs *SV Ziatov*?'

'With each side captained by a Sensky?' said Detty joking, she was astounded when Mara appeared to take her seriously. 'I don't see why not although David would have to captain the opera house side and his singing voice only comes into its own with raunchy dressing room songs.'

5
THE MATCH

Football is an art more central to our culture than anything.
the Arts Council deigns to recognise.

GERMAINE GREER AUSTRALIAN JOURNALIST

The match was billed as a Charity Match between a *Staatsoper Königshof 11* and *SV Ziatov*. The designation *Staatsoper* was applied loosely and the *Staatsoper* had acquired several players from the *FC Königshof* whose musical qualifications also only extended to dressing room *repertoire*. The *Staatsoper* team was captained by David Sensky who might just, tenuously, qualify by being a close friend of the undeniably musical Bernadette von Ritter. The President's daughter, now *die Frau Ministerin Oblova Senska* was billed as captaining the Ziatov side. It was expected that she would merely do the kick off then be substituted for a regular player from the bench. This was the normal and expected role of a VIP starting the match. The VIP, who does the kick off, usually was supposed to make an anodyne tap to his/her striker and then retire gracefully to the stands. She didn't. Mara had appeared in the strip of *SV Ziatov* which was deemed entirely appropriate as she was wearing the club colours of the constituency that she represented in the *Hansetag*. No problem there.

However, rather than the traditional bloodless ceremony, Mara passed to her colleague, the regular Ziatov striker who, clearly pre-briefed, passed back to her. She then dribbled neatly round the bemused Königshof striker and then her opposing husband. After accomplishing that manoeuvre, now well inside the opposition's half, she made a long accurate pass to the advancing Ziatovian midfielder. She was clearly enjoying herself and showing no signs of retiring onto the bench but was obviously eager to remain part of the game. It took an accurate save from the Königshof keeper, a talented amateur goalie and scene shifter, to prevent the village side going one up. Mara had clearly not been following the normal script but the packed *Hansestadion* loved it and burst into rippling applause. Mara remained on the field until nearly the end of the first half taking part in some accurate one – two passing which, truth to tell, was of a much higher quality than could usually be expected from a village side. Towards the end of the half, she allowed herself, reluctantly, to be substituted and, wreathed in smiles retired to the Ziatov bench.

At the end of the game, after the presentations, she was on the way to her lonely female dressing room when she was stopped by the opposing captain who lifted her high into the air with a bear hug and a kiss:

'I knew that you could play but I have never seen you do it.'

'Was I all right?' asked the breathless Ziatov captain.

'You were superb and I really mean it, although I suppose that I am a bit biased.'

The sporting press coverage had a field day. When interviewed by the sports' service of the FSL (*FreiSenderLivonias*), Mara's comment was,

'I had always dreamed about playing football in front of fifty thousand people and given the opportunity, I was not going to pass it up.'

'But where did you learn to pass like that?'

'That's a very long story but I did have to go and practise incognito with Ziatov's training sessions to see if I still could. They were sworn to secrecy. They were rather surprised but, bless them, they kept quiet.'

'Still could?' asked the interviewer.

'That's right' she said but no more was forthcoming.

The match had finished one all with the Ziatov goalie saving a penalty struck, perhaps a bit modestly, by David Sensky. The Trophy consisting of a double magnum of *Spezial Reserve von Ritter Sekt* was quickly doubled so there was one for each team. The presentation was made by *Die Komturin Bernadette von Ritter* on behalf of the *Weingut* donors. In her presentation speech she remarked that it would be good to arrange a charity rugby match against Ireland but she feared that Livonian rugby would have to put in a fair bit of practise first as, as she asserted proudly, her birth country was currently rather good.

The theatre restoration fund, from both tickets and donations, however, had benefited from the match to the tune of five million thalers (two million €).

*

Inspektor Kunz sat at his worn beech wood desk and wished that he hadn't given up smoking. He stared pensively at the score marks on the desk made by generations of his predecessors. He didn't think that they were actually initials or messages of unrequited love, although some of the scratchings appeared to be in Cyrillic and could have been either. However, policemen, particularly old-style policemen, wouldn't do that, would they?

These musings didn't help him with his present dilemma. He had received a visit from Kommissar Weiss. Usually this was not a problem. His relationship with his boss, the Kommissar, he would describe as 'normal' – this didn't go as far as friendly, that would have been unusual, even irregular, but they had a mutual understanding. Weiss respected the long, loyal service of Hans Kunz and usually left him alone in his undemanding country post. After all he was within five years of retirement and had distinguished himself showing a dangerous regard for humanity and local justice during the dreadful days of the fascist regime. This time however Kommissar Weiss had something more on his mind:

'Do you have room for an additional agent or two here at Ziatov, Herr Inspektor?'

'Not really, without building on, but why do you think that I need them Herr Kommissar?'

'Well, you know the Polish *Dwor* and its adjacent cottage by the river. I think that they may have found buyers for them.'

'What both of them?' Kunz was surprised. These properties had been on the market for some time. Young people now liked modern apartments in town and they were too remote for the elderly. In addition, they needed full restoration. However, he was glad:

'I am delighted to hear that. It is a lovely traditional house and the cottage is sweet. It has been terrible seeing them empty and deteriorating. It will need some money spent on them, though. Tell me more, Herr Kommissar.'

'Well, the reason for my question was the prospective purchasers. I don't think that the funds for restoration will be too much of a problem but security may be.'

'Security?'

'Yes, I should put you fully in the picture and explain why you might need to accommodate more officers.' Hans Kunz raised a quizzical eyebrow. 'You see you will have on your patch in your delightful *Dwór* and its Keeper's cottage, two – no I tell a lie, four VIPs.'

'Go on, Herr Kommissar' Kunz was now intrigued.

'Probably, for different reasons, four of the best-known people in Livonia have indicated that they will buy both properties. David Sensky, his wife Tamara Nikolaevna née Oblova, Marc von Ritter and his wife Bernadette Niamh née O'Neill.' He stumbled over Detty's second name but made a brave try to give all four of the VIPs their full titles.'

There was a stunned silence. Inspektor Kunz could see his cherished dream of the short Livonian summers being spent on his allotment with its cosy shed, receding into the distance. Not that he had anything against the four people, who had been dropped like a bombshell into his tranquil life. Like many, he loved, from a distance, Tamara with her troubled history, ready ceremonial phrases and pretty ingenuous smile. He wasn't a football fan but still was able to see David as a Livonian icon. As for Marc and Bernadette their achievements for their adopted country were part of its enduring mythology. But to have them suddenly dumped on his quiet rural patch, that was something different.

Mara and Detty had visited the properties with the agent two weeks before. In both cases it was done without any initial enthusiasm and just provided an added strain in their crowded lives. Detty however felt guilty that she had ignored the call from the agent on the day of the fire. After all it wasn't a cold call, she had contacted the agent first. A week or so before the turmoil caused by the fire, she had visited him with Mara, and they had spent some time explaining their requirements. After considerable delay and some grumbling, they had found time to make a visit to the properties after Mara's constituency 'surgery' in the Ziatov *Rathaus*.

They loved it, or rather them, at first sight. They ran about like a couple of kids in the long unkempt grass that stretched down to the small river talking about picnics and barbecues. Mara with more local knowledge than Detty announced that she thought that the main house was properly described as a *dworek*. This was somewhere between a cottage and a manor house. A *dwor* proper was a grander building with a distinctly aristocratic provenance. This one, had, in addition a genuine cottage which the locals referred to as 'the Keeper's cottage'. In spite of the Polish name and the overall traditional Polish design it appeared that the history and details of the house owed a good deal to several long-term occupiers, Russians, Swedes and several lots of Germans had all owned it, as well as the recent Moltravians. These last had contributed little as the house had been empty for some time since the upheavals of German and Soviet occupation. Traditionally these houses were made of timber which stretched from the roof tiles via the walls to the foundations. In time the main walls of this house had been replaced by brick and the wooden roof had been retiled with ceramic tiles. The characteristic gabled front porch, however, which was large and measured almost one third of the frontage, with two windows from the main bedrooms, was still timber. It was in such a poor state of repair that the four massive timber supports seemed in danger of impending collapse.

The agent had another appointment and the women readily agreed that having arranged access, he would leave them to look over the two properties in their own time. They could return the keys from such doors that had workable locks, to his office later.

The main hall was behind the portico. Empty it seemed vast with only small piles of rubbish to break up the echoing emptiness. Behind was the abandoned kitchen with a larder or storeroom to each side. Off the main hall in the front on either side were smaller rooms perhaps suitable for studies, libraries, or a music room. Detty's imagination ran riot. She found herself wondering if her mother-in-law could supply the necessary timber for restoration. Then she told herself not to be ridiculous – Livonia had plenty of timber and the expertise to use it without imports from hundreds of kilometres away. The steep mansard roof was double and, as well as the windows over the porch and through the roof alongside, there were, intriguingly, two very small windows in the upper part of the steep roof.

They tried to explore the upstairs and got as far as the two grand bedrooms with two smaller ones on the main floor without falling through the rotten floorboards. Detty hoped that the little windows in the roof led to small rooms suitable for the children. The staircase up from the first floor was there but was so seriously unsafe that it was impossible to go up. Even in its terrible condition it clearly had signs of old beauty and dignity.

'I don't think that we can go any further without killing ourselves,' said Detty, 'let's go and have a look at the cottage.'

The Keeper's cottage was much smaller but in much better repair. It gave the impression of having been lived in much more recently. Plumbing was there but distinctly archaic as was the wood fired boiler. The ground floor was in one room leading through into the kitchen at the back. The first floor consisted of two bedrooms, small but comfortable with an old fashioned but seemingly functional bathroom in between. 'This would be plenty big enough for us' Mara added as an afterthought '- at present,'

Detty smiled. 'We will get the experts onto it, find out who owns them. Then we can get an idea of restoration and costs.'

'*Jawohl*, Frau Ministerin' said Detty aware that almost for the first time since the dreadful journey to The Farm, Mara had taken command.

There was a hint of irony in her '*Jawohl*' but most of it was admiration.

'And, when you have finished winding me up, Frau Komturin, we have to start working on how to restore your opera house.' The riposte, using Detty's formal title, evened the score. Detty notice that it was now 'her opera house' that needed restoring. 'Thursday – tomorrow is too soon, we need to get everyone there.' Mara had been determined to fit everyone into her tiny office at the Ministry – it was a question of status, prestige. However, eventually with reasonably good grace she had to agree there was no space and had transferred the meeting to the Committee room on the first floor of the Hansehaus. From her father, she had asked permission, very formally, to use this room. He had, of course, formally but graciously granted it. It was only Detty who privately noted the surreptitious wink that the President had given her with a proud smile twitching round his face. It was the only sign of his immense pride in his Minister daughter.

Mara duly took the chair and welcomed everybody. Most knew each other, however, she, very properly, did the round of introductions:

Dr Lev Ivanov – Architect
Dr Viktor Manin – Consultant Surveyor
Dr Eng. Michael Santini -Structural Engineer
Dr Alphonse Peyer – Director of Works
Dr Birgitte Frankland – Finance Officer
Dr Helmut Rosen – Electrical Engineer
Dr Richard Strauss – Acoustic Engineer
Professor Dr Hans Neumarkt – Minister-observer
Professor Dr Helge von Grunstand – Direktor Königshofer
    Philharmonica
Frau Komturin Bernadette von Ritter -Direktorin Schliessen O'Neill
    – Musik Hochschule
Frau RitterinTamara Oblova Senska MinisterinPräsidentin Projekt
    Staatsoper Königshof

After everybody had introduced themselves. Dr Strauss provided some light relief by pointing out that he was no relation of the distinguished musicians who bore his name. Mara thanked them for coming, particularly at short notice.

'As you will see from the agenda that I have prepared, I think we should start by getting our expert members to outline the situation and the problems in their fields. If you agree we might start with Dr Manin.'

'Thank you, Frau Ministerin. I have prepared a preliminary printed report on the state of the theatre after the fire. I have copies for everybody but to save time I will just summarise my findings. The theatre behind the forward proscenium arch has effectively been totally destroyed. Subject to my architect colleague's opinion, I would recommend demolition and a complete rebuild. Thanks to the brave and most intelligent intervention of Herr Ludwig of the stage staff in lowering the safety curtain, the auditorium, although suffering considerable water and dust damage, was almost completely spared. Unfortunately, the safety curtain did not protect the orchestra pit which was badly damaged before the *Feuerwehr* fighters were able to extinguish the fire in that section. Beyond my scope, but happily, I gather that no instruments except the large *immobili* were in the pit at the time as the orchestra was about to go on tour. Is that correct Herr Maestro?' He turned to Helge who nodded '*Genau.*'

'The second problem, if we follow the course that I would like to recommend, is that of grafting the new build onto the preserved auditorium. This is of course technical and I look forward to meeting with Dr Ivanov to discuss the solution to this problem.'

'Before I finish, I would like to suggest, Frau Ministerin, that a vote of thanks and if possible, a gratuity is awarded to Herr Ludwig whose bravery and foresight undoubtedly saved a large part of the theatre which would otherwise have been completely destroyed.'

Mara nodded. 'Thank you, Herr Doktor, I entirely agree with you about Herr Ludwig and I will set the wheels in motion to appropriately express our appreciation of his outstanding service, nay valour. I will report back to this committee when we have sorted something out. Perhaps we should hear from Dr Ivanov next.'

'If you don't mind Frau Ministerin, I think we should hear what Frau Dr Frankland and Frau Komturin O'Neill have to say first, then my contribution will make more sense,'

Mara indicated Birgitte Frankland. 'I can give you a very broad provisional report on the financial situation subject to detailed revision later. In very rough terms' she stressed 'the German insurers will contribute up to €30 million for the rebuild of the destroyed stage and adjoining areas. There is still discussion about the insurance position regarding the damage to the auditorium and some of the stage fittings and fixtures. I gather that electrical work would be included if it is deemed to be restitution and falls within the overall capped amount. Work that is deemed to be incurred by additional improvements and features which were not part of the original structure is not included in their estimate. At this point, Frau Präsidentin, with your permission, I would like to give way to Frau Komturin O'Neill whose contribution at this stage will be highly relevant.'

'Frau Komturin?' Mara, looked expectantly at Detty,

'First, thank you for inviting me, as I feel that my role is only on the periphery of these deliberations. Second, I think most of you here speak English and will know what I mean when I say that I want to "put a spanner in the works." Please though, don't take that too literally. I will try to be brief. First, *meine Damen und Herren*, the destruction of your lovely theatre is a tragedy of huge significance. Those who were either with me in the theatre at the time of the liberation '*Fidelios*' or who saw them on TV will not need convincing how important that event was to all of us and perhaps most of all to me personally. I could go on but I won't.'

'However, every disaster of this kind provides opportunities as well as grief and I think that here we have a series of opportunities which are unlikely to recur in our lifetime. As I partially recovered from the shock of the fire, I said to the Frau Ministerin that the one thing that I insisted on when the theatre was restored was having a decent coffee maker in the staff canteen.'

She got the expected laughter but then became serious. 'The coffee maker started my thinking. I believe we have the opportunity of providing Königshof with one of the finest medium sized theatre complexes in Europe which means in the world. I won't break you in gently. I would like to see, in addition to the restoration of our beautiful auditorium with state-of-the-art facilities, a second studio sized theatre, a second and third stage with an additional rehearsal room (particularly with our dancers in mind). Also, we need a complete scene preparation and painting flat behind the new fly tower with costume workrooms, props facilities and armoury (my colleague *Kammersänger* Henry Schliessen is particularly keen that we have a good armoury.)

Hank's live sword bearing intervention to stop the attempted kidnapping in Florence was well known and there were smiles all round.

'That is a broad outline of my megalomaniac fantasy but I am sure that it will change over time. Now I understand that to achieve any of this will take very large sums of money although a little of it may be subsumed under 'normal restoration.'

6
MUDDLE

Lo! thy dread empire. Chaos! is restored.
Light dies before thy uncreating word:

ALEXANDER POPE: *THE DUNCIAD* IV 653

Detty felt that she was a juggler with three plates spinning in the air, wondering which one was going to crash and shatter on the floor. She wondered how to cut herself in three. She realised that Mara was hardly better off. She had her normal duties as a congresswoman plus the huge task of guiding the opera house rebuild. For Detty, there was her megalomaniac desire to develop the ruined theatre into a state-of-the-art multi-stage modern opera house. Then there was the half-rehearsed production of *Tristan und Isolde* with no theatre in which to perform it. At the back of her mind was the fact that it had been deemed unproducible by several theatres after its composition to the despair of the composer. Notably Vienna had abandoned it after, reputedly, over one hundred rehearsals. Now many theatres world–wide had produced it successfully many times since then and she had revelled in learning *Isolde*. However, for all that, *Tristan* made heavy demands on cast and orchestra and was by no means the easiest show to put on. Finally, there was the pending purchase of the Polish house which she found, and so did Marc, appealing. When she had mentioned this last to Marc, he was immediately extremely enthusiastic but each project needed work. Regrettably the *Dwor* and its cottage, although exciting, had to take a back seat.

The indefatigable Karl Staufen, following his miraculous, but, highly irregular, escape via the theatre service lift, had organised two temporary cabins in front of the forlorn, dirty but largely undamaged portico of the theatre. Detty made for the first one to be greeted by Paul, the long-standing doorman. After a few conventional phrases about how terrible it all was, Detty found Staufen's secretary in the cramped temporary office. She looked at her watch. It was 3 pm -OK – 9am EST that would do assuming Hank was in the EST zone. She had no idea:

'Laura, can you phone Kammersänger Schliessen's *Handy* and see if I can have a word with him. You probably won't get him but leave a message on his voicemail to ring me, if you can.'

She gave Laura the scribbled number. Miraculously he was on the line almost immediately, probably from somewhere either in the Met or his New York apartment. Detty knew that he had an apartment in West 61st Street a short way from the Lincoln Centre.

'Detty, I have only just heard – how bad is it?'

She rapidly filled him in with the details then added. 'I am worried about the *Tristan* – all was ready – there was, ironically, only a week for us then the technical week to go before the *Generalproben* but of course you know that.'

'We must sort something out. I am coming over anyway for next week. Have you ever thought of an open-air *Tristan?*'

'What in a Baltic winter?'

'I tell you what, perhaps we should book Madison Square Gardens and put the show on ice.'

Trying unsuccessfully to be tragic and serious, Detty giggled. 'Just one problem, I can't skate.'

'Don't worry, I can always carry you round the rink over my shoulder.'

'And how would I be supposed to sing?' Despite the absurdness of his suggestion Detty felt her mood lift after talking to Hank. He always had that effect on her. She returned to the Hansehaus.

Mara had beaten her to it. Bath time was underway with Gianna, now returned, presiding. But Mara hadn't been allowed to be let off. Apparently there had been insistent pleading from Niki and the journey of Bill the Polar bear and the Hansa cob, after many adventures, was making progress through the Northwest Passage.

Detty laughed. 'There seems to be a lot of fantasy around this evening. I have just had a mad American tenor saying that we should do *Tristan und Isolde* in the open air in a Königshof winter. When I pointed out that our climate here didn't really favour open air shows in winter, he said perhaps we should go for an ice rink in New York.'

She was taken aback when Mara, temporarily relinquishing her role as the Polar bear *Schiffer* said.

'Well, it's not like that but I do have an idea for you but perhaps it had better wait until after bedtime and our supper.'

Gianna was making up for lost time after her absence and had cooked them *Penne all'arrabbiata*. They got the children into bed then decently replete from *Penne* and *Chianti*, they settled comfortably. Detty raised a quizzical eyebrow at Mara, following her hint before dinner.

'Well,' she said 'I had a phone call from my favourite bishop, Dieter Höfer, this afternoon. In fact, he was looking for you but hadn't got your *Handy* number on his phone so he called me. He asked whether we were looking for a theatre. And how! I said. Then he said Bialovsk might have a solution. Apparently, there is a cinema there but it's more than that. It was built in the 1920s during the German Weimar period by a wealthy Austrian enthusiast with an estate on the other side of the Bial River. He seems to have had a lot of money and wanted the theatre to be a sort of Austrian operetta Bayreuth. Well, surprise, surprise it never worked. The old man died, his heirs in the family weren't interested and anyway the operetta craze was dying, swamped by politics, and changing tastes, and the cinema was taking over. The theatre was changed into a cinema and a Welte organ was imported from Freiburg and installed. Then the talkies arrived and they stopped using the organ but amazingly it is still there, apparently. The theatre is now used only for casual cinema showings about twice a month. It is right at the back of the town – almost outside so it wasn't really in the front line and the relatively minor damage caused by the war has apparently been repaired.'

'I think I've seen the building from a distance and wondered what it was,' interpolated Detty.

'Bishop Dieter was very diffident but did wonder, if there is no other suitable Königshof theatre, whether it would be of any use as a stopgap.' Mara paused – eyeing Detty who was deep in thought. After a time, she roused herself.

'How big is it?' she asked peremptorily.

'Apparently over fifteen hundred seats – if the old orchestra pit seats are included it has nearly two thousand.'

'Wow – that's big for a provincial theatre. The old man must have had delusions of grandeur. What's the stage like?'

'Detti – hang on – I have no idea. I only heard about it this afternoon and from a bishop at that, not a man of the theatre.'

'No, I'm being unreasonable- I'm sorry. But one more question – do you know who owns it now?'

'Apparently *Agricoop Livonia* who bought it as a possible warehouse site but found another one that was more suitable, access problems for HGVs or something, so they let it continue its role as an occasional cinema.'

'I know about them or rather their predecessors' HGVs. They bring back nightmares.' Detty smiled. 'Right – we need a visit – yesterday. Hank will be here next week and his opinion would be valuable unless he wants to turn it into a skating rink. However, I think we should make some sort of visit first. What's the minimum that would be useful, Frau Ministerin? I think we should keep the first party as small as possible. However, I will stand them all *Abendbrot* at Die Dame in Rüstung if we can finish while they are still serving.'

'Helge is essential, as housing the orchestra is likely to be the main problem. Viktor Manin, the surveyor, Michael Santini, the structural engineer, Alphonse Peyer the director of works and Richard Strauss, the acoustic engineer.'

'OK I'll ring Helge now. I know that he's teaching at Krenek today and will be staying there.'

She got out her phone. 'Helge hi, we have been having some thoughts about how we manage without a theatre.'

She went on to describe all they knew about the Bialovsk cinema. Then she put the phone on voice so Mara could listen.

'It's an unusual idea, Detti, but we've had some of those. I see two immediate problems, first how to house the orchestra – from what you say there must have been some sort of pit – but what is it like and what is there now? And second what's it going to sound like? Without being too arrogant and stuffy about it, after a lot of hard work on everybody's part, we now have a very fine orchestra – I would be embarrassed to quote some of the terms that have been used about it.'

Detty interrupted, 'I'm not. I will save you the trouble, Helge, and quote the FAZ.

'*The Königshofer Philharmoniker has, in a few short years since it's re-foundation, become one of the great orchestras of Europe.*'

'Yes, well, be that as it may,' said Helge clearly embarrassed to have the *Frankfurter Allgemeine Zeitung* quoted back at him, 'it is all down to the girls and boys, they have splendid talent, don't fight – much (the much he added after a pause) and work prodigiously. Now I cannot ask them to play in a ghastly space and this venue, even if it is basically suitable, will need some exploration and possibly diplomatic selling. To which end, can I bring Luisa Stocken with me, I think that you may have met her, Detti? However, just to remind you and Tamara about her, she is our principal oboist and cor anglais player, quite important in the forthcoming production of *Tristan* as I am sure that you will agree. She is a fabulous musician. However, none of that is the reason that I want to invite her. She is also President of the Orchestra Committee and my principal co-auditionist. She has immense respect from and influence over the orchestra and, I need hardly add, that if we get her on side, it is half the battle. However, she is not a pushover and behind a charming exterior defends her troops like a tigress.'

'She sounds terrifying,' said Mara.

'She is, but fair. I would also like to bring Michael Storen, the senior Concert Master. I know that you are trying to keep the party small but I think that these two are vital if we want to get the orchestra on our side. By the way they are friends and allies so they won't fight with each other. You note that I call Michael 'Concert Master', I don't usually use American terms but I do agree with Daniel Barenboim when he says that the British 'leader' translates dubiously into German.'

'Very well – certainly bring them.'

*

They set out climbing into a government MPV for all the world like children on a school outing. Detty took care to sit next to Luisa and they had some general enquiries about each other's families and the difficulties of having young children with a demanding and irregular career. Luisa had a five-year-old daughter and a husband who was an accident and emergency consultant at the university hospital.

'It's horrendous,' she confessed 'he works all hours and most of my work is in the evening – with rehearsals during the day as is normal. We have a Greek girl and she's lovely but it isn't the same as having mum or dad at home. Your husband's a soldier, of course, so you must have similar problems.'

'It's probably slightly easier for us though there are now two of them, but it's a bit similar. Marc gets quite a lot of leave and I'm not singing every night but I have a lot of homework to do, plus teaching at Krenek, and so I imagine, do you.'

'At least I have a score to work from.' laughed Luisa.

Detty realised, after Conservatoires, overseas engagements and work at home that it was unusual to get real fellow feeling from an instrumentalist however eminent. There was always, in the background, the feeling that eighty to a hundred or so very talented musicians toiled in the pit while the banner posters and 'bravos' went to two or three singers. In her heart Detty had always thought that it was unfair but really didn't see how she could alter it, above always seeking to treat her orchestral colleagues with the maximum courtesy and consideration. They then got onto a mutual enthusiasm for horses which was completely neutral ground.

As they reached the site via the new Bialovsk bypass, Detty's heart sank. The road that they turned into was at the back of the cinema which was surrounded by several jerry-built temporary buildings, rubbish and disintegrating concrete.

She whispered to Mara in front of her. 'We already have three ruins – we may be about to acquire another one.'

However, once they turned round to the front of the building spirits rose slightly. There was a portico, not hugely different from the one at the Hoftheatre in Königshof but clearly in a poor state of repair. The local guide found a key and opened the grand double doors of the main entrance while a cloud of dust fell on everybody's heads. Once inside they faced the elaborate nineteenth century doors which led into the stalls, while on either side elegant but filthy staircases led to the upper tiers of seats. They went through into the stalls. The whole party had acquired a sensation that they were visiting a relic of the artistic endeavours of a bygone age. They stood silent and impressed looking round the old theatre, over the filthy velour stalls seats and up to the three horseshoe shaped tiers reaching up to the gallery. It wasn't difficult to imagine live popular shows of years gone by, with cheering or booing the talent of the day. They eventually found a door which led behind the cinema screen into the old stage space. It was surprisingly big but filled with enormous amounts of rubbish.

Mara brought everyone to order. 'OK folks, I know it's impressive but can we make anything of it?' Victor the surveyor, Strauss, and Michael the structural engineer started to have a deep technical discussion aided by pen knives being stuck into various parts of the auditorium.

'I think' said Detty tactfully 'we will let you folk get on with the auditorium while the rest of us try to decide if we can make music here.' She winked at Luisa who grinned back.

Luisa then rapidly went over to Michael Storen. 'Michael, I think that we may have slipped up. Have you got a violin with you?'

'No, have you got an oboe?'

'No' 'Well, how the hell are we going to find out what the place sounds like?'

Detty was smiling in the background. 'Well, lacking a better trial, *Professori,* I have brought my instrument with me and, although it won't be the same as orchestral sound, I can, if you want, give it a go, if I can get onto the stage in front of that terrible cinema plasterboard or whatever it is.'

'Carry on, Detti, what are you going to give us?'

'Oh, a bit of *Tristan,* after all that's what we are hoping to do here.'

Helge said, 'I'd offer to accompany you on the organ but I am sure it's not working from first inspection. Sadly, if we come here, I think we will have to get it moved.'

'OK, as long as you turn your tape recorders off, I'll do it unaccompanied.'

'A real musician from the vocal ranks.' said Michael.

'That sounds a bit backhanded and you haven't heard it yet.'

'No, no. I'm very impressed – genuinely.'

Detty scrambled onto the stage in front of the primitive cinema screen. She cleared her throat from the pervasive floating dust and sang a scale. Then she paused concentrating for a moment and began.

Mild und leise
wie er lachelt
wie das Auge
hold er öffnet
seht ihr's Freunde?
seht ihr's Freunde?

And on she went until,

unbewusst
Höchste Lust!

They all stood back and applauded her. 'Thank you very much, I am very touched. However, to bring everybody back to basics, was it OK? What was the sound like?'

'I think that it is possible.' said Strauss 'It's a bit difficult with a creaky, empty theatre but first off, I think it's not bad. There were no obvious faults.'

'Are you talking about the acoustics or my *Liebestod*?' teased Detty.

'Would we dare, Frau Komturin?' they said in unison.

'Well, I think it's about the strangest venue that I've ever sung in.'

'OK' said Mara, staying serious, 'now what about the pit. Do you think that you, Helge, Luisa, and Michael will you be able to get your orchestra into it and what will it sound like then?'

'Well, we have no idea what is underneath until we get that crap off the false floor. However, from the surface area there might be enough space for double wind particularly if we can filch some space under the stage and 14,12,10,8,6 strings. It's a bit slender for *Tristan* but as long as Luisa can do her virtuosa bit on the cor anglais we might get away with it.'

'That's on stage anyway so probably not a problem – not sure how I get back into the pit though,' said the latter.

Detty was so glad that Helge had suggested bringing Luisa and Michael. They were throwing themselves into the challenges with enthusiasm and having the orchestral players rising to the task gave a great sense of solidarity.

Mara deferred to Alphonse. 'How long is it going to take you to get rid of, what the Herr Professor Maestro refers to in refined technical language, as *die Scheisse* and make the pit usable?'

'Not long – tomorrow if we have the owners' permission.'

'I've got that already' said Mara 'they seem rather tickled that we might be able to use the old place and want to cooperate. They will need paying but I have stressed the limits and they seem happy. Fortunately, the current CEO of the Agricoop is an amateur musician. Can you get contractors to open and clean the stage at the same time?'

Detty was amazed that Mara had made all these contacts in a couple of days but she knew that Mara could be very persuasive and the Oblov name helped.

'When can you come back?' Mara turned her attention to Luisa, Michael and Helge.

They conferred. 'Probably not until after the weekend. Problem is that we have concerts at the *Konzerthaus,* Berlin on Friday and Saturday next.'

'No pressure – nothing too important then.' teased Detty which was greeted by a satisfactorily broad grin from Luisa.

'No, it can't be important – no soprano participation.'

'*Egalité* – deuce 'said Detty laughing – she was going to enjoy working more closely with these folk.

'When you two have finished' said Mara 'can we say Wednesday week – at least provisionally? Alphonse, can you get a team to open the pit and the stage, and try and tidy the place up a bit if there's time?'

'*Jawohl!* Frau Ministerin.'

*

They drove back after the promised visit to Die Dame, largely in silence. As they reached the Theatreplatz with the singed wreck of their former home staring reproachfully at them, it was a more sombre mood.

Preparing to leave the MPV, Detty said to her neighbour Luisa, 'What are you playing in Berlin?'

'Brahms, Tchaikovsky, Waldhüter and Bruckner. There is a different programme for each concert.'

'I wish I could come' Detty wistfully 'but with all this on, it just isn't possible.' She had made a friend. 'We might have to get you in as assistant orchestra librarian. I am delighted to say after the FAZ and various other press and radio comments the concerts have been sold out for some time. I'll get you a recording. We are trying to start publishing them but with all these other snags, it has got a bit lost,'

'That would be great' said Detty 'anyway *toi,toi,toi.*'

7
PROGRESS

luce intellettual pieno d'amore[8]

DANTE *PARADISO* XXX vs40

Detty had breakfast with Gianna and the President after feeding the children. Mara had dashed off at the crack of dawn to her office, despite her avowed dislike of early mornings. Hard working conscientiousness, she had undoubtedly inherited from her father. She had left David, who had a match with a late kick-off in bed. As she went, she had said to Detty. 'I can't believe that I have been privileged to get this job *and I'm going to bust a gut to do it well'*.

The second part of the statement was in English and Detty knew that it was one of her own English expressions which Mara, working hard at her English, had picked up. Detty just hoped that her friend didn't trot it out inappropriately. I suppose there are worse phrases, she said to herself.

Nicklaus was keen to know how the post fire plans were going. She described their visit to Bialovsk and the hope that they had to have

---

8 Light of the mind, full of love

found an alternative provisional venue. Niki junior had announced loudly from the floor during this breakfast discussion that he wanted a trumpet. Nicklaus senior tried hard and not very successfully to control his smirk behind his hands. Niki's mother had suggested that he might wait until he was a little bit older. That didn't go down at all well and Detty was quite relieved to leave her grumpy four-year old in the capable hands of Gianna.

She went off to a meeting with Mara and the restoration team that morning and then hoped to go on to Bialovsk. She had burnt the midnight oil studying the European Neighbourhood Policy with a view to getting help with the €30 million that was needed for the second stage of the re-development. She reckoned they needed half the additional €30 million from outside sources including the ENP, private and commercial donors mainly in Germany and the USA and the other half, they would have to raise themselves.

At the meeting Mara reported that *Agricoop Livonias* had offered to pay for the temporary restoration of the rather pretentiously named *Alhambra* as long as they were acknowledged in the publicity and retained the freehold. It was agreed that these were completely reasonable requests and that Mara should brief the lawyers about the proposed lease and write to thank the *AgriLiv* for their offer. Clearly, they had to wait to go further on Bialovsk until the orchestra were back and the pit in the theatre, at least, cleared. Detty hoped that they would soon have the huge experience, with not a little wisdom, of Hank whose presence, in spite of his joking, Detty felt was going to be very useful.

In the hiatus, she was able to turn her attention to the Polish house. Mara had little time available as it was taken up with working hard to get enough money to make the extended rebuild of the opera house a possibility. Detty had reported that she had done some research on external funding. Clearly, though, Mara's official status (and name) placed her in a better position than Detty to work on the actual contacting of official sources. In a rather ministerial manner, she had told Detty that, in the matter of the houses, she should go ahead 'but keep her informed'. Detty smiled to herself at this evidence that her young friend had donned, not only her official mantle, but had also adopted official language with enthusiasm. After Detty had outlined her modest but promising external funding resources, Mara finished by saying some of the preliminary drawings for the rebuild would be ready in about two weeks. Satisfied they adjourned for coffee at Cafe Daina.

She had made a start on the Polish houses. Over a very late lunch in 'The Woman in Armour' she had buttonholed Lev Ivanov, the architect and asked him whether his studio undertook domestic work. He said that yes, they did. Detty then tactfully explained that they needed architectural advice on the restoration of the *Dwor* and its cottage. She added hurriedly, in case she had been misunderstood, that she realised this would not be the sort of work that he himself would do. However perhaps he had a more junior colleague who might be interested in old Polish buildings and who could help them? He had smiled:

'I think that we might have just the chap. Jonas Rabikis who came originally from Vilnius in Lithuania is doing his doctorate here in Königshof at the university and practical work with us. His thesis is on domestic architecture during the Commonwealth. Would that do?'

'Sounds too good to be true.' Detty had said.

*

"I think that it's about time we involved the men in the restoration of the Sviatov houses, Frau Ministerin.'

Detty said as they were finishing coffee, 'Do you know David's timetable for the next couple of days? Marc is coming up tomorrow and I thought that we all might go down with them both to get their thoughts, before we start to brief our Lithuanian friend. It's a window of opportunity while the orchestra are wowing Berlin and before whirlwind Hank arrives.'

'I'll ring David now. I think he's got a short first team training then time with the youth team today but tomorrow may be possible.'

They then went their separate ways. Mara had meetings and Detty had to go to Krenek to teach. However, David confirmed that he could fetch Mark from the airport early on the morrow and they could all meet at Cafe Daina with the young Lithuanian before going on to Ziatov.

Detty finished her teaching and drove to Bialovsk. She stopped at Die Dame in Rüstung for a quick chat with Falk and a dish of his signature *Barszcz und Brotchen*.

It had been several days since any of them had seen the *Alhambra*, Detty decided to have a sneak preview of the progress, if any. As she approached the building, she was taken aback to hear the sound of a large tractor. She watched for a few minutes as the machine ploughed up the derelict waste ground in front of the building while a digger with the name of a well-known UK racing sponsor on its side collected the large concrete pieces, whilst the smaller bits and multiple brickbats were thrown into a skip by a huge black man stripped to the waist.

Eventually he noticed the watching Detty and came over to her,

'*Guten abend, meine Frau,*' he said in accurate German '*kann ich Sie hilfen?*'

'I was just wondering what was going on' she answered.

'Well, it's the boss, Herr Belken, he says that the old *kino* is going to be an opera house and you have to have nice flower beds in front of an opera house, don't you?'

'I suppose you do' said the gobsmacked Detty, thinking of Bayreuth. It crossed her mind to add 'or a marble fountain à la Metropolitan, New York,' but she didn't dare for fear one would be installed instantly, so she just added 'but you see I am with the opera company and came really to have a look inside again.

'However.' she added after a pause 'I am sure the flower beds will look very fine and it is very good of Herr Belken to take the trouble.' 'I am sure that it will be possible to look inside if you are involved and have identification, ma'am. The restoration site manager will be back from his lunchtime sandwich at any minute.'

He was as good as his word. The site manager arrived rapidly, greeted her courteously and said that there was no need for identification as he recognised her from the TV. With Detty, feeling like a movie star, they moved inside. For the second time Detty was astounded. The scarlet velour seats were clean if still showing a bit of wear. The stage was opened up – clear, clean and cavernous. Best of all the orchestra pit gleamed with black matt paint and stretched wide and deep across the stalls area and back under the stage. The *Alhambra* had come to life and almost justified its pretentious title. People had been working very hard and it showed. Detty stammered her thanks.

'Well' said the site manager 'the boss said it was important – priority, he said.'

'Is he in?' asked Detty 'I must thank him personally.'

'Well, he lives in Bialovsk – it's a big house on the road up the river but I believe he has gone to Berlin this week -some sort of concert he wanted to go to. Something about hearing our orchestra play.' She liked 'our orchestra.' 'Does he have a partner and might he/ she be at home?'

'Yes, he is married and yes, she hasn't gone to Berlin and is probably at home, they have two school age children.' said the puzzled site manager.

'Do you have her number?' He rummaged in a folder. 'Here it is.'

Detty pulled out her *Handy* and phoned the number. A woman's voice answered.

'Frau Belken, this is Bernadette von Ritter. I believe your husband has gone to Berlin to hear the Philharmonica play. No, no there is no problem – only I am so grateful for all the work he has got done at the *Alhambra* that I would like to organise a VIP ticket for him for the Philharmonica concert tomorrow and an invitation to the evening post tour party. Can you tell me where he is staying?'

She scribbled the address down. She then rang Regina, her secretary at Krenek.

Breathlessly she said. 'Can you find out where the orchestra are staying and try and leave a message for Luisa Stocken to 'phone me as soon as she is free. They are not playing today and they should have finished the morning rehearsal.'

A few minutes later, her *Handy* rang.

'Detty, it's Luisa. No, no I was just off to the *KaDeWe* shopping. Is there a crisis?'

'No, far from it. Belken, the CEO of AgriLiv, has organised miracles at the *Alhambra* but is in Berlin to listen to you. It would be great if you could get him a VIP ticket and an invitation to meet the orchestra after the concert. Is there the normal party? There is – wonderful. He is staying at the Westin Grand, *Friederichstrasse* – strangely enough I've stayed there – a long story.' 'Fine, I'll get our associate manager, Tom, on to it right away – he's only just been appointed and he's keen and wonderful. He can fix anything.' 'Fine. See you Wednesday.'

By mid-afternoon, Detty received a text message. 'All fixed. Found him. Coming to concert+party. Well done you! We will have to include a soprano solo in the next concert. Love L x'

Cheeky bitch,' exploded a delighted Detty, convulsed with laughter, somewhat startling the Site Manager who was still within earshot. 'Can we bring the orchestra down next Wednesday?' she asked him. 'Sure, that's what we've done it for. How many are there?' 'Give or take 80-90 maybe 100 – depends on whether they all come.'

He seemed rather surprised at the number. Detty started texting again to Louise.

'Rehearsal at *Alhambra* next Wednesday? Can your MOLA[9] folk find seats and desks and the other things we need? Were the parts for *Tristan* saved?' 'Hang on Detty. I'm an oboist not a magician but I'll get Evgeny, the orchestra librarian, to phone you and discuss it first-hand (I think that the parts were saved or most of them anyway). Fortunately, the library wasn't at the theatre – no room. As you probably know we have a house for auditions and individual instrument rehearsals behind the *FreiSenderLivonia's* building and we keep the library there. Some of the girls and boys might have taken the parts home to practise but that wouldn't be a problem. Detty was fascinated that Luisa always referred to her distinguished colleagues as '*die Mejaleis und Benjeis*' 'the girls' and boys' in the *platdeutsch* of the Königshof streets where she had grown up. Political correctness only went so far. Luisa was as good as her word, and Evgeny phoned as she was on the road back to Krenek. Fortunately, it was a stretch clear of the woods and she was able to pull off the road and get a reasonable signal. He thought all the *Tristan* parts were available as there was no particular reason why any player should have had left theirs in the pit at the time of the fire, but he would check. Regarding seats and stands, he thought that he could hire them OK and would attend to it as soon as the evening concert was over and he had sorted out

---

9 Major Orchestras Librarian Association

the hotel and transport home. Not for the first time Detty wondered at the complicated work of running an orchestra and the behind-the-scenes heroes and heroines who went completely unrecognised by the audiences. Even she, at one time, had thought that an orchestra librarian just put out the conductor's score and the parts and that was all. She now realised the myriad of difficult and often highly technical work, particularly about bowing etc, that came his or her way. On this occasion it appeared that only four orchestral parts were missing and the indefatigable Evgeny thought that he could photocopy them or if all else failed get them from the Internet.

Wednesday dawned sunny but very cold. They had moved to Krenek the night before and Detty had run round the lake to clear her head from sleep. She felt tense as she left Gianna and the children and set out for Bialovsk. She was the first at the *Alhambra* and she tucked herself into the Dress Circle. It had been agreed that the first rehearsal should be for the orchestra only. The orchestral sound was considered to be crucial. It was exciting but worrying. If there were major flaws in the sound, it would present a huge problem. First, there was no obvious alternative and then there was the considerable amount of effort and expense that AgriLiv had already incurred. She was woken from her reverie by a soft *hochdeutsch* voice beside her saying,

'Do you mind if I sit next to you?'

'No, of course not' she stammered. 'Perhaps I should introduce myself and say thank you.'

Detty was puzzled. Who was he and why did he need to thank her? He resolved her dilemma.

'Helmut Belchen, CEO of *AgriLiv*' her neighbour explained 'we haven't met but I gathered you organised the wonderful time that I had in Berlin, so thank you. It was a great thrill. They played magnificently and I was so proud.'

'I think that I should be thanking you' she broke into a broad smile 'your people have done wonders.'

'I just hope it works' he echoed her own thoughts.

'We will know in a few minutes.'

'Well, the stage looks fine' said another voice behind them.

'Herr Belken, meet Anna Strolz, our *Regisseurin*. Anna this is Helmut Belken who has produced this magical transformation.'

They chatted for a few minutes. Fortunately, the *Tristan* sets were minimal and Anna and her designer had already started on acceptable replacements and modifications but they were all holding their breath knowing that everything depended on how the sound was that morning. The orchestral players were trickling in chatting excitedly about their unfamiliar surroundings. A few minutes later Luisa stood, looked round the pit and played her oboe 'A' for the final tuning before picking up her cor anglais.

Helge took his place on the original, cleaned up, podium. '*Bitte Takt Eins, meine Damen und Herren*' He was very proper – no girls and boys for him this time, and he gave no clue that it wasn't just another rehearsal. But the old theatre came to life. The cellos whispered *pianissimo* before the sounding the famous chord and surging into the erotic crescendo of the *Vorspiel*. Helge went straight to the orchestral cue after the unaccompanied seaman's taunting song. Detty had to restrain herself not to sing.

'*Wer wagt mich zu höhnen?*'

Instead. she turned to her neighbour and gave a surreptitious thumbs up. He grinned happily. Helge completed Act 1 and they broke for coffee. He came up to Detty.

'How was it?' he asked slightly anxiously.

'To my ear it was fine' said Detty 'I think under today's conditions with an almost empty theatre it was on the 'wet', reverberant, side but that should allow for the absorbent effect of a full audience. It is probably worth getting the acoustic boys from the University down to have their say but I would be very happy to sing in it just as it is. The circles are shallow so we don't have a problem of cavernous under balcony spaces. I would suggest we get on and do the '*Tristan*' with it just as it is and then we may have a chance to do some fine tuning, if necessary, afterwards.'

At that moment Luisa joined them. 'How was it in front?' she asked.

'Very good' said Detty and then with a wicked grin added, mixing her languages to Luisa.

'*Bravissima vollendete Kunstlerin*!

Luisa for a moment looked puzzled then broke into a broad grin.

'You are getting your own back, *mein Irisch Kind,* aren't you?'

She then added 'I am glad to see you have been studying your score.' Thereby letting Detty know that she was familiar with the score direction that 'the English horn in *Tristan*, demands a very accomplished artist.'

Detty thought that she had to some extent evened the score after the cracks about soprano solos. It was great fun.

Anna and Mara had joined them.

'OK' said Detty 'All systems go. Anna, can you, they, manage the 'technicals' in a week?'

'We will give it our damnedest. It might be OK, the set is minimal and the stage is only fractionally smaller than the Hoftheatre. The guys from *AgriLiv* have done wonders with the basic electrics and our guys should be able to fix the rest. It probably won't be perfect but we have public goodwill and they realise that it's a miracle that it's happening at all.'

'I'll get the box office on to substitutions and if necessary, refunds.'

There was no need for any refunds and the touts were offering tickets for all four performances on their nefarious outlets for eye-watering prices. Mara's department colleagues had managed to get Bialovian school and college music students into the dress rehearsals. Briefly *Tristan und Isolde* had replaced the top German pop groups as the main talking point amongst the students.

*

The weather was crisp and wintery. Bialovsk had put on a show and was determined to make the most of its unusual opportunity to compete with Königshof. The rivalries of second cities were notorious. Detty arrived in good time for warm up and costume in her newly decorated and surprisingly spacious dressing room. She thought of Cork's rivalry with Dublin. Certainly, Bialovsk was going to make good use of its great evening to outsmart the capital. The cathedral and the *Rathaus* were floodlit on one side of the grass square. Just behind them, the front of Die Dame in Rüstung was also brightly lit and, on the flagpole above the inn sign of *Bradamante* and *Brünnhilde*, was displayed a huge green and white Chalice and Falcon flag. Detty reflected that the last time she had seen a flag flying over the old inn, it had been at half-mast for Liese and her companions' death. This, however, was a festive occasion and the town deserved it. Excited crowds were already gathering along the road to the theatre awaiting the President's and Tamara's arrival. She floated her final F sharp *'Lust'* drawing out her last bar and sank at Julia's feet waiting while the orchestra at last resolved the '*Tristan*' chord as the curtain slowly closed. There was a respectful silence until the applause broke with the curtain, old but newly cleaned, rising to reveal the full cast. After their own bows, Detty led Helge on stage to renewed cheers. Here had been an argument, Detty had said firmly. '*Maestro*, after all they have been through, I want the whole orchestra on stage for a curtain call, at least on the first night.'

'You can't do that, Bernadette, it's not the custom.' She knew it was a serious argument when Helge called her 'Bernadette' but she wasn't going to give way and entered full *Valkyrie* mode. Hank joined in the fray and said he also wanted the orchestra on stage. Finally, they won and led by Michael Storen up they came to receive their cheers. However, Detty hadn't finished her scheming, at the right moment she nudged Hank who turned into the orchestra ranks and emerged leading Luisa, cor anglais in hand and smart in her black trouser suit, reluctantly, out to join the other soloists in the front row. Rather out of character she was blushing but that wasn't visible to the audience. At her interview for *Der Osthansa Kurier*, Detty was asked about Luisa's unusual curtain call.

'It's only right' she said 'the cor anglais player is as much a soloist in *Tristan* as the singers. It was only right that the audience was given the chance to acknowledge Frau Professor Stocken's superb performance. I hope that it becomes the usual custom.'

There was also a comment about it in the FAZ in an article headed 'Phoenix in Livonia'. After the performance the five leading principal singers plus, Helge, Luisa, Michael, and Anna adjourned for supper in Die Frau, which was a mass of flowers, to renewed applause from the customers who had been in the audience.

8
THE PHOENIX

Her ashes new create another heir
As great in admiration as herself

SHAKESPEARE *HENRY V* ACT 5 SCI

They had a theatre and they had a *Tristan* – no mean feat but the main problem of the rebuilding of the Hoftheatre remained, to say nothing of the private enterprise of the Ziatov houses.

It was confirmed that the insurers would pay the cost of restoring the theatre as it was which left the €29.5 million to find for the improvements. The expatriate Livonians in the USA were launching extensive fund-raising activities including a concert tour for Hank and Detty which the best estimates came out at about $5 million. A similar tour was in the early planning stage for Germany but negotiations were on going and nobody was sure, how much if anything, it was going to raise. A corporate patron scheme open at home and abroad was launched together with a seat naming scheme at €5,000 to €10,000 a seat depending on the location in the theatre. This might raise €2m to €4m but this still left a long way to go. The quintet drove to Ziatov on a sparkling winter morning with a sprinkling of snow falling on top of the deep older snow. They called at Inspektor Kunz's little office to collect the keys which they had left there after their previous visit.

'A man came about the extra electrical wiring that you wanted done' said the Inspektor 'but I said that I had no instructions about letting anyone else in so I sent him away. He wasn't very pleased. I hope that I didn't do wrong.'

They looked at each other from one to one, each puzzled. After a pause Mara said what they were all thinking and, one by one, they shook their heads. Nobody had arranged for a contractor to visit the houses about new wiring.

Mara broke the silence.

'*Vielen dank,* Herr Inspektor, you did quite right. None of us has authorised entry to the houses. It might have been a genuine mistake but several of us have had problems with this sort of thing in the past so please continue your good work and don't give access to anyone without authorisation from one of us. Although your prompt action stopped this visitor entering the houses, I shall notify Frau Major Lopokova, the head of military intelligence, and ask her to send a surveillance expert to check the entire site particularly the outbuildings. I will get my office to let you know when the inspection is to take place. They will ring you and then you ring them back on this number. This is normal security.'

She took out a card from her handbag and handed it to Kunz.

A bit thoughtful, they left and went to the houses. The rest of the visit went well. Jonas Rabikis made a lot of notes and was entirely in tune with restoring the main *Dwor* without spoiling the traditional character. He would consult with the structural engineer about making the building safe, renew the timber staircases and rotten floors and consult about modern services and bathrooms. During all the discussion the unauthorized 'electrician' was always at the back of their minds. Tanya's surveillance team would have to go over the house and outbuildings with a fine-tooth comb.

On this visit, when they got to the cottage, Jonas suggested that it would be entirely possible to add two single ground floor rooms in character at the back to give an office and an extra reception room (or children's playroom thought Detty but knew that it was more than her life was worth to voice this.) It was good that the young Lithuanian was throwing himself into the task with enthusiasm. He said that he would have the preliminary drawings ready for their approval in two weeks. They left feeling reasonably content.

Back at Königshof, after a couple of days Tanya's team reported that they had examined all the buildings extensively and found no bugs or evidence of other intrusion. They hadn't moved all the wooden floor which lay with an airspace over the stone foundation layer but this would have been a huge task and there was anyway no evidence of recent disturbance. There were no more strange happenings and gradually it seemed that the unauthorized visit might have been a genuine mistake.

*

It was the beginning of spring. The snow was gradually clearing. On the conference room table of the Ministry the plans were laid out. They had got a long way with the restoration of the proscenium, the pit, and the stage but they could go no further until they knew if the great extension could go ahead. That was the problem, they had done everything that they could think of to raise money. They had sucked the well and the well-wishers dry. The US tours had raised $6m – more than they had hoped for as it included a windfall of broadcast rights because of Hank's home reputation. The seat naming had raised €3m. The football match produced another €3m. Sundry donors had chipped in €5m. The government had provided another €7m which was as much as they could without a political scandal in a cash strapped country recovering, albeit fairly well, from a disastrous civil war. Even this sum might produce opposition fury – they held their breath. They looked at each other round the table. Lev Ivanov, the architect, scanned the anxious faces. He had done his best. He had been conscious of the need to save every thaler from the start but his commission was to produce a fine, state of the art theatre and he had done his very best to find an impossible compromise. Santini, the engineer, the acoustic engineer Strauss, Mann, the surveyor and the others looked from one to the other. Detty stood at the back – silent. They all knew that it was not their shout. The responsibility was elsewhere. Neumarkt looked straight in front of him, deliberately not looking at anybody. After a long pause, he spoke.

'*Meine Damen and Herren*, I must and will take the responsibility for the decision that we will take this morning. As you all know after our most extreme efforts, we are still around €5 million short of our target. Failure to go ahead with the project will result in massive abortive costs and a political scandal but starting Phase Two and failing to complete will also result in a political scandal and damage the morale of those involved with the arts in this country. I will take responsibility. It is, of course, my job which is on the line if there is, as there very well might be, a disaster either way. However, much of the work and the huge amount of money that has already been raised has been due to another person.'

He paused and Detty, completely powerless, felt dreadful. It had been her idea; she had been too light-hearted about it and now her friends – and one very dear friend were looking down the barrel of a destructive gun. €5m was a huge sum, a small proportion of what they had already raised, to be sure but massive. They had no apparent way of closing the gap and it loomed threateningly over them. The sources had all run dry.

Neunarkt started to speak again. 'My responsibility, it is to be sure but Frau Ministerin I think you should make the decision. Please tell us what you think.' Mara stood silently for a minute which seemed an age. She was wrestling with her conflicting thoughts. It might be Neumarkt's responsibility but he had really made it hers. For a moment she hesitated then she spoke remarkably calmly:

'*Herr Minister, meine Damen and Herren*, I have been learning my English and they and the Americans have an expression '*we are between a rock and a hard place.*' Despite the problems that my *Chef* has outlined with both courses of action, I think that to cancel the second phase, as we have no further source of funding, would be the safest course of action and carry with it the lesser risk.'

She paused and looked round the sad faces gently nodding. Detty, embarrassed, wiped away a tear. Mara was speaking again:

'However, the courage that took us across the Fojn, subdued the *Zehnheiligenweg Weg* and besieged *Der Winterburg* was not the result of looking for the safest course of action. With your permission, Herr Minister, which you say I have for this decision, we go ahead. I instruct you, Herr Peyer to start work according to Herr Doktor Ivanov's plans for Phase Two of the reconstruction and extension of the Hoftheatre Königshof.'

Everybody started applauding, Mara held up her hand for silence.

'I don't think that I need to remind you, *meine Damen und Herren*, that you may be applauding prematurely – we will see.'

It was a drained Mara and an almost equally drained Detty who crossed back to the Hansehaus. When they had summoned up the strength to deal with bed time, Niki seemed at least briefly to have abandoned his trumpeter's ambitions, and with the help of Gianna, they had sat down to *Abendbrot*. Nicklaus raised a single eyebrow looking at his daughter. She just said three words:

'We go ahead.' He nodded gravely. 'Hans rang me and said he was going to leave the decision to you. I thanked him for phoning and said that of course it was entirely up to him.'

'Did I make the right choice?'

'We will see,' he paused for some minutes then added quietly, 'I would have expected nothing less from an Oblov.'

Equally quietly, Mara said. 'Thank you, *Vati*.'

Detty decided to chip in,

'What she won't tell you, is how well she did it. She had us all on the edge of our seats,'

Nicklaus laughed loudly. 'Well, she has a friend who is a *prima donna* you know. She must have learnt.

9
THE PRECIPICE

wie im Traum ich ihn trug,
wie meine Wille ihn wies,
stark und schön
steht er zur Schau;[10]

WAGNER: *DAS RHEINGOLD* SC 2

The work went ahead but it gave no pleasure to Mara and Detty and the time dragged. Their mood wasn't helped by the campaign from the opposition press, with the *Livonian Democrat* running banner headlines wondering how the junior minister in charge of the Hoftheatre rebuild was able to spend large sums upon her riverside 'villa' in Ziatov, when the state clearly could not afford a decent rebuild of a national monument. This contradicted their previous stance that the opera house project was a wasteful indulgence but they had conveniently forgotten that. Despite her determination to be a tough politician, these comments hurt and made Mara more miserable. First, was the obvious unfairness

---

10 As my dreams designed,
    as my will determined
    It now appears strong and fine

of describing her run-down cottage at Ziatov as a 'villa' but more important, it declared far and wide their intention to move there.

On a brighter side, one morning *The New York Times* devoted a two-column article on the Phoenix of Königshof together with helpful bank details for making donations. Detty was pretty sure that a certain American tenor had called in a few favours to get this printed. It raised $750,000, the bulk coming from one anonymous contributor.

After this the campaign quietened down and there was only the sound of excavators and bulldozers carrying out Mara's instructions to begin phase two, which began to sound like a funeral dirge. The background noise was a reproach to the small anxious group wondering how the hell they were going to pay for it. They were facing disaster and day by day the abyss yawned ever wider in front of them. Detty was aware that Mara was looking more and more drawn, anxious and grey. She worried desperately for her and felt it was all her own fault for pressing for the upgrade. And yet, and yet, deep down she still felt this was a once in a lifetime chance which should not be missed. She wracked her brains – where on earth could they find the €3.5 million now still needed to complete.

Mainly Mara was silent, often going out early to bury herself in her constituency business. One day she stayed to have breakfast and announced calmly but sadly:

'We have only enough money to meet the bills and wages for ten days. I have tried the bank again but they told me bluntly that they were sure the project was going to fail and they could not waste any more money on it,'

After this bleak announcement, Mara left miserably for her office.

Gianna had gone back to Italy for a week with her parents. On an impulse Detty dressed up the children in their warmest clothes and bundled them into the lift. Reaching the ground floor,

Falk was on duty and called out. 'Do you want a hand, Frau Komturin?'

'No thanks, Falk, it's a nice morning, I thought that I would take the children for a walk.'

It amused her to be addressed as 'Commander' when she was, like hundreds of other mums, just performing her domestic maternal duties. She got the double buggy out from the back store and prepared to get the children into it. Reasonably enough, Niki, who was on half term, said that he was too old for the double buggy. He insisted on walking. They then slipped out of the back door of the Hansehaus. The melting snow had been cleared from the footpath although it had frozen again overnight and she had to guide the heavy buggy over the resulting skating rink with care whilst keeping an eye on Niki slipping around in the frozen snow. Struggling a bit, she eventually got them round the square into the Cathedral close. As she pushed the buggy, the children were unusually silent taking in the still snow-covered surroundings. At least temporarily, Niki's trumpet ambition was still in abeyance. She thought about Mara's gloom and anxiety and the overriding problem causing it. The prospect of having to abandon the great opera house project when it was ninety per cent completed, was very depressing. The abortive work, the waste and the inevitable storm of criticism would be far worse than the present recurring headlines in the *Livonian Democrat* which indicated that they were closing in for the kill. This might even bring down the government as well as indelibly tarnishing the reputation of the Oblovs.

In addition, there was still the nagging worry about the real nature of the unauthorised 'electrician' who had tried to gain access to the Ziatov properties in the owners' absence. The four of them had hoped to move to Ziatov quietly but their intended move was now all over the national press in the most unfortunate light. Detty hesitated under the entrance arch with its supplication to the Virgin, *Mater Dei Ora pro Nobis*. Then muttering to herself 'we need her prayers'. She hesitated at the great west door before making up her mind and adding 'suffer the little children'. She turned resolutely and pushed the buggy through the door and into the nave.

The cathedral seemed deserted and she quietly pushed the buggy up towards the choir and the High Altar. Moving to the side she lit three candles, one for Liese Zahnsdorf, one for Mara and the last one was she supposed for the suffering theatre which was so very dear to her. She was just lighting the theatre one when her *Handy* went off with a loud squeal. Feeling very guilty that she hadn't turned it off before entering the cathedral she just suppressed an oath, remembering where she was. She looked round and heaved a sigh of relief that there was still nobody in sight. She thought to herself – the damage is done now I might as well answer it. The screen said 'Ännchen' and Detty smiled that Mara still used her code name from the civil war.

'Hi Detty, I've just had an odd text message. It was from Helmut Belchen, CEO of *AgriLiv* saying that he would like to talk to me as soon as possible. Could I ring him to fix an appointment when I could see him? I rang back. First, it was a genuine call (I needed to check that), second, he said that he would like to meet with me as soon as possible, so I suggested this afternoon at 4 pm at my office. He then said that if possible, he would like you to be there too. So, I said that I would ask you. Are you free?'

'Yes, Niki's at play group this afternoon and Lotte, Falk's wife will look after Liese – it was already arranged so I could go shopping.'

*

Helmut Belchen, immaculate in a dark grey suit, thanked them both for sparing the time to see him.

'I know you are both very busy so I will come straight to the point. If you are able, I would like to talk to you about your opera house.'

Detty's heart sank. There must be a problem with the *Alhambra*. Perhaps Belchen had had a change of heart and they would no longer be allowed to use it. All manner of catastrophic thoughts flooded through her mind.'

'It's your opera house not ours,' she muttered.

'No, no, I'm sorry. I didn't make myself clear.' said Belchen 'it's not the *Alhambra*, I am talking about, it is the Hoftheatre. I hope that you will forgive my impertinence for interfering. You see I happened to be sitting next to Lev Ivanov at a *Hansa Stiftung* dinner last week and he was talking about the project. We talked a bit about the finance problems then the design. Before he finished, he said that although the design was complete as it stood, the foundations allowed for one or two more levels at the back above the rehearsal stage and the ballet studios. These extra floors could be added later if required. That set me thinking. You may or may not know that AgriLiv has a smaller fisheries division as well as the much larger land based one. Although our major processing and storage facilities need to remain at Bialovsk, the Board have thought for some time that it would make sense to move the head office to the capital where both the branches can, to some extent, be united. This would produce economies, ease communications, and increase the prestige of our rapidly developing enterprise. To come straight to the point, would you and your committee consider granting us a lease to build our head offices over your rehearsal stage and dance studio? We realise that this is a lot to ask and that it is a prestigious situation. It would add a lot to the profile of the company to have a head office in such a prominent situation. Of course, we would expect to pay the going rate.'

There was a long pause then Mara broke into a smile.

'I can see no possible objection' she said 'however you will appreciate that the final answer must come after our board had considered it and the lawyers and architect have had their say. If you could possibly put an outline proposal in writing I guarantee that we will consider it without delay.'

'You will have it by the end of the week. The preliminary work has already been done.'

He was as good as his word. The draft proposal came in on time. The Board accepted it subject to terms and conditions and it was passed to finance and the lawyers. They all held their breath. They had to wait for ten days. Then one morning Mara, at breakfast, got the scrambled phone call. Her expression was enough but, very properly, she said nothing except:

'*Vati*, may I have the downstairs conference room here for a meeting tomorrow morning at 10 am? My own office is not big enough.'

'I think that will be possible. Assume yes, but I will ask Petra to check with admin to make sure that it doesn't clash with anything.'

Promptly at 10 am the following day they gathered – the whole board, Helmut Belchen, his secretary and the AgriLiv finance director. Detty represented the opera company. It didn't take long. Mara with remarkable calmness announced that they were there to agree to the addition of 4,000 square metres of office and administration space to be added on two storeys behind the fly tower and above the ballet facilities to be leased to Agricoop Livonias Gmbh (the Company) for an initial ten years with an option on both sides to renew. The additional building and equipping of this accommodation were to be at the expense of the Company who had agreed a rent of €6.3m to be paid annually in advance with immediate effect from the signing of the contract.

Equally calmly, she then said. 'I shall now put the proposal to the vote – Board members only of course, please. Those in favour.

A group of hands went up.

'Those against,' There were none. 'The motion is carried unanimously. I shall now sign the contract on behalf of the Department and then perhaps Dr Belchen will sign on behalf of the Company.'

Signatures duly made; it was time for congratulations all round.

'Just one more thing, Frau Ministerin, if you would be kind enough to let our Finance Officer have the relevant bank details the first payment can be in your account before the close of business today. There is no point in delaying.'

'Of course, could you please see to it straight away, Anna?' addressing her secretary.

'*Sofort. Frau Ministerin*'

Detty smiled inwardly at her little schoolgirl friend being addressed so respectfully with the dignities of her office. She had earned it. Then her thoughts came back to Belchen. What a man – he knew just how urgent it was but had dressed it up as normal routine. As she went down the stairs behind him after the meeting, she whispered to him. 'You are an unusual sort of guardian angel.'

'I can't think what you mean, Frau Komturin' but with a slight smile he added 'but it was a good concert and party – thank you.'

As they left the Hansehaus to get into a taxi for Golabki for lunch, Detty was sure that the diggers, concrete mixers and dumpers across the road on the Opera house site had changed from a minor into a major key, David was waiting for them at the restaurant.

'How was it? he said, then looking at his wife's face he added 'I don't think that I need to ask.'

Detty got out her *Handy* and rapidly typed a message to Marc in Ingolstadt.

> *wie im Traum ich ihn trug,*
> *wie meine Wille ihn wies,*
> *stark und schön*
> *steht er zur Schau;*
> *hehrer, herrlicher Bau!*[11]

She showed it to Mara and David before pressing send. 'Perhaps it is a bit premature, but not much.'

'What's the quotation?' asked Mara.

'*Das Rheingold, Wotan* gazing at *Valhalla*.'

---

11 As it came in my dreams
    As my will saw it
    Strong and fine
    On view to all
    Sublime, lordly pile

10
DER WONNE SAAL

Alles die es möglich gemacht haben

Vote of Thanks

It was finished. After all the traumas, disappointments, disagreements, there it stood. The new fly tower soared magnificently into the lowering Baltic sky. The two side stages, the back building with its third stage, the studio theatre, the scenery workshop. The Green Room had its state-of-the-art Italian coffee machine ruled over by Olga, the presiding genius of the Staff Canteen, rejoicing in her new palatial premises. The dance studios and rehearsal rooms stretched out the back. For two floors above the dance premises, the Königshof head offices of *Agricoop Livonias*, which had at the eleventh hour made it possible, were all finished. All that was lacking was music – and that would come.

There had been long arguments far into several nights discussing how the re-opening was to be celebrated. The huge work had been completed in just over two years – a massive achievement, and by the end of September the final work on the services had been completed and the theatre handed over to the in-house technical team. Everybody involved held their breath until Alphonse Peyer, the director of works came back to Mara and her Committee and announced with a smile from ear to ear,

'Yes, Frau Ministerin, we will be ready to let you mount an opening gala by 6th December, the Feast of Sankt Nicklaus, our national day. You will have rehearsal time Frau Komturin but I suggest that you don't make it too complicated,'

'*Vielen dank,* Herr Doktor.'

All that remained was to fix the number of shows, the actual days, and the programmes. It was agreed that there was to be a week of gala performances with variable starting times to suit young and old. First, there would be the formal opening Gala with the President and all local and foreign guests, the programme was left to Detty. She was determined that the only appropriate first music to be heard in the arisen theatre was Elisabeth's greeting to the Hall of Song. Thinking more deeply she realised that they could do the whole of Act 2 of *Tannhäuser* – semi staged, as they had no sets and anyway the *tecnik* was not ready for a fully staged performance. Otherwise, it was ideal – plenty of tenor, bass, and baritone solos– great chorus pieces and sparkling orchestration. This would be Part One – now for Part Two. Here she had a stroke of luck. Trudi Meyer had already been booked, before the fire, to accompany Hank in *Die Schöne Müllerin*. Detty phoned Trudi's agent in Munich and asked him to get Trudi to call back. The call duly came as Detty was savouring the coffee from the new machine in the Green Room.

'Thanks for calling. How do you feel about Rachmaninov 2 or 3 for our gala opening?'

'I would love to do either' said the ever-enthusiastic Trudi 'Is it only one performance?'

'I wondered about three – the first, third and fifth, with Eugenia Provoska, the key board prize winner from the College, doing the *Emperor* on the second, fourth and sixth.'

'Fine by me. We will go with the Rachmaninov third, if Helge agrees.'

'You are a devil for punishment,' laughed Detty.

*

The technical team had left the house and some stage lights on for an extended test while they went to lunch. There was only one guardian technician high in the new lighting box. Wide-eyed and alone, Detty passed security and entered the theatre. She saw it then for the first time without the clutter – all the builders' rubbish had been, like magic, cleared away. She climbed up on to the stage with its state of the art revolve via the rehearsal walkways, already laid out for the opening Gala rehearsals, and looked out over the huge new pit and into the auditorium. Suddenly, it came over her. For the moment, she was oblivious of the magnificent technical building stretching behind her. She just saw her auditorium, her temple, and it looked, cleaner and brighter to be sure, but as it had been when she had sung *'Abscheulicher'* on the most emotional day of her life. Suddenly, on compulsion, she knelt in the middle of the deserted stage and prayed aloud. She then still on her knees, sang, on an impulse, not *'Abscheulicher,'* but *'All'mächt'te Jungfrau hör mein Flehen!'*[12] to the empty theatre. It seemed a correct vote of thanks for the achievement after the dark days following the fire. She suddenly remembered the solitary technician up in the lighting box, felt embarrassed and wondered if anyone elsewhere in the building had heard her.

Her last fight had been the strangest. She had been faced with a determined looking Mara.

'My father will do the opening,' she said.

'Of course,' said Detty, not really concentrating,

'The renewed theatre is to be called 'The National and Hof Theatre'.

'Fair enough' said Detty her mind elsewhere.

'The two auditoria are also to be named. The studio is to be, with his agreement, the Schliessen Theatre.'

'What about the main space?' asked Detty, absently.

'It is to be named the O'Neill Theatre.'

'No, No, No!' screamed Detty, stamping her foot like an infant 'it is completely inappropriate. This theatre belongs to the public, the nation, everybody – not me. It can't be named after me.'

---

12 Almighty Virgin, hear my prayer
    Tannhäuser Act 3

'OK, Detti, then you can go before the entire Council of Ministers and the President, a few weeks before the next election, and tell them that they have all made fools of themselves. In addition, I should tell you, there was a computer ballot which we kept from you, of a thousand random citizens with five name choices and ninety-one per cent voted for this title.'

It stopped Detty in her tracks. 'What did the remaining nine per cent choose?' she said, suddenly having regained her sense of humour and laughing,

'They were scattered among the remaining choices.'

'Nine sane people amongst the ship of fools.'

'Perhaps you would like me to forward that quote to *The Livonian Democrat*? Or perhaps better would be a shot of the heroine of Livonia behaving like a naughty child and having her bottom smacked by *die Ministerin Oblova Senska.*'

'You and whose army?' Detty towered over her friend, adding 'Marc doesn't go in for that sort of thing.'

'You'd be surprised at the strength of small packages. "Though she be but little, she is fierce!"'

'Your Shakespeare is coming on, Frau Ministerin! OK, as usual, you are right.' Detty had said at last, 'and you are telling me that I am being childish. I do have one request, however. I accept the name as long as long as there is a plaque, prominent on the outside front of the portico, saying the following:

This theatre, which has arisen from the ashes, is dedicated by all the free people of Livonia in honour to those who have suffered so much and our heroic dead.

'It would be difficult to refuse you that,' said Mara thoughtfully 'and you will take part in the opening ceremony?'

'OK. Keep me away,' Detty, who laughing, had recovered her composure, 'I won't let anyone else sing the National Anthem.'

*

In the event she didn't sing it. She stood watching from her luxurious new dressing room window high in the refurbished theatre wing as the President's motorcade arrived and The Swans Guard of honour played the National Anthem from beside the dedication plaque mounted as she had requested. As the outside band finished, she relaxed and waited until after a time, when the audience had settled, the Assistant Stage Manager came over the intercom. *'Frau O'Neill, funfzehn Minuten bitte.'* How often had she heard that in various theatres?' she thought, but it was still always exciting and more so tonight of all nights.

It had been agreed that Hank should sing the name part in *Tannhäuser* on the first evening and then hand over to Lev for the other nights whilst he concentrated on *Die Schöne Müllerin* in his sold-out eponymous studio theatre. She waited for the:

'Frau O'Neill zur Buhne, bitte'

and then, tingling, she made the short walk through the still paint-smelling flats into the wings, waiting for her semi-staged entry cue, while Helge's orchestra surged from the new pit below her. Then she was off peeling her greeting to her 'beloved Hall'. It had been a difficult taskmistress but now it was all worth it. She adored it. The orchestra and chorus were great and her fellow soloists weren't half bad either, she decided. Walter Liebig who seemed prepared to do anything that they demanded at Königshof sang a magisterial *Wolfram* and Hank was as magnificent as ever as the delinquent troubadour. How lucky they were to have an international star cast on hand for the opening. Her voice soared over the men in the final *'nach Rom'*, She then took her curtain calls with a smile of pure joy.

After that she dashed off like a teenager to change, with the help of her faithful dresser, Elena, into her burgundy Lanoure model with its fabulous, ruched skirt, before hurtling into the staff box to hear Trudi's Rachmaninov. After that Julia Kitze closed the proceedings with Gluck's *'Chiamo il mio ben cosi'*. Julia's voice had matured and a glorious stream of dark contralto sound filled the new theatre.

Even as the celebrations were going on, Detti was still concerned with the lack of repertory for the new season. It had been impossible to arrange contracts until they knew that the theatre was definitely going to be ready. As soon as Julia had finished and acknowledged her applause,

Detty shot out of the box and down to Julia's dressing room knocking hard before going in.

She didn't beat about the bush:

'Congratulations – that was fabulous, Julia, now then do you want to do the whole thing? Do you know it all?'

Julia looked surprised and then produced a strangled 'Yes' and 'yes' then 'when?'

'I thought the end of January, if we can cast the other parts. Is that OK?'

'Sure.'

*

The snow was falling again, gently visible, through the long new picture windows looking down from above the portico over the forecourt to the square below. The invited guests filed into the post-performance reception in the grand hall which had been opened up from the old bars and stretched right over the top of the portico. Once the guests were all lined along the walls, the trumpeters of the Philharmonica appeared in front of the Grand Tier boxes, stood to one side, and played again the *Entry of the Guests* trumpet fanfare from the Second Act of *Tannhäuser* that they had just heard. The curtains at the back of the boxes were pulled aside and Mara wearing a long dark olive-green skirt with a cream silk blouse with high ruff collar came forward. Detty in burgundy was slightly behind on one side and Trudi in the black silk dress in which she had played, on the other. Behind them came Helge, then the other principals and chorus masters. All took proffered glasses. Vigorous applause broke out. Mara, tiny but authoritative, took another pace forward and motioned for silence.

'Herr Präsident, Herr Minister Präsident, *meine Damen and Herren*. I will be very brief and only propose two toasts. The first echoes the greeting in song so wonderfully sung by Komturin O'Neill a short time ago, – a bit modified – *Dich, teure Halle, grüss wir wieder, froh grüss wir dich, geliebter Haus!*[13] Raise your glasses to our wonderful arisen *geliebter*

---

13 You, beloved hall we greet again, joyful we greet you, beloved house

Haus. After mutters of approval and the drinking of the toast, Mara continued. 'Now my second toast *Alle, die es möglich gemacht haben – herzliche Dank.*' 'To you all who have worked so hard – all who have made it possible.'

She raised her glass again followed by all the gathering.

After a short pause, Max Schäfer, smiling broadly, called for silence again.

'Herr Präsident, Frau Ministerin, *Meine Damen und Herren,* It is not usual for you, Herr Präsident, to fall short or shirk your obligations, however, for some unaccountable reason,' he said with a smile, 'you have asked me to propose this vote of thanks in your place, I can't think why. First, on behalf of everyone, I wish to thank Komturin O'Neill who, as always for this country, has worked tirelessly on behalf of the restoration project. However, the chief vote of thanks from me, everyone here and the whole community who are grateful for the re-birth of our precious national monument must go to the *Direktorin* of the restoration project. I ask you to raise your glasses to die Frau Ministerin Tamara Nicolaevna Oblova Senska. Massive applause and the clinking of glasses followed.

After a considerable pause Mara again signalled for quiet:

'Herr Minister Präsident, Thank you. My wonderful footballer husband, David, has taught me a useful English expression which is suitable for this occasion 'Team Effort.' It is my prayer that this theatre will still be sending music here and all over the country when none of us are still alive to witness it.'

Applause followed with everybody crowding round Mara, almost burying her in the bustle. Later that night, the official cars arrived. Everybody fetched their thick coats and went out into the bitter snowy evening, just pausing to look back at the elegant old floodlit facade and the new proudly floodlit fly tower reaching massive towards the jet-black sky. Later that week, the other performances. booked out, were reeled off as the snow continued to fall.

There was one more charming interlude when Mara and Detty were invited for the official opening of the new premises for the Ballet Academy attached to the new theatre complex. With ceremony the director presented them both with Honorary Fellowships of the Academy in recognition of the work that they had done to realise their splendid new premises. Detty who spoke her thanks first said that she greatly admired the staggering artistry of dancers, but that she hoped there was no practical part for her envisaged in the award. If anyone doubted her lack of dance ability, she would refer them to her (joint) performance as a *Rheintochter* at Bayreuth which she assured her distinguished hosts resulted in a lot of bruises but not much dancing talent. Perhaps, however, her blushes would be saved, she said, as danseurs nearly two meters tall were, to say the least, unusual. She did point out that, at a modest level, her companion, Mara, had danced. The latter then forcefully claimed that she also had been passed over by Terpsichore. Together though they said how touched and honoured they were.

*

Detty had one more task before they left for Oberdorf. She had been made a Governor of St Paul's School at Sovils for her support after the terrible explosion. In this capacity she agreed to take part in the Christmas concert. She sang solo verses in the choir favourites, Es *ist ein Ros'entsprungen*, *O Tannenbaum*, *Alle Jahre wieder* and *Oh du Fröhliche*, and at the end they together they sang a rousing *Adeste fideles*. Her first verse was solo then she listened attentively to the choir. The girls and boys of the soprano section swirled into a glorious descant over the last verse which was a complete surprise to Detty as she had not heard it sung like that since Oxford.

'You did that really beautifully,' she announced after they finished, 'Can I book you to come and do it next year in the restored Hoftheatre?'

They laughed thinking that she was joking.

'No, I am absolutely serious,' she said, 'the restoration was too late to arrange a *Weinachts Fest* this year. However, we will do one next year and I really want your choir to take part.'

The Head of Music admitted afterwards over *Gluhwein* and *Stollen* in the staff lounge that the choir had worked hard at the unfamiliar descants as a compliment to their distinguished visitor.

*

It was going to be a hard winter. There was nothing more practical that she could do. It only remained to bundle the increasing von Ritter entourage into the car and head through the snow towards Germany and Oberdorf. Detty though had a problem. She now had the official rank of programme director for the opera. Because there had been no certainty about the date of completion of the Hoftheatre, there was still the problem of lack of repertory. The *Alhambra* had been booked for a Christmas *Hansel und Gretel* and the ballet company were already prepared to do a *Casse Noisette* also at Bialovsk. However, bookings for the main theatre were scanty. It was far too late to book international artists. As she gazed at the snow, she had an idea. As well as Julia's *Orfeo,* they would do *Die Zauberflote* with their rich supply of emerging artists. They were short of basses but most of the other parts could be double cast. It would be a tremendous idea to let the youngsters do the first staged show in the new theatre. She had already mentally pencilled in Leif Rohren as *Papageno*. He was the young baritone who had been runner up in the first college voice competition a couple of years before. Detty knew that, although he had a good voice and fine stage presence, like many newly fledged professionals he was not finding it easy to get work. If Walter was still available and could do it, it would be good to have him as *Sarastro* and anchorman. It would be great for the youngsters to perform with an internationally famous artist. Immediately she fished out her *Handy* and phoned Walter. She found him in Paris preparing to do five *König Markes* in the first half of January and left a message for him to ring back when he had a free moment. Half an hour later he rang saying that he had a *Wotan* in Berlin during March then was free for April. He had wanted to go home to ski but he could put that off.

'When do you want to stage Die *Zauberflote?*'

'April will do fine.'

'OK then, I hope that I can still get that low. I do more baritone parts these days but I'll give it a go if I must. Why don't you ask Dieter Tinsel. He has a lower tessitura than mine and he seems to be back on form after making a success of *Waldner*. I'll do *The Speaker* and direct, if you like.'

'Good idea, I'll ask Dieter and let you know.'

'If that doesn't work out, I'll try *Sarastro* but it really is too low. If I have to, I might be able to do it. I think that the bottom notes are still there. I am blessed with a good range. I'll try it out in the bath just in case.'

*

The snow continued to fall and the drifts got higher. They took the south route through Poland and Prague. All along it was slow going with Marc occasionally muttering oaths in military German as he struggled to keep even the jeep on the half-cleared road. They stopped, still in Poland at a mountain village in Silesia just before the Czech border. The children were bundled into bed and Marc and Detty sat down for a welcome meal of *pirogi*, venison and local vegetables while the nascent *Odra* thundered over the rocks into the valley. Their Polish host was very concerned and helpful. With a twinkle in his eye, he said he would even forgive Marc for being German as he had an Irish wife and such delightful children.

It was just as cold the following day but bright and sunny. Everybody was travel-weary and the children had had enough, as with relief they passed through the village and up to the *Schloss* to be greeted by a beaming Hildegard. Inevitably she took more notice of Liese and Niki than the adults. Eventually she round got to saying that Herr Max and Frau Sophie were both still at work but knew they had arrived and would be back soon. The *Altes Herren Haus* was heated and ready for them but that Frau Sophie had said that perhaps they would like to have dinner all together first and stay at the *Schloss* at least for the first night. Detty looked dubiously at Liese and Niki but the excitement of arriving seemed to have banished all tiredness. As the children warmed themselves on hot milk, Max and Sophie arrived almost together.

Max immediately opened a bottle of champagne and proposed a toast to the restored theatre which he had read about in the FAZ.

'After all,' he said, 'It is not every lucky man who has an opera house named after his *Schiegertochter*[14].'

---

14 Daughter-in-law

'It's not the whole opera house only one auditorium,' protested Detty.

'That seems to me to be enough,' said the irrepressible Max.

At that moment Detty's phone rang.

'Sorry, I ought to have turned it off' she said disentangling the phone from her capacious travelling handbag and casually looking at the screen. Suddenly she was more interested.

'It's Walter' she said 'probably wants to wish us *Frohe Weihnachten*. Do you mind if I take it.'

'Who's Walter?' asked Sophie.

'Just another of your daughter-in-law's male admirers,' said Marc grinning.

'He is just a greatly esteemed colleague – bass baritone – with a sense of humour.' Detty protested and pushed the 'accept' button.

'Hello' she said.

'I'm driving down from Berlin on the 21st to spend Christmas at home in *Kirchsee* and shall be coming near to *Oberdorf*.'

Detty pressed the 'voice' button so the others could hear.

'My neighbour at *Tegensee* carves beautiful wooden animals and I've got a couple for the children for Christmas which I collected the last time I was home. As I'm passing, I wondered whether I might drop them in.'

'You'll be coming down the A9 then?'

Detty looked at Sophie who gave her a thumbs up. 'Yes, of course you can come in and see us on 21st for *Mittagessen*– it's just a short trip from 31 – the Berg junction –just over the border in God's own country.' Detty made a face at Marc.

. 'Your Sat Nav will take you straight here – of course I forgot for the moment that you are also a Bavarian – a member of the clan – you will be amongst allies – will you sing the *Bayernhymne* before lunch or leave it for the *Liederabend* afterwards?'

'Are you sure you wouldn't like my version of '*O soave fanciulla?*' Detty burst out laughing.

'I tried *Mimi* in the car after we met- it was horrible.'

'*Carissima*, nothing that you sing could ever be horrible.'

'See what I mean?' Marc mouthed to his parents.

'We expect the *Bayernhymne* sometime, if not on the doorstep. See you on 22nd – Ciao.'

She rang off then and had to explain her first meeting with Walter. 'We thought that he might be a disaster but realised that by good fortune we had the talent and loyalty of a great singer but I have a surprise request for him after the port.'

On the 21st, after a leisurely breakfast there was a disturbance in the carriageway in front of the *Schloss*. Then from the doorstep a powerful and tuneful bass voice was singing, not the *Bayernhymne*, but the more seasonal *Tannenbaum*. Hildegard, although familiar of course with the Christmas carol, was not expecting it in this context and looked thoroughly startled.

'There's a gentleman singing very loudly in *die Vorhalle* he's by himself and doesn't sound like *die Sternsinger* from the village' she announced.

'Don't worry Hildegard that will be a colleague of mine who is coming to visit us' reassured Detty.

'Let me go and let him in.' 'Ach, I thought he had a good voice and that explains it.'

'You are a sound judge – he is one of the best bass-baritones in Europe.'

Walter was introduced all round and they toasted each other with the family *sekt*. Walter, after suitable protests, was persuaded that he should stay the night, enjoy *Abendbrot* and not have to complete his long drive after the constraints on his meal. There was a lot of banter and Walter struggled to control his glass of *sekt* with a young von Ritter sitting on each knee while he told them he was a friend of *Der Weihnachtsmann* twitching his moustache. At last, they were able to sit down to pike quenelles and venison.

At the end of the meal Detty proudly produced a decanter of late bottled vintage port Taylor 1983:

'This was a present from Ben Charles, he sent us six bottles apologising that it wasn't vintage but he said he realised that it would have to travel.'

'Who is Ben Charles?' said Sophie again looking puzzled.

'He is a leading light in Nutt Bros the St James Vintners in London' said Detty.

'And another of your admirers?' said Max with a twinkle in his eye.

'Just an old friend from Oxford.' said Detty.

'You may wonder that I get a look in,' said Marc smiling, 'but the contact with a leading wine firm can come in useful.'

'I am sorry but I would like to talk shop for a couple of minutes with Walter,' said Detty, 'I must trap him while I can and realise that delay may be fatal so my apologies, but here goes – Walter what are your plans for November and December after next?'

'What's coming now? – I know,' he said fishing out a diary from a deep pocket, 'you want me to sing *Rodolfo* for you debut as *Mimi*.'

'Not exactly but you are on the right lines.' He looked at his diary. 'I have four *Amfortas* in Munich at the beginning of November twelve month. After that I told the agent not to book anything until the New Year as I thought that you might want me for the *Nicklaus fest* as I seem to be a bit of a fixture.'

'You are a thought reader' exclaimed Detty 'are you sitting comfortably?' He smiled. 'Come on – what's coming next?'

'Well, you know that we have not been able to book soloists far ahead because we didn't know if the theatre would be ready, so we just arranged two ballets, a *Fledermaus* and another *Hansel and Gretel* which we could do at Bialovsk or at Königshof, if it was ready, and cast from locals. However now the theatre is ready and we will have already done a few productions to see if there are any snags before next winter.'

'Come on – I can't stand the suspense,' said Walter.

The port circulated and the men refilled their glasses and so, after hesitating and deciding that she wasn't singing for a bit – at least not professionally – did Detty.

'How do nine *Wotans*, strike you?' she said looking at Walter anxiously at last.

'Oh, is that all?' grinned Walter, 'I thought that you had something much more difficult in mind. That's OK but I do have one question. I assume that I shall be kissing you to sleep otherwise I won't agree.'

Detty blushed 'Yes, I hope so. I can do *Siegfried* and I am quite well on with *Die Walküre* but I've got a lot of work to do on *Götterdämmerung* and I need Eileen and Haydn to help. We have home-grown singers for *Siegmund*, *Erda* and *Waltraute*. We might have a *Sieglinde* and *Hagen* from the College although both are rather inexperienced. Provisionally, we thought that it would be better to audition for a senior outsider for *Fricka*, rather than overload Julia, promising as she is. She'll be a splendid *Erda* and couldn't do *Fricka* as well. We need to audition for the others but there are some good candidates still available, I think. But I wanted to try and nail you first. I will get Karl Staufen to contact your agent re fees and expenses – I hope that we can still afford you,' she smiled, 'but please bear in mind that we are on a reasonable financial footing now so don't be too charitable.'

'You know what I said last time, Detti, I have no objection to being paid, although for you lot, I would do it for nothing. After the expression that I have learnt from the English it will be "mates' rates" – you know my debt to Eileen, Helge and you. Do they use that expression in Ireland?'

'I have heard it; you are very generous.'

'Who is the lucky girl then?' said Marc laughing, 'kissed to sleep by Walter and kissed awake by Hank. Where do I come in?'

'You have already taken me over the hill and I whispered, "I will" some time ago and look at the result,' she waved towards the children playing unconcernedly in the adjacent room 'anyway there is always *Götterdämmerung* to follow.

Mich musste
der Reinste verraten,
dass wissend würde ein Weib![15]

---

15 The purest of men
    Had to betray me
    That a woman might become wise!
    Götterdämmerung 3iii

Now that is enough shop and time for a concert party.'

They spent the rest of the afternoon and early evening with a mixture of Christmas carols, folk songs and a few operatic pieces. Niki accompanied by his mother gave them:

Weim Gott will rechte Gunst erweisen

Which he had sung at school, the adults applauded loudly. Detty then wanted to rush the children towards Gianna who was to supervise bath and bed. She wasn't allowed to get away with it and Niki protested loudly that he wanted to stay and hear Herr Walter sing the *Bayernhymne* as he had promised. Walter went to the piano and said solemnly. 'You must all stand.' He then started.

Gott mit dir, du Land der Bayern,
Heimaterde, Vaterland!
Über deinen weiten Gauen
ruhe seine Segenshand!
Er behüte deine Fluren,
schirme deiner Städte Bau
und erhalte dir die Farben
seines Himmels, weiß und blau!

Gott mit dir, dem Bayernvolke,
dass wir, unsrer Väter wert,
fest in Eintracht und in Frieden
bauen unsres Glückes Herd!
Dass vom Alpenland zum Maine
einig uns ein jeder schau
und den alten Ruhm bewähre
unser Banner, weiß und blau!

Although he stopped his voice down for salon use, the great bass baritone voice intrigued Niki who immediately asked.

'Will you sing some more for us?'

'Perhaps tomorrow – but I think that its bedtime now' said Walter with a tactful eye on Detty.

'That was the Lutz version of the hymn. I think it's better than the present official one. I see Niki is following the family tradition – he sang really well' said Walter to Marc as Detty, Gianna and the children left.

'No encouragement from us' said Marc 'Neither of us think that you should start them singing too early. He just came home from nursery full of the folksongs and Christmas songs he had been singing with the class then we went to a concert given by all the seven-year-olds. It was very sweet. When nursery finished, he said he wanted to sing a special song for *Oma* and *Opa* when we visited them before Christmas.'

'That sounds great and if they have that sort of enthusiasm, you can't stop them and why should you,' said Walter.

'At least for the moment he seems to have forgotten about the trumpet but he's developed more than a touch of Königshof platdeutsch argot since he has been at school' said Detty as she came back in carrying a music case 'but I suppose that is inevitable.'

Walter laughed '*Platdeutsch* with an Irish accent, that sounds interesting.'

Once the children had left they continued singing and laughing – first some Christmas carols, then some folksongs which degenerated into the raunchier ditties of *Der Oktoberfest*. After another pause for refreshment, Walter teased.

'Come on Detti, if you won't sing *Si, Mi chiamano Mimi* for us – at least give us some Irish input.'

'OK' said Detty getting her banjo out of its case 'I am afraid I've only got the short five string here – the long one is a bit bulky to travel with.'

She started by singing *The Fields of Athenry* then lightened the mood by playing jigs and reels one after the other. After a time, she put her banjo down and sang unaccompanied and gently *Ceol a'phiobaire* and then the love song *An Clàr Bog Dèil*. The family audience was spellbound but uncomprehending. After that, she picked up her banjo again and changed into English and sang *The Cliffs of Dooneen*.

'I would like to finish my contribution with the song that I mentioned earlier. It could have been written for Marc and me, and she began *The Roads of Kildare.*

When she finished, she changed back into German while the others applauded.

'It's not quite us; there are a few differences, I'm glad to say that you, Marc's family, are a bit broader minded than Johnny's but I am sure you agree that it's close. We could adapt it.'

'You must do it for the others and the children. We will learn the chorus. You had better stay for a second night, Walter.'

The latter protested loudly but eventually said, 'I suppose I could – Carla is not coming from Bologna until Christmas eve.'

'And who is Carla? asked Detty suspiciously.

'She is a soubrette from Venice who I promised to do some teaching with while we were both free at Christmas.'

'Oh really – over Christmas?' said Detty 'You are beginning to make me jealous.'

'Nobody could ever take your place, *meine Retterin*' he laughed.

11
JAN

the stables are the real centre of the household.

GEORGE BERNARD SHAW: *HEARTBREAK HOUSE* ACT 3

The week after Christmas was taken up with tobogganing on the meadow slopes beside the orchard at *Oberdorf* and visiting lots of people in the village with the usual treats and remarks about how much the children had grown. They arrived at Silvester and Max lovingly presided over *Der Feuerzangenbowle* for the adults and a cleverly produced second one with the same ceremony but no alcohol for the children. There was disappointment on the faces of the children as they prepared to leave to go back to *Königshof* for work, school and for Marc's return to Ingolstadt. The theatre Gala had been a triumph but, Detty as the now officially newly appointed, *Intendantin*. had a great deal on her plate. Her job, in practice was one that she had been doing for some time. However, with the restored Opera House, the Minister Neumarkt had decreed that the job should be advertised and the winner formally appointed. There were several other applications from suitably qualified people which made Detty feel nervous. She chided herself but she really did not want anyone else to take over 'her' opera house. She need not have worried as a unanimous vote of the appointments panel gave her the job 'on account of the unique position that she occupied in the cultural life of the country.' Flattering as that was, it still didn't fill the performance schedule of an opera house that had only re-opened for business long after most good artists already had full engagement diaries. In addition, they still had the dilemma of security at their Ziatov houses. The restoration was nearly finished but they were conscious that the houses were surrounded by extensive wild grounds, currently only modestly fenced. True there had been no other incursions after the spurious electrician but both Mara and Detty realised that, even with the increased police presence, the houses were vulnerable. It was one thing to secure an apartment in the President's residence, quite another to secure two remote houses in hectares of forest, pasture and water meadow.

Detty made frequent visits to the Ziatov houses to judge progress, sometimes with Mara when the latter could spare the time. Her own schedule was a bit more relaxed as, although she had teaching commitments at Krenek and quite a lot of work arising from her *Intendantin* job. For the first time in years, she was not actually preparing any immediate new roles and although conscious that the *Götterdämmerung Brünnhilde* still needed a lot of work, it was fairly distant. She had arranged an intensive visit to Manchester later. She usually called in at Inspektor Kunz at Ziatov. Sometimes it was just social; sometimes she needed to collect her keys if a spare set had been used by the workmen. This time she had brought with her Niki who had no school that day, as he had begged to be allowed to come and visit 'their new house'. As they entered Kunz's cramped office, she had a surprise. She didn't like dogs. She tolerated, amused, her aunt Deidre's Irish Setters but otherwise her fear of dogs had been determined by the guard dogs at the Farm and her terrifying escape from the Tuscan farmhouse. However, she knew at once that the two little worms with enormous paws that had nestled round her ankles were different.

'You can tell how big they are going to be from their paws —unlike human babies they grow into their paws.'

Inspektor Kunz had imparted information with the air of wisdom. The puppies were now nuzzling Niki whose face was wreathed in adoration. 'These are the last two puppies. There were originally six, the others have gone to two farmers down Bialovsk way. For my book, these are the best pair though and my wife said that we should ask for a bit more for them. That may have put the farmers off.'

An idea was forming in Detty's mind that a major part of the solution to the security problem was playing with Niki on the floor in the form of two lovely *Schäferhunde* puppies.

'*Mutti,* can we have them – please!' pleaded Niki voicing what was in the air.

'It may be possible but I need to speak to the others first. Herr Inspektor, don't sell them to anyone else – can I give you a deposit?'

'Don't worry, Frau Komturin, that won't be necessary. I would love to see them stay on the estate here – just let me know when you have had a chance to talk to the Frau Ministerin and your husbands.'

Detty was sensible enough to see the problems and realise that there were a lot of people who needed to be consulted. When they got back to the Hansehaus, the first was Gianna. Her answer was immediate and positive.

'Not a problem, *Signora,* I grew up with two *Marremanas* so a couple of *Pastori* will seem like home.'

It was a new idea to Mara but she saw the security point. 'Perhaps I would rather have two fierce hounds on our side than various brigands against us.'

*

Almost as soon as they were back at the Hansehaus and after her brief conversation with Gianna, Detty had just had time to get the children into bed when she was met in the drawing room by a rather nervous looking President.

'Detti, you know that we never got that Charity Ball that you wanted.'

'No, I'm sorry. We never got round to it,' she brightened, 'but the restored opera house now has the facility to put a dance floor over the stalls. We could do it now.'

'Like Vienna – could it be?' 'Yes, pretty much – probably not quite as plush but fairly smart. If you want, I will find out from the technical crew.'

She raised a quizzical single eyebrow, looked at the President and waited. 'Well, you see,' he looked embarrassed, 'I have rather a personal announcement to make and I would like to have a colourful occasion to make it.'

Detty hadn't a clue as to what was going on. She decided to be professional and matter of fact. Later that evening, Mara came in from an official engagement. She sat her down in the drawing room, Detty proffered the standard pre-prandial Jameson's, and raised an eyebrow when Mara refused it.

'Mara, what is going on in this house? I have just been accosted by the President looking like a schoolboy planning a first date and now you are refusing whisky which I find highly suspicious.'

'Well, as usual you are not far wrong. I do know what my father is up to but I have been sworn to secrecy and had better let him tell you himself. As for me, I am not sure yet but I am late. I am going to see the wonderful Frau Professor next week and have a scan. A bit different from last time I visited her, I am delighted to say.'

Detty broke into a huge smile and hugged her friend lifting her high off the ground.

'That's so wonderful. What does David say?'

'He is thrilled to bits but worried because of the difference in our statures.'

'I am sure that the Frau Professor will help you cope with that.'

*

Detty was excited and threw herself into hyperactive mode. She called a meeting with the technical department and explained that she needed a dance floor over the stalls in six weeks. She was met with a few shaking heads. Apparently, the design of the restoration had allowed for this but there was no actual flooring. Putting on her most winning smile, she asked whether she could have details of quantities, dimensions, and suitable type of flooring yesterday. The shaking heads continued but there were smiles and a look of determination on the face of the tecnicos. They came back with the recommendation that an international firm who supplied the ballet companies of the world could do the job. It would be triple layer yellow pine with dual density elastic blocks underneath. Detty could see multiple euro signs sprouting on all sides. However, she called in the Belgian European manager of the company and in best *Valkyrie* mode pointed out that this was a prestige order and the publicity would benefit their company hugely. After a period of consideration, the manager agreed and quoted a considerable discount. Detty pointed out that this was a country with a huge musical tradition which, however, was just recovering from a civil war. There undoubtedly would be more contracts in the future, but at the moment funds were very tight and that they were approaching an Austrian firm who were said to be very competitive. The discount was then increased to a level which was a small percentage of the original figure, and the training of the local team in fitting and dismantling the floor were to be included at no extra cost.

Feeling quite pleased with herself, she then got the rehearsals for a *Cosi fan Tutte* rescheduled to a backstage. It was some time before she managed to get back to Ziatov to check on the restoration, but one morning she had time after Niki had gone to school. She told Gianna that she could have the morning off and then meet Niki later if she wasn't back. She bundled Liese into her seat in the back of the car and set off for Ziatov. The puppies were still in Inspektor Kunz's tiny office occupying most of the floor space.

'They have grown a lot.' she said, rather obviously.

'They have. I bring them with me in the morning – it's better than leaving them on their own until lunchtime. When I have a break, I have been training them to follow a scent – important if they are going to be security dogs. I shall miss them when you move in.'

'Well, you will still be able to see them. They will be around and perhaps we can come to an arrangement for you to look after them when we are both away.'

He visibly brightened. 'That would be a great pleasure.'

*

Even on the Baltic, late winter will celebrate the occasional day by bursting prematurely into spring. This was one such day and as she made the short drive from the village to the *Dwor*, she gloried in the sudden sunlight and the sparkling melting snow although it was still far too early for the appearance of wildflowers and green shoots. She was to meet Jan at the house for a detailed inspection and a discussion of his routine which would later be confirmed in a formal contract. The first problem was where he would live. Detty had discussed it with Mara and they both felt strongly that he should live on the estate. However, there were no other habitable buildings besides the *Dwor* and the cottage although there was one decent outbuilding that Detty had earmarked as a stables.

Jan's appointment was not yet due so she drove round the house sliding her four-wheel drive through the snow and slush and stopping from time to time to make a few notes about lay-out and improvements to the grounds. Liese was dozing in her car seat so she woke her gently and together they then went into the house. She made a note of jobs that still needed doing, and furniture and fittings that she had to get, on a clipboard. After a bit she had to relinquish the clipboard to Liese who had insisted that she wanted to draw a picture of Niki's ship. Detty couldn't, for the moment think what Niki's ship was. At last, she remembered that it was the Hansa cob skippered by the Polar Bear Bill. It was the intriguing invention of Mara's bedtime story and had been repeated many times and much loved.

Detty and Mara had interviewed six people the week before to try and fix someone for an important job of Estate Manager at Ziatov. What they had had in mind was a *faktor* who was to be to be a right-hand man and supervise the renaissance of the run-down estate. There were two locals whose experience was only in small holding agriculture, although their references were good. Then there was one ex FWL from outside Bialovsk – great guy but no relevant experience. There were two Germans who were promising with some experience of running properties but they had no local knowledge. Marc was consulted while they debated the choices.

'My fellow countrymen can still be viewed with suspicion in this part of the world.'

'I think that you have done a certain amount to correct that.' objected his wife.

'I hope so, however...'

'I am sure that there would be no problem and, after all, David and I am impeccably Livonian born – as long as I keep quiet about my German passport of which, may I say, I am immensely proud.' chipped in Mara who still maintained her dual nationality and was more patriotically German than the Germans.

'I still think that to appoint a German *faktor* with one Irish boss who is married to another German would not be tactful and, as you say Mara, your dual nationality might give the media a field day if they fall out of love with your family – no, sorry, but better not.'

They looked at the last of the six applications. Detty's heart leapt. Jan had six years' experience running an estate which included a small mixed-race Latvian and Arabian stud outside Poznan. More important however, he had been a fully trained groom at the world famous Polish Polaski stud. Now Detty harboured the semi-secret ambition to have horses of her own and had even discussed with her uncle-in-law, Christy about taking retired chasers of his. He was quite enthusiastic. She knew that her champion mare, Firebrand would have to stay with Christy, at least as long as she was racing, but there were always other, less eminent, horses who needed retirement homes at the end of their careers. Then there was the prospect of ponies for the children – it was exciting and Jan seemed exactly the right man to head up the team.

For the form of it, they had interviewed a short list of three and gave them each a brief visit to Ziatov but the result was never in doubt. Jan was told that he had the job with a probationary six months to be confirmed afterwards by both sides. Detty asked Jan to arrange a longer visit to Ziatov to talk further about the job and try to sort out housing. Hence his appointment.

'When can you come down here to have another look round with me – or both of us if I can prise Frau Senska away from her ministerial duties? Perhaps a weekend might be best.'

However, it had been arranged for that morning at ten, and on the dot of ten Jan arrived. The first problem was language. The interviews had been conducted in the *platdeutch* of Livonia and Jan had told them with a wry smile that he was comfortable in German and Russian as well as his native Polish. Detty, in German, congratulated him on his punctuality and to her surprise he replied in excellent, albeit accented, English.

'I am always punctual, Madam. Stable work always makes you punctual and old habits die hard.'

'How did you get your good English?' asked Detty as they walked through the slush round the house.

'It's a long story,' said Jan continuing in English 'my mother died when I was ten and my little sister was nine. My father was desperate. He had no accommodation at Polaski Stud where he worked and his hours didn't lend themselves to being a single parent looking after motherless children. On a recommendation, he applied for a job at Coolmore. He got it. His English then was rudimentary, but there was a house and he was assured the children's care would be OK as there were people and facilities to look after them. So, the three of us went to County Tipperary. We went to school locally but in the holidays, we worked and watched. I was stage – or perhaps I should say stable struck. To have, perhaps one of the greatest studs in the world on your doorstep with kind people was amazing. Unfortunately, it didn't last. My father had a riding accident and had a compound fracture of his ankle which was slow to heal. He couldn't work. Then my grandmother had a stroke in Poland and needed looking after. After two years we had to go back. We were able then to live with my uncle, who fortunately had moved up from *Klodzko* in Silesia, and was working at Polaski. He could just about squeeze us in to his small house where he lived with his wife and afford to feed us. My father got some light part time work at the Post Office and as soon as I was old enough, I signed on as an apprentice at Polaski. They liked my Irish knowledge and I worked hard and tried to keep up my English. That's my story, Madam.'

'There is nothing about Ireland on your CV' said Detty thoughtfully.

'There couldn't really be, Madam. I was a child at Coolmore. I had no contract and if I had claimed experience there, at that great stud, I would have been seen as a pretentious fraud and laughed at, or worse.'

'You are probably right. Your English is excellent but I didn't detect a Tipperary accent.' she smiled.

'I might have had one at school but at the Stud they came from all parts of Ireland and abroad so it was a mixture.'

'Why do you want to work here – it seems a bit of a come down after two international studs?'

'Two reasons or perhaps now three. I fancy the idea of a private estate – being in charge, easier hours and more friendly. Also,' he blushed, 'there is a young lady from Bialovsk who I met on holiday and who I would like to see again. Added to this now, if you will forgive me, Madam, but the idea of working for an Irish boss had its appeal. Your country saved my childhood and still means a lot to me. However, I didn't realise that you were Irish when I first applied.'

Detty laughed 'You don't know me yet – I'm a terror. My soldier husband says that I have the military capabilities of an armoured division.'

'Ah, but you may find yourself facing a winged hussar.' He had relaxed and laughed in his turn.

'Not a bad ally to have.'

They arrived at the outbuilding and Jan agreed it would make a good stable with potentially six boxes and storage space.

12
SIEGLINDE AND SIEGMUND

des frech frevelende Paars [16]

Die Walküre Act2 Sc1

'The floor needs a total remake, Madam. We need a rubber compound but we must make sure the floor underneath is right first. Best let the contractors clear all the rubbish off the top and then we can screed it properly. Will you let me know when the preliminary work is done then, if you let me, I can get some estimates? There may be a local firm that can do it or else we can go to Poland, or even,' he smiled his cheeky smile again, 'or even Ireland. If you don't mind me asking, do you know what is in the floor above?'

'No idea' said Detty 'We hadn't got that far but from the outside I realised the roof needs relaying. I think that we need proper insulation. I imagine once the loft was used for storage – hay or something. Let's adjourn to Die Dame to try and find some lunch.'

---

16 Impudent outrageous pair

They arrived at Die Dame in Rüstung and Jan looked startled at the inn sign bearing a good likeness of his companion. Kurt bustled out and was introduced to Jan. Detty explained he was going to work for them at Ziatov.

'I have been here before – with Irina – but we were just ordinary customers –not treated like royalty,' mused Jan.

Kurt smiled. 'I hope that you were treated well, all the same.'

'Yes, with great courtesy and the food was excellent, but tell me how Frau von Ritter's portrait finished up as your inn sign?'

'I detect from your excellent German, but slight accent, that you are not from these parts, so you may not know the history of our civil war that well. It is enough to say that the outcome of the war was largely due to the efforts of two women and one man. You are going to have the privilege of working for the man and, as well, for probably the most important person in the whole war, who is now standing beside you. The third person – the other woman tragically gave her life for her country. However, even before Frau Major Zahnsdorf's terrible loss, I had decided to name the inn after the two soldier heroines of the civil war and they graciously gave their permission. Hence *Die Dame in Rüstung, The Women in Arms* as a name. It only remained to get the inn sign painted in England, where they are good at these things, with their portraits on either side as two of the great military women of the mythical past – Liese as *Bradimante* and Detti as *Brünnhilde*.'

It was the first time that she had ever heard Falk use her first name let alone its diminutive – he was getting carried away by his enthusiasm.

'Now I understand,' said Jan.

'Now enough about me. Don't take any notice of Falk, Jan, he enjoys embarrassing me. It's all a myth.'

'Ask any other citizen of Livonia and they will tell you it's all true.'

'Frau Bernadette told me that her husband thought that she was an armoured division, so perhaps that explains it.'

'Let's get back to the barn loft.' said Detty, embarrassed, and changing the subject.

'Why did you want to know about the loft?' Detty asked when they were comfortable.

'Well, Madam, I wondered whether it could be converted into a flat for me. I could do a lot of the work, I could live in a caravan as spring is coming on and anyway, as Poles we are used to a bit of cold weather, and it could be ready for next winter.'

'I like that idea. If you don't mind, I will get Jonas Rabikis, our architect on the restoration of the main houses, to look it over and see if he spots any serious snags. He might make some useful suggestions about services. I think you will get on with him. He is a Lithuanian, almost a compatriot of yours.'

'Ah the old Commonwealth, those were the days – but we haven't been quite as close since then – we argued over Vilno, they call it Vilnius. Still I am sure that I will get on with him.'

Jan thought that there was room for a good-sized bedroom, a living room cum kitchen and a bathroom. The first thing would be to get the water and electricity laid on. They would need it anyway for the work and the stables. Detty agreed to talk to the plumber. There was no mains water at the house – it all came from a deep well. Detty didn't know if there was enough to supply the barn or whether they would need another well. If there was any long run of pipe work needed, it would have to be deep because of the hard winters although near to the river the water table was probably not that low. They sat down to their *pirogi* and *kalte braten* in the side room that Kurt seemed to reserve for Detty and her guests. The log fire blazed in the grate.

Afterwards Detty sought out Aleks, the site manager of the restoration to ask him to get an estimate from the subcontractors for the electric and plumbing works for the barn. They settled the position of the electric points and the water outlets. The following day, Jan lost no time in getting to work on clearing the accumulation of rubbish from the floor of the barn.

'The base layer is concrete, Madam, but it's in a poor state and I think that we should reckon on re-laying it, otherwise we will be putting an expensive rubber floor on top of rubbish. We will need a proper wooden staircase up to the loft. Should it be in the middle or at one end?'

'The middle would be best. It should still leave room for four horseboxes. We can plan to build the tack room on behind.'

*

Detty set out for Krenek thinking about the session with Jan the day before. The flash of spring had disappeared and the lowering clouds massing from the East towards the Russian border threatened further snow. Marc was in London for a NATO security meeting, He had gone straight from Ingolstadt, but they had spoken on the phone the night before. It had been agreed that he should go to Henley after the meeting and give their house a brief airing after its long empty winter although their Irish friend, Grace, did keep an eye on it. She was pleased with yesterday's day at Ziatov and was increasingly convinced that they had made an excellent choice in the enthusiastic Jan.

She stopped at the Lodge hooting her horn at a student who was standing outside the library concentrating only on her *Handy*. The student looked up, realised who the irritated driver of the four-by-four was and tried to scuttle off rapidly. Detty wound down her window and called to the departing girl.

'I hope your viola is getting the same concentrated attention as your *Handy*, Roberta.'

'Yes, Frau O'Neill.'

I'm beginning to sound like a proper old school ma'am, thought Detty. She must remember her vow to respect the young. The girl blushed. Detty laughed and drove on to park the car and to leave her case.

Her first session was with a talented, but rather disorganised undergraduate mezzo soprano. Sorting her out was hard work but at the end of the session Detty felt that they had made some progress.

For the rest of the morning, her session was with one of the stars of the Conservatoire, Hanna Leiden. Hanna was a thirty-year-old dramatic soprano who clearly had a major career in prospect. They were women of approximately the same age albeit separated by status and experience. They had a collaborative plan. Hanna was studying *Sieglinde* and although, for the moment Detty had kept it to herself, she hoped that Hanna would be advanced enough to sing the part in the following year's *Ring*. To this end they had arranged to go together to Manchester after the Easter vacation to be coached by Eileen Vaughan. The plan that Eileen had suggested was that they would sit in on each other's sessions as Detty worked on the *Götterdämmerung Brünnhilde* and Hanna on her *Sieglinde*. That morning they went through, Act3 Scene 1 of *Die Walküre*- the 'prophecy' scene where *Brünnhilde* and *Sieglinde* are together, with Hanna producing a sparkling:

> '*O hehrst Wunder*
> *herrlichste Maid,*'[17]

They were with Ernst Hemel, who had come down from the opera house in Königshof, where he was the Head of Music Staff, to assess Hanna's progress. He was acting as repetiteur, they both stood back and applauded, to Hanna's obvious delight. They talked a bit about the trip to Manchester, fixing the more mundane arrangements. Detty had agreed readily to the joint sessions suggested by Eileen, who was always keen to work with new singers but hadn't arranged the actual dates. Eileen's secretary said that she was out of the college for the day but had got Detty's message asking for dates for some intensive work after Easter. However, unfortunately Professor Vaughan was judging a competition in Korea after Easter. Was there any chance that they could both come before Easter?

Detty looked anxiously at her diary for some time. Hanna was used to her young *Professorin* being a bit unpredictable but her next remark completely took her aback.

'Do you know anything about horse racing, Hanna?'

'Not really, Frau O'Neill.'

'Well, do you mind learning?'

'No, I suppose not, Frau O'Neill.' She waited for an explanation.

Detty grinned and the explanation came.

'Two things. First, I think we know each other well enough for you to call me Detty. The other is a bit more complicated. You see I have a wonderful horse. No, really, I don't mean *Grane*, although I suppose

---

17 Oh greatest wonder, miraculous woman

they do have something in common. Seriously, this mare will be running in the Champion Hurdle at the Cheltenham Festival just before Easter. This race is the most important in the world in its class. She has already won the race twice. If she were to win it again, it would stamp her as one of the greatest hurdlers of all time. In short, I can't miss this race. We can still get to Manchester for Eileen if we start straight afterwards but it would be easier and quicker if you came to Cheltenham with me. Now you could languish in a hotel room or even in our house in Henley, while I go to the races, but collecting you to go to Manchester would take longer and it would be very boring for you. If you are willing you could come with me to the races and it would save time. It might be a new experience.'

'Sounds fascinating. I'll always go for a new experience. Count me in.'

*

Just as they were finishing Detty got a message from Regina, her secretary saying would she ring Jan on his *Handy* when she had a minute. He was at Ziatov working. She rang him at the end of the morning teaching session.

'Good morning, Madam, I have got on well with clearing the floor but I have discovered something that I would like you to look at before going any further.'

'OK, I am going back to the Hansehaus this evening. It might be after dark. Have you got adequate lighting?'

'Yes, I have a rechargeable pole floodlight that I have bought to continue working when the light goes.'

'OK, see you later.'

Detty drove up to the barn and noticed that there was a caravan parked near with an electric cable leading from a point outside the main house. Jan hadn't wasted any time. The snow was melting and the road up to the barn was clear and gritted – also presumably Jan's work. However, there were still piles of snow from drifts both at the side of the drive and elsewhere in many places. A bright light was shining through the cracks in the barn door, which was still original and, in old age, a poor fit. She went up and shouted to Jan who promptly opened the door. He had been busy. Three quarters of the floor had been cleared of the poor-quality concrete that had previously covered it revealing a stone slab, carefully laid years before by some former work men or *Bauer*.

'This is what I wanted you to look at, Madam.' Jan indicated a large flat stone in the part of the floor that his clearing operation had just reached. The stone was about seven hundred millimetres round, much like all the others surrounding it, but in one respect it differed from its neighbours. Let into the surface of one side of the stone was a thick metal ring, recessed in a cavity. The ring and the cavity, although old, were clearly more recent than the rest of the floor. Something must be underneath. Detty stood looking at the find for some minutes wondering what it meant and what to do.

'The first thing, Jan, is that we make sure that it is safe. I don't need to tell you that at least three campaigns have passed through these parts in the last hundred years and each have left their traces. This find could be booby-trapped; I think that it probably isn't but we don't need to take any chances.'

Despite Falk's panegyric at lunchtime, he looked surprised.

'My thoughts exactly, Madam. But forgive me if it seems impertinent, but I am surprised that a lady singer should have appreciated this so quickly.'

'That *is* patronising, Jan, be careful – but at least you didn't imply that my Irish origins would make me familiar with explosives – some would have done and it has happened before.' Detty was thinking of her Spanish experience. 'However, you probably have forgotten that one of my other occupations was as a captain of intelligence in the FreiWehrLivonias.'

'I am sorry, Madam, I was just impressed but that explains it.' he looked only mildly contrite, smiled and then went on 'Do you want me to report this to the police?'

'No, I think that I can do better than that – I think that it would be a bit beyond Kunz. Wait here a minute,' she went out and crossed over to her car, rummaged in her handbag and fished out her *Handy*. She went back and joined Jan then punched in a number and put the phone on 'voice' so Jan could hear and join in.

'Is Major Lopokova available? She is – great. It is Bernadette von Ritter, can you put me through, please?'

'Tanya hi. How is Eva Maria?'

'She is fine – exhausting my wheelchair skills. You haven't seen her for a bit – come round but I don't suppose that is why you are calling. What can I do for you?'

'Can you spare me a bomb disposal expert?'

'Detty, what on earth are you up to now? Is this a new opera?'

'No but come to think of it – it might help the *Götterdämmerung* production that we are doing next year. No, it's like this...'

She went on to explain the current problem. Tanya suddenly changed and became very professional. 'Secure the site. Is anybody resident yet?'

'Yes, our *faktor* elect Jan Kowalczyk.'

'Right ask him to be ready to meet a squad led by Feldwebelin Brigitte Neuland at Ziatov tomorrow morning at 07.30 hours.'

'OK, I think that I must teach at Krenek tomorrow but I could come to Ziatov at lunchtime.'

'OK, I'll get Brigitte to send you a text when they have got an answer.' 'Fine,'

'Love to Eva Maria.'

Jan was laughing. 'You ladies are a funny lot. Half chatty mother talk then high-powered military planning with hardly a pause.'

'What is wrong with that? That's the way it is here – you had better get used to it.'

'*Jawohl, meine Frau.*' Detty noticed the significant ironic change into German and laughed.

*

It was a new bike. It was a late birthday present. Mum and Dad (he had decided for now that they should be 'Mum and Dad' at least at home as he was becoming intrigued by his Irish ancestry) had decided that it would be dangerous to have a bike in the middle of Königshof, although he grumbled that he didn't know why, as there were plenty of parks and open spaces. However, he accepted philosophically that that was *die Eltern* for you and agreed that the bike would go to Ziatov. The bargain was that Dad would try to get him a ride on a tank at the next open day at Ingoldstadt. The bike would be delivered when they moved, or were about to move, to Ziatov.

It had arrived, but for the moment he could only ride it when he was off school and when he went with Mum or Dad on a trip to the 'new' house where the bike was kept in the barn. He was assured that it was closely watched by Jan who wouldn't let anyone steal it. He was almost satisfied as he liked Jan. He liked the twinkle in his eye and the way he talked to him like a grown-up. Jan, without being asked, had offered to clean the mud off the bike when he had had his ride and see the tyres were pumped up properly. Mum, in a severe mood, had said that he must wash the mud off himself and learn from Jan how to pump up the tyres so that he could do that himself. She also laid down the rules. He could only ride the bike in front of the house while Mum, Dad or Jan was watching until they were sure that he was safe and knew how to ride it. He would be tested, Dad said, a bit like a driving test that you had to take before you could drive a car on your own when you were older.

Several weekends before the great day had arrived. Dad, with a clipboard stood on the steps of the house. He told Niki to put on his helmet and checked that he had done it properly. He then instructed Niki to ride up and down, get on and off, turn round, park the bike against the curb. Then he had to check the tyres and demonstrate how he would clean the bike. When it was all finished Dad had put on his best military manner and told him that *Kadett* von Ritter had passed his cycling test. He could now ride on the roads of the estate, always with his helmet on, but on no account should he go beyond the gates.

For the last couple of weekends, he had plied the tracks of the estate amidst the melting snow and was now becoming bored with the small number of accessible tracks. It was a fine day; still quite cold but warmer rain was promised later. There was only morning school on a Friday and as soon as it had finished Gianna picked him up and they set off for a cold lunch at Krenek before going round to the *Dwor*. As they were finishing lunch, Detty's *Handy* rang with a scrambled number.

'*Frau Komturin?*'

'*Ja*'

'*Ich bin Feldwebelin Neuland.* We have finished the examination of the stone in your barn. There is no explosive device attached but it is a very heavy stone and although we had to lift it partially to complete the examination, we thought that either you or one of the other co-owners would like to be present when we finally lift it to explore what is underneath. As far as we could see there is a large hole going somewhere underground.'

Mum had disappeared with Jan and the army lady. They were going into the barn to look under a stone. It sounded pretty boring. He wanted to do something more interesting. He put his helmet on. He didn't want to be court marshalled which Dad had said would happen if he was found riding without a helmet. The thaw had opened a few more paths including quite a long one which wound tortuously from the main path towards the southwest side of the estate, away from the little river to the furthest point of their grounds. He couldn't see far down it; it was very twisty but he wanted to explore it. There were still snow drifts on either side of the path – some quite high, but the path itself was clear enough for his bike. He set out. After several hundred metres of winding path, he came to a sizeable downhill slope.

*

There were not many hills in Livonia and none that he had seen before at Ziatov. Water from the melting snow flowed down the path but it was still cyclable and he would have to clean the bike anyway when he got back. He started off down the slope. He was over halfway down when he decided that he was going too fast. He braked. The bike didn't stop and started to slide faster and faster wobbling from side to side. Miraculously he stayed on the bike. In front of him was another sharp bend still covered by a high snow drift but fortunately no trees. He was scared but thought that if he ploughed into the snow drift at the bottom corner, he would stop. He didn't. The drift was not very thick and he went straight through it onto an even steeper slope on the far side. Now he did come off the bike and was thrown over a fallen tree into thick undergrowth while his bike hurtled on straight into a pond at the bottom where it disappeared with a splash. His first thoughts were for his precious bike now submerged in the pond. He cried, but as he did so he realised that his right leg was very painful and he couldn't move it. His shoulder hurt too. He was stuck. To add to all this at that moment there was a crash of thunder and the heavens opened with torrential rain – it was warm enough for rain not snow. To make matters worse, a fierce wind was now crashing through the trees. He was very cold and wet. He shivered and wept.

*

Detty went into the barn with the others. Brigitte was quite short with her dark hair in a bun, a ready smile but an authoritative manner. For the moment she concentrated on the work in hand giving her orders in a clipped speech which was clear and concise. She was dwarfed by the three men in her squad that she commanded but she certainly had an air of authority. It was apparent that she was treated with respect. Detty also noticed that she smiled quite a lot and the crinkly lines round her eyes probably indicated a sense of humour, reserved for more relaxed occasions. Together the team lifted the massive stone by the thick ring bolt. Underneath a vertical shaft led down. With their torches they were able to see the bottom of the shaft perhaps five or six metres down. The capable Brigitte said that she would stay around with her two colleagues in case there were any unexpected finds at the bottom of the shaft. It appeared that a passage led off from the bottom of the shaft. Now they struck a problem. They had no ladder. If the underground chamber had been used there must have been a ladder originally but with the fighting that had taken place in years gone by, to say nothing of previous owners, all trace of a ladder had disappeared. The nearest likely supplier was in Königshof but Detty thought that there was a good chance that Inspektor Kunz had one that they could use until they could buy one.

She rang him –yes, he was in the office and he kept a suitable ladder nearby in his allotment in order to prune trees and pick fruit. 'I will come for it straight away,' she had said and set off in her four-by-four, telling the others that she would not be long.

Inspektor Kumz was as good as his word. He was in his tiny office which was almost filled by the two dogs. He had unearthed the ladder and parked it ready against the wall outside. Detty loaded it into the back of the four- wheel-drive. She suddenly had a thought.

'May I take the dogs? It would be a chance to introduce them to their new home, I will bring them back this evening.'

'Of course, Frau Gräfin, after all they are your dogs.' Without a second thought she encouraged the dogs into the back of the car and they jumped in rapidly settling comfortably alongside the ladder. Off she set back to the *Dwor* and the estate.

As she drove back with the rain beginning to sheet down, she was aware that something was worrying her. For the moment she couldn't focus on it. Then she realised what it was. She thought, with some disquiet that she hadn't seen her son for some time. She had last seen Niki go off on his new bike as they went into the barn to explore the mystery stone, but when she left to get Kunz's ladder there was no sign of him. Surely with the weather deteriorating and the heavy rain falling, he should have come back? When she arrived back beside the barn, she immediately asked. 'Has anyone seen Niki?' They all shook their heads. She phoned his *Handy* – no signal but mobile signals were always patchy in this locality.

'He's been gone an awfully long time.' She was now getting quite anxious. 'I must find him – he might have fallen off his bike.'

She unloaded the ladder then set off in the car with the dogs still on board. She started by looking round the cottage. No sign. There was also no sign that another vehicle had entered through the gates although they had been left open because of the various comings and goings. This was reassuring, as after her own experience, kidnapping was never far from her thoughts. However, she was now getting really worried and visions of the little girl by the roadside outside *Neudrossenfeld* kept coming back to her. It was illogical – the little girl had been used as bait to trap her and was, to some extent, part of the plot, not a victim. She searched the main tracks – there was nothing to see except the odd tyre mark where the heavy rain had not yet penetrated. The marks were now being obliterated by the rain, but those that were still there seemed to be heading to the far corner of the grounds leading away from the main drive. She followed this side track and got to the junction of an even narrower side path, leading right into the far corner of the estate. It was too narrow for the four-wheel drive. She searched down it, but after several hundred metres there was a bend and from the junction she could see no further. On the spur of the moment, she showed the dogs Niki's parka to sniff which he had left in a heap in the car. She then let them out of the car. They snuffled around but clearly the rain had obliterated any scent. Anyway, if he had passed this way on his bike, little if any scent would have reached the ground. She set off down the path looking for tracks or fragments of Niki's waterproof or shorts. It was slow going and as she reached the steeper part of the descent, she slid about on the water covered ice and nearly fell twice. Surely, he couldn't have cycled down this water slide. She wished that she had brought a stick for herself but she was so keen to find her son, that she had set out without much forethought.

The *Schäferhunde, Siegmund* and *Sieglinde*, lolloped along, sometimes behind her sometimes in front. Occasionally one or other sniffed to the side of the track but rapidly lost interest and gave up. Neither the rain nor the thaw had been enough to clear the snow but had made it messy and had almost certainly obliterated any sign or scent which might have indicated that Niki had been that way, if indeed he had. She came to a sharp corner in the track. She was despondent and thinking that she was completely wasting her time and should be back looking in more likely places. She tried to ring Jan on her *Handy* to see if they had found anything, but again there was no signal. Opposite the tight bend the undergrowth was thick and the trees above had shed a lot of snow, blocking the path round the sharp corner, making the path beyond impassable. Better to turn back, she thought.

She had already turned round when she heard wildly excited yapping. *Sieglinde,* the young bitch, had disappeared from view under the scrub but her excited barking was clearly audible. She had found something. Detty turned and, heart thumping, forced her way through the thick undergrowth towards the loud barking. Panicky now, she wondered what she was going to find. There, halfway down the slope towards the pond lay a shivering, blue and soaking Niki. The first thing he said between his chattering teeth was,

'My bike's in the pond, *Mutti*. Can you get it out? You see I can't move my leg it's a bit sore.'

Detty quickly took of all her outdoor clothes and covered him up. Not much good as he was still soaking underneath. She tried her *Handy* again – still no signal.

'*Schatzi*, I must get help. Don't try and move. I'll be back in a few minutes.'

'OK, *Mutti*,' English seemed forgotten in a crisis 'but can you get my bike out when you come back?'

'Yes, of course we will, as soon as we can, but for now stay still.'

She forced her way back through the undergrowth and started to run up the path. On the slope it was still glacially slippery and she fell over twice. After the second fall she slowed down saying to herself 'if I break my ankle, it won't help Niki' so she slowed down and was more careful. Reaching the level surface, she began to speed up – running faster, she reckoned, than she had done in the 1500 metres at the Stadium opening. She reached the car and tried her *Handy* again. This time there was a signal – not good – but a signal. She rang Jan.

'Yes, Madam,' came the answer.

'I have found Niki. He has had a fall. He is very cold and I think has broken his leg. I am about 1200 metres down the southwest path and he is another five hundred metres down a side path. Can you send for an ambulance and get one of the others to come up here to the junction so I can go back to Niki?'

'Yes, Madam, at once.' There was a short pause.

'I can come at once with two of the squad, Feldwelbelin Neuland says she will stay at the barn to direct the ambulance crew with a stretcher, but she doesn't think they will need directions. They won't take long to get here.'

What on earth does he mean? thought Detty, it's a good forty minutes from the university hospital ambulance station in Königshof after they have alerted the crew. Of course, they would find it difficult to locate the right spot on the tortuous path. Her earlier assessment of the Feldwelbelin's competence must have been wrong, she thought. As she dashed back to Niki, she reckoned that the ambulance would probably take an hour to get to the estate, aside from the need for directions to find the remote spot where Niki had fallen. She was wrong – in about five minutes, she heard the familiar noise that anybody who has been in a modern war zone instantly recognises, often with fear. There was no fear this time and as the helicopter clattered to hover overhead Detty could see the Falcon and Chalice of the *FreiWehrLivonias Sanitätsdienst* together with the ambulance red cross clearly on its side. Brigitte Neuland had apparently wasted no time fiddling with civilian ground-based ambulance services. There was nowhere to land even for a helicopter but rapidly one after another two military medics and a stretcher were winched down beside Niki. His left leg was rapidly splinted and the stretcher winched up to the helicopter.

The remaining medic saluted Detty,

'We can land the helicopter next to the house. There is room there to pick you up to go with the little boy, Frau Hauptmann, it is just as quick as winching you up and probably more comfortable. I will come with you.'

Detty had no idea where he had got her military rank from let alone correctly using it – maybe Brigitte had used it to give force to her request for a helicopter – but how had even Brigitte known her former rank? She thought that she should have saluted the medic back but her drenched, torn and muddy shirt and jeans hardly seemed appropriate uniform and she just said a civilian.

'Thank you – you are very kind.'

The emergency medical consultant examined Niki as soon as he was taken into the Accident Department. Detty watched him do the examination while he chatted to Niki about how the accident happened. Detty was amazed how grown up her seven-year-old sounded.

'I fell across a fallen tree when I came off,' explained Niki in answer to a question, 'I think that a bit of the tree caught my leg awkwardly as I fell.'

'That looks about it' replied the doctor 'that's why the skin is a bit mucky over the break, but you were lucky the piece of bone has stretched the skin but hasn't gone through. We just need to clean you up a bit and get you ready. Then we will give you a short sleep while we straighten your leg out and put it in a splint. You will need the splint for about two months – depends a bit on how it heals – OK?'

'That sounds fine. Will I be able to ride my bike again – if we can find it in the pond?' replied Niki.

'Oh, yes, we aim to make a good job of it for you.'

'That's very kind of you.' Detty had a feeling of déjà vu, Niki having this adult conversation sounded exactly like his father. She felt redundant – the entire conversation had been between Niki and the doctor; he had not referred or deferred to her once.

Niki was duly taken into the prep room and Detty used her waiting moment to ring Marc at Ingolstadt. She rarely phoned him at work but she hoped that he had finished giving his lecture. He answered promptly and confirmed that he was free and merely tidying up some papers. He listened attentively.

'But is he OK?'

'I think he is fine. He was hypothermic, not surprisingly, but the medics from the FWL seem to have gone a long way to correct that. He has closed mid shaft fractures of his tibia and fibula which a very nice casualty surgeon is correcting and splinting as we speak. Apparently, he will need to be in a splint for six to eight weeks but then should be fine. He seems to be more worried about his bike than his leg. It's at the bottom of the pond – I think that it's a dew pond so I hope it's not too deep.'

'Apparently he is following the family tradition that the non-combatant members of our family seem to get wounded more often than the combatant.' 'Marc, please don't make that joke. I know that you think it's funny but it scares me stiff. By the way, when he was discussing his case with the surgeon – leaving me out of the conversation – he sounded exactly like you.'

Marc chuckled. At that moment, the surgeon came out so Detty explained that she must ring off.

'*Entschuldigung, Schatzi*, I'll come straight back. I know that a Luftwaffe friend is flying to Berlin this afternoon so I'll hitch a lift and then I'll talk my way onto the evening flight to Königshof, give Niki my love.'

The surgeon smiled reassuringly. 'He will wake up in a few minutes. He is fine. It has gone back nicely and is straight. We will need to see that it stays straight but the cast fits well and with this age group, there is usually no problem unless they go mad and get over active, but it was a nasty break and he was lucky that it wasn't compound – through the skin – which is much more difficult – infection and non-union can be a problem.'

'Well, he has had – is having, superb service – thank you so much.'

'Not at all. All part of the job. By the way, I gather you know my wife.' Detty peered at his name label – Robert Zachow – it meant nothing to her and she raised a quizzical eyebrow.

'Oh sorry' he said 'Luisa Stoken – she plays the oboe in the Philharmonica. She uses her birth name professionally.'

'OK right. Yes indeed, I remember her mentioning that her husband was a surgeon. She's wonderful. She was responsible for getting the opera house restored.'

'She never told me about that.'

'It's quite a long story. Look could we meet socially? You have a daughter I believe.'

'Yes, Anna, she is about the same age as Niklaus.'

'Great, Niki likes girls. He takes after his father.'

'She's fierce like her mother.'

'They should make a good pair,' they both laughed.

They waited for a couple of hours for the nurse to check Niki's circulation after the cast had been applied. Then they were allowed to return from the hospital to the Hansehaus. This had elements of musical comedy. The ambulance was, this time, the usual terrestrial sort (boring – exclaimed the patient, who had rather hoped that he would go back by helicopter as he had come). The crew unloaded Niki who had been instructed not to weight bear until the cast was changed to a walking splint. They hoped this would be at the next visit in ten days. The crew got him into the lift in a wheelchair but didn't realise that the lift didn't reach the penthouse on the top floor. When they arrived at the floor below the penthouse, Detty called on her resourcefulness and tried to lift Niki with the Fireman's Lift that she had learnt in her teens in her Convent Catholic Guides. She remembered how to do it but the trouble was that Niki's left leg, which she needed to grip to get him over her shoulders, was the one with the long splint. She decided to reverse the whole procedure and start with her left arm gripping Niki's right leg. It was clumsy as she was right-handed but eventually, she made it. The trouble didn't end there as the wriggling patient kept hitting the wall of the staircase with his encased leg as she struggled to climb up, as it was not very wide. Triumphantly, they eventually made it onto the penthouse landing. They were greeted by a round of applause and the sudden appearance of two figures, Marc at the bottom of the staircase, newly arrived from Ingolstadt and Nicklaus senior coming out of his small upstairs office on hearing the commotion. Detty was furious that her struggling efforts had been watched and applauded by the two men. She then calmed down and realised that both men had only just come on the scene and were too late to do anything to help. She started laughing too.

Marc was the first to speak from the bottom of the staircase.

'I think in future that I had better do the lifting and carrying up the stairs.'

'That's sexist and patronising,' said his wife, fury boiling up again. From the top of the staircase came the calm reasoned voice of Nicklaus, 'I have a better idea. You all go into the Diplomatic Apartments on the floor below until Niki has his cast off. There are large showers in the en-suites and the lift reaches that floor so no carrying is necessary.'

'No, Sir' said Marc 'that is really not necessary, I can manage to carry him OK.'

'Marc, when you address me as 'Sir', I know that you are going to be insubordinate. I am used to being bossed around by your wife but after all she is *Die Oberkomturin* of the principal Order of Chivalry in this country but I am not going to be bossed around by a mere *Brigadegeneral* and I would remind you that in relation to that rank, I am your Commander-in-Chief. You will occupy the Diplomatic Quarters downstairs and I will ask Petra to make the necessary arrangements. That is an order.'

'*Jawohl,* Herr Präsident!' said Marc smiling broadly. Detty noticed that Nicklaus had used Marc's, now only honorary, FWL rank rather than his substantive *Bundeswehr* one. Nicklaus was in bubbling good humour. In the last few weeks, it seemed that a great burden had been lifted off his shoulders. She knew from Mara, whose lips were sealed, that something was going on – but what?

*

As soon as they got organised in their palatial apartment and could sit down with a glass of wine each, they reviewed the day's events.

'I think that we have had two heroines amongst others today – one on four legs and one on two. The four legged one is back being spoilt by Inspektor Kunz so she's all right but I think that I should ring Tanya to thank her and send thanks and congratulations to Brigitte Neuland – in fact, I'll do it now. She fished out her *Handy*. Tanya's adjutant answered the phone.

'*Frau Major Lopokova bitte. Ich bin Bernadette von Ritter.*

Detty put the phone on 'voice' for Marc.

'*Eine moment bitte, Frau Komturin.*'

'Detty, is all well?'

'More than well. We have a son with a splinted leg and your Brigitte Neuland was magnificent. Please give her our thanks and congratulations.'

'That's great and will go on her record. It couldn't have come at a better time. She is before the Board for a Commission next week.'

'Well, she thoroughly deserves it.'

Marc came over and gesticulated to Detty to pass him the phone. 'Tanya, would a personal endorsement from me help?'

'Wow- I'll say,' came the reply, 'I'm pushing hard because we need another junior officer. Jurgen, my husband, has got his commission but we thought it was a bit dodgy, almost incestuous, for him to continue in my unit, although it's not illegal here, reluctantly we decided that he should transfer to the Engineers, which was, in fact, his first unit before I led him astray. But I miss him and not only for the obvious reasons but as a colleague. It has left us very short staffed at officer level. Really today's exercise shouldn't have been left to a NCO but Irina is the only junior officer that I've got. She was away on another job and anyway Brigitte is, of course, exceptional.

'I'll send a note directly to Sergei Malinov and I hope it does the trick. How's Eva Maria?'

'She's fine, thank you.'

'When we've got the house sorted, we must have you down.' He gave Detty her phone back, pulled out a pad and started writing. How's this?' he asked Detty, who had finished the call.

An Herr General Sergei Malinov, Abwehrminister, Personal Feldwebelin B Neuland today performed a difficult rescue operation for my family. She showed leadership, organisational skills, and empathy (Führung, Orgsnisationsfährigkeit und Empathie) at an important level. I would like to support her application for a Commission in the FWL
    Signed: Marc von Ritter
    Brigadegeneral, Freiwehr Livonias (Ruhestand)

'That should help.' agreed Detty. It was several weeks later that Marc received a handwritten letter addressed.

Privat, an Brigadesgeneral Marc von Ritter.
Residenz Republikspräsident, Hansehaus, Königshof.

It read:

Dear General von Ritter,
My very grateful thanks for your great help with my recent application for a Commission.

As you will be able to see, I passed the Board and your efforts were successful.
With very respectful greetings.
    Brigitte Neuland
    Leutnant
    Military Intelligence and Security Corps
    Freiwehr Livonias

They sent her an e mail with their congratulations.

13
THE CHILDREN OF LIR

And a stone was put over them, and their names were written in Ogham. And they were keened there, and heaven gained for their souls.

LADY GREGORY IRISH MYTHOLOGY BOOK 5
THE FATE OF THE CHILDREN OF LIR

After the excitement with Niki's mishap, it was a few days before they got back to the hole in the barn floor. Brigitte Neuland, who was awating her promotion Board, said that she would bring her squad back when they explored underground 'in case they met any unwelcome surprises'. Marc was still with them, not being due back at Ingolstadt for some days.

They gathered for flask coffee and then arranged the ladder. Brigitte went down first with a powerful torch. One of her colleagues, then Detty, Marc and Jan followed. There was a short passage, narrow in Stygian darkness only relieved by the restricted but powerful beam of Brigitte's torch. The passage led away from the bottom of the shaft at right angles and after a few metres opened into a larger chamber. The four of them gathered just inside while Brigitte swept her torch round the chamber walls. Piled in one corner was a collection of terra cotta plates and beakers with some old-fashioned knives and spoons. Then the torch swept on and suddenly they all gasped. On one side of the chamber a broad shelf of stone protruded from the wall. On it were crumpled a few rugs. Brigitte put on rubber gloves and gently drew the rugs to one side. All their jaws dropped in horror. On the shelf, still covered by rags of clothing were three small skeletons – each one smaller than the other. They had obviously once been three children. The largest skeleton, from her clothes, belonged to a girl and the other two seemed to have been boys.

Brigitte was the first to recover from the shock.

'We need to get Forensics up here straight away and find out what this means. Tragically, it looks as if the children were entombed down here – it is horrible. Knowing what went on in this country before the war, one must wonder whether it was done deliberately. It seems hard to believe it was an accident but we will have to wait for an explanation if one is even possible. It has clearly been a long time.'

This dreadful finding cast a gloom over the von Ritters' pleasure in their 'new' home. Brigitte said that she would notify the civilian police, and shortly afterwards Detty received a call to tell her that a Scene of Crime Team was on its way and would she be present to answer any questions while they investigated. They duly arrived accompanied by a Commissar from Königshof, a tall fair, good looking young man but with a patronising manner and an expression that suggested that he had an unpleasant smell under his nose. Oddly, he was called Mousse and as this was certainly not a Livonian name, she wondered where he came from. He spoke in what passed for high German, fairly fluently but with a strong rather unattractive nasal accent. He abruptly motioned Detty into his police van and started to interrogate her. It was obvious that he regarded Livonians, women and all people of dubious foreign origin as a sort of under-class. Detty realised that she fell under at least two of the despised categories.

He started to question her abruptly and sarcastically. What was the purpose of her uncovering the chamber? Did she intend to keep horses down there?' – smirk. Had she intended to store contraband or stolen goods there? She was a foreigner, wasn't she? What connections did she have with people smugglers on the coast? He mentioned a couple of names of notorious gangs who had been in the news very recently. Detty realised that, incredibly, he had no idea of her rank and status in the country but decided it would not be appropriate to enlighten him. She discovered later that he had been seconded on an exchange arrangement from the Belgian police as part of the preparations for Livonia to join the European Union. This accounted for his ignorance but not, she thought, his appallingly bad manners. Detty, trying to keep her temper, quietly suggested that you hardly let an unexplained manhole go without investigation in a newly purchased and restored property. You would also hardly involve a military bomb disposal squad if you were pursuing criminal activities.

'We will see, won't we' was the supercilious young man's only comment. He then continued his questioning. Why did she need this large property? Livonia was hardly a usual situation for a holiday home, he said, with another smirk. Then he asked if her name was von Ritter, why did she have an alias? What, in fact, was her nationality? It so happened that she had three choices of citizenship but at this point she decided to reply 'Irish.' This led to the usual questions about connections with the IRA or other illegal organisations. She now realised that he was digging a hole for himself and began to feel less cross. What nationality was her husband? Why was a German buying a house here – after all following WWII, Germans were not very popular in these lands? As Detty struggled to control herself, Marc, who had had been in the city for an interview with a banker about routine changes to be made to their accounts, arrived. The young Commissar now started to ignore Detty completely and address his questions and conversation entirely to Marc. Marc, of course, did not know about the morning's events and found the questions extremely puzzling. He excused himself, ignored the Commissar's instruction not to leave and left saying that he wanted to see how the Scene of Crime team were getting on. Just as Detty felt the comedy had gone far enough. Jan came to the van, apologised for interrupting but said Inspektor Kunz had arrived and would like to speak to Detty. 'Is that OK?' the latter had asked the Commissar, 'I suppose it will have to be,' was the surly and brusque reply.

Kunz entered. 'Excuse me, Herr Kommissar, Frau Komturin, but I have just had Frau Ministerin Oblova Senska on the phone wanting to speak to you but your phone was switched off. She said that both she and her father would like to know what was going on. The Commissar's ignorance began to unravel. Why was this odd foreign woman referred to as 'Commander' and what connection did she have with a Minister. Clearly nobody had briefed him about the joint purchasers of the Estate. Now Commissar Mousse gradually began to realise that he might not have done himself any favours and might be in a hole, but unwisely he didn't stop digging.

'I don't like having my interviews interrupted even on account of some politician' he said pompously, especially not a female one, thought Detty 'Tell the Minister that Frau von Ritter will phone her back when I have finished with her. What has it got to do with her father anyway – it isn't a domestic family matter?'

He had led with his chin and this time Detty delivered her knockout blow.

'Herr Kommissar, you seem unfamiliar with this country. Are you not from here?' she said, smiling.

'I don't know what business that is of yours, but since you ask, I am on an exchange secondment from Antwerp to prepare this country for joining the European Union.'

'I see – well perhaps you should know that most things in Livonia have to do with Frau Tamara's father. He is President of this country but also, by coincidence, happens to be a very dear friend of ours.'

The deflation was immediate and total, 'I am so sorry, Frau Komturin, I didn't know.'

'You mean that you would have felt that you were justified in being extremely discourteous to your interviewee if he or she had been an ordinary citizen and not a senior officer of the national order of chivalry and a friend of the President?'

'Of course not, Frau Komturin.'

'Well, that's the way it appears to me. How long does your secondment to this country last, Herr Kommissar?'

'Another two months, Frau Komturin.'

'I think that it might be shorter than that. I shall discuss the matter with the Minister of the Interior. Let me have a copy of your report when you have prepared it.'

Detty knew that she had no right of access to his report but thought it unlikely that her routed enemy would query it.

Jawohl, Frau Komturin! She left suppressing her smile until she was well clear of the van. She had no intention of reporting him to Klaus Heber, the Minister of the Interior. She could fight her own battles but there was no harm in letting this ghastly man stew for a bit. She was quite capable of dealing with this on her own.

When a worried Commissar Mousse returned to the *Präsidium* in Königshof, he asked several of his colleagues what they knew of Komturin Bernadette O'Neill; he was not reassured as one colleague filled in the details.

'I thought that she was an opera singer?' asked Mousse.

'She is an international opera singer but that is not the main point. Here, she is a national icon and credited with the success of the war of liberation which she turned in our favour, almost single handed, by several exploits of unbelievable courage and difficulty to say nothing of ingenuity. Why do you ask?'

'But she said that she was Irish, was that a lie?'

'Frau von Ritter does not usually lie and why should she stoop to lying to a minor official?' He winced at "minor official" 'She is Irish.'

He muttered '*Heilig schijt!*' but fortunately nobody was near enough to hear or was, at least, not near enough to understand his Flemish, although it didn't need much translation. The rumour circuit rapidly ran round the *Präsidium* about the events at Ziatov. The junior ranks, who didn't care much for Kommissar Mousse, who bullied them, sniggered behind their palms. His more senior peers accosted him directly:

'I gather that you have had a run in with Bernadette von Ritter' one said.

When Mousse nodded miserably, he went on. 'You don't want to do that here. Better to take on a Bengal tigress or a Great White Shark. People who cross her are usually found three miles out in the Baltic in a concrete overcoat. Even her husband says that she has the military capability of a fully equipped Panzer division and he knows, he is a high-flying German officer, who also served with us during the civil war.'

This was the woman that he had patronised, mocked and insulted. Occasionally his peers gave him a weak smile of sympathy but most just grinned. He didn't believe them about the concrete overcoat but it still didn't make him feel extremely comfortable.

For the rest of his time in Livonia, he treated all witnesses with elaborate, perhaps overdone, courtesy. Every day he expected to be expelled with his career in ruins.

*

At Ziatov, as Detty and Marc waited for information. Mara and David joined them. When the report came it consisted mainly of things that they already knew or guessed. The skeletons were indeed an older girl of about ten and two boys of eight and six, Carbon dating came through and this did cause some surprise. The skeletons were seventy years old which meant that they were alive in the nineteen forties and had lain in their weird, improvised sarcophagus since World War II, undisturbed during all the recent upheavals. None of this solved the problem of how they got there and why they were there. They thought that the most likely explanation was that they had died elsewhere of some illness and then, in the turmoil of wartime, had been laid to rest under the barn when no more appropriate grave could be found. But all together and fully clothed? This didn't fit with the theory. Crime, it might be but at least it was not a recent crime. They felt puzzled and rather flat. As there was no way yet of eating or sleeping at Ziatov, Detty suggested they 'phoned Gianna who was in charge of the children at the Hansehaus and said that they wouldn't be back that evening and could she do bedtime. That arranged, they could all go to Krenek to dine in Hall and use the two rooms in the lodge flat for the night.

It was Friday night which had become a traditional Dining Night at The College. As many as possible of both students and staff were expected to dine in. Before the meal there were aperitifs, more often than not provided in the form of Sekt from the Von Ritter suppliers at a very competitive or almost non–existent price. These were consumed around the huge fire in the Great Hall amidst a gale of chatter, which was mainly about music, but also any other topical subject. After the initial reception, the kitchen staff produced their best menu from seasonal foods. After the main course had been served, Detty had introduced a tradition that as many as possible of the kitchen and waiting staff came into the Refectory to the applause of the assembly. They then sat down and had their own meal at a special table reserved for them alongside the students and academic staff. Detty, Mara, Marc and David had joined the press round the great fire and had contributed to the chatter. Inevitably everybody wanted to know about Niki's accident and then the conversation moved to the strange findings at Ziatov. There were gales of laughter when Detty recounted her interview with the police officer. She then explained about the sad discovery of the three little skeletons and the puzzle of how they got into the vault like chamber. 'Nothing really seems to fit.' she mused.

It was Helge who made a suggestion.

'Have you tried asking Ludis, the gardener, to see if he can throw any light on the problem?'

It appeared that Helge lived his bachelor life in a flat in one of the College's surrounding cottages, These, years before, had been occupied by estate workers. They had become very run down when Krenek was deserted but had been restored for use by students and some of the members of staff into decent little bungalows and apartments. Helge, who had responsibilities both for the College and the Philharmonic Orchestra had a very busy life and found it convenient to live near the College and take most of his meals in Hall. It saved him cooking for himself or having a housekeeper. Living nearby he had struck up quite a friendship with Ludis the gardener, who appeared, rain or shine, cycling from his bungalow in a tiny hamlet halfway between Krenek and Ziatov. Helge often met him and chatted to him as he walked his adored pointer bitch, *Die Soufleuse,* round the lake every morning and evening. Helge often stopped for a gossip and he soon realised that Ludis was a fund of knowledge on local history and traditions. Helge had learnt a lot of local facts and a fund of anecdotes from him. Detty knew Ludis a bit and was always amused that, uniquely, he always referred to her as *'Fräulein'*. However, unlike Helge, she had never really plumbed the depths of his knowledge of local lore.

'Can I join you on your next walk and we will see if Ludis can throw any light on the Ziatov mystery?' For the next two days the heavens opened with heavy spring rain which rapidly cleared the remaining snow but was unsuitable weather for chatting. However, the third morning was still cold but bright and Detty was able to meet Helge for his walk. Ludis was trimming the reeds from the path round the lake. He was being helped by a young man with dark wavy hair, wearing a blue coverall. Detty knew that the Works Director for the College had finally persuaded a reluctant Ludis to take on two school leavers to help him with what was a sizeable, albeit wild, estate. They had been interviewed and appointed by the Personnel Manager and Detty had not met either yet:

"*Morgen, Fräulein, 'Morgen Herr Professor'* said Ludis, putting down his clippers. This was the expected greeting. Notwithstanding that Detty was Ludis's ultimate boss, she got the usual *Fräulein*. Detty didn't mind a bit, in fact, she loved it. She found all the Livonian deference, at length somewhat tiring, and being the unadorned *Fräulein* was refreshing. It made her feel young, as she was. She had dressed that morning with a liberated scruffiness, perhaps consciously playing into the role assigned to her by Ludis. Her hair was in a bun, she wore a multi coloured woollen pompom hat and faded fleecy jogging bottoms, topped off by an elderly vintage water proof riding jacket, which had been her pride and joy when she bought it for herself as a sixth form teenage school girl but which was now, unsurprisingly, showing evidence of more than a few years of hard wear. She was proud that after a number of years and three pregnancies, it still fitted her pretty well. Got up like this, she reflected, she looked more like an impoverished student or stable lass than the Co-Director of a prestigious music Conservatoire.

The chatter with Ludis started about the capricious spring weather and the plans for the further development of the lake. Detty wanted to restore the summer house in the middle of the lake so, in the warm weather, concerts could be given by the students and staff to an audience on the bank. It was an attractive idea but had hit a major snag – the island was a predator-safe sanctuary for a number of different waterfowl who could not be disturbed. The idea therefore was in abeyance while the resourceful Co-Director tried her best to work out an alternative. Would a wooden landing stage let out from the bank serve for the musicians? she asked. Helge was anyway unconvinced of the desirability of open-air concerts, although Ludis thought that such a stage could be built and indeed there was a master joiner in his village who would probably be able to do it for a reasonable price.

'But it would need piles driven into the lake, *Fräulein*, he would need some outside help with that.'

'I might call in a favour from the FWL.' said Detty.

They left the topic for the time being and turned to the subject that they were really there to discuss.

'Ludis, do you know what went on at the Polish house during the World War? You see my husband and I have just bought the main *Dwor*, and Herr and Frau Sensky have bought the Cottage, However, during restoration, we have made a very disturbing discovery.'

She went on to describe the finding of the three skeletons. 'Now you have been in the neighbourhood for many years and we wondered if you had any information, even guesswork as to the events at the *Dwor* all those years ago. I know that you must have been only a child then but perhaps you might have heard something.'

She had to be careful not to imply that he was in anyway involved in what might have happened. He nodded then was silent for some long minutes as he stared into the distance and his eyes became moist with tears. It was as if he was scanning through the years to reach his small boy's memories and they were not good. At last, he spoke:

'It was a terrible time, *Fräulein*, – there were so many people died and perhaps they were the lucky ones. Others just disappeared; it was rumoured they died too but more horribly. Even as a child, I was confused as to what country we were in, what country I belonged to – first it was Germany. then independent, then Polish, then German again, then Russian. It is hard to remember anything clearly. The second lot of Germans were terrible. They shot twenty young men on the road to Bialovsk in reprisal for killing one German soldier. Each small town had a police barracks – Gestapo police – they called them. In the barracks they tortured people so you could hear the screams in the square outside. They pushed people into barns and set fire to them. They rounded up all the Jewish people and loaded them into cattle trucks. They all disappeared into the south to be murdered, we thought. The couple who owned the *Dwor* and the Estate were Jewish. They were quite rich, he was in business, timber, I believe. They were good kind people who would always help if anybody local was sick or had an accident. They had three small children, I think. The rumour went round that the children were sent off to England before their mother and father were rounded up but we didn't really know. Maybe they were murdered or rounded up with their parents and murdered with them- we just didn't know. Eventually the Russians came. Everything was destroyed in the fighting but we were so pleased to see the Russians and, despite the wreckage we were happy. We should not have been, more people disappeared; soldiers were billeted in the houses and ran amok stealing and breaking up what they couldn't steal. They destroyed everything they laid their hands on. They raped our women – some of them very young girls, just children. They were different from the Germans but quite as horrible. At last, we had a few years peace then we had Travsky, but you know about that……' he tailed off and stared into space again with tears running slowly down his rugged cheeks.

Detty wished that she had not asked him and got him to tell this appalling history. Particularly with her charity work, she had heard some terrible stories from recent times and she realised that before that there had been horrors in the more distant past. However, this vivid story, simply told by a countryman who had lived through it, albeit as a young child, was starkly horrific and real. She stood silent with Helge. Neither felt that they could say or do anything. Then as they stood, speechless and appalled, a young voice came from behind her:

'*Entschuldigung,* Frau Komturin.' Detty, still pre-occupied, hardly noticed that unlike his boss, the youngster addressed her with her title. 'I overheard what you were discussing and wondered whether I might be able to help.'

Ludis stirred himself from his reverie. 'This is Kurt' he said 'who is one of my new assistants. How do you think that you could help, Kurt? These events that we have been talking about happened years before you were born,'

'I know that, Herr Ludis, but you see my great grandmother who is still alive, worked for Frau Feldstein when she was young and knew the family well. My great grandmother had a bad time in the World War, I think, but so did many but she came through it. She might be able to help you. She is ninety now but quite fit. She lives in the retirement home run by The Sacred Heart, she knows your story, Frau Komturin' he blushed, 'and I think would be honoured if you paid her a visit. I go to see her quite often on my day off and could come with you, if you wished.'

'I would like that very much. When could we go? Who is in charge – should we get permission?'

'Sister Inge, who was a teacher at the school but is now retired, is the Warden. I think we should ask her.'

'I know Sister Inge. She grew up in Naila, local to my parents-in-law's village, before she joined the order, so we have something in common. We talked about it at the Sacred Heart celebration.'

Sister Inge was duly approached and said that she would be delighted for Komturin O'Neill to come with Kurt when he was visiting his *Urgrossmutter*. Kurt was such a nice lad and so kind to the old lady.

Ilse Steinmetzin was planting lettuces under an improvised cold frame resting against the wall in front of her apartment when they arrived.

'I do it each year' she said, 'There is nothing like a bit of home grown when the better weather arrives.'

'But the snow has only just gone, surely it's a bit early.' expostulated Detty, even though she was, assuredly, no gardener.

'Ah well' said the old lady, getting up from her kneeler as straight as a lamp post 'You see this is a special place. The wall gives some shelter but the main thing is that the main drain from these six apartments lies right underneath. It is of course watertight and well buried but just enough heat filters upwards as the hot water passes to start and protect the lettuces. They say that they spend a fortune heating the hot houses in the Botanical Gardens outside Königshof but I get the heat for nothing,' she chuckled. 'You will take tea.'

It was an instruction more than a question. They went into the apartment. An antique Samovar was already hot and from it came the scent of blackcurrant leaves. Detty inhaled the scent.

Frau Steinmetzin smiled. 'Blackcurrant leaves – dried. They are an essential part in the *zavanka* –the hot water' she explained as she poured the hot scented tea.

'I see' said a puzzled Detty who didn't see at all. Boldly she sought an explanation, 'Frau Steinmetzin, please forgive me for asking but you have introduced me to classical Russian tea making although you have two names of apparently German language derivation. I am being impertinent, but I wondered how that came about?'

'Not at all, Frau von Ritter, many people have been puzzled by that.' she chuckled again and had changed into the *Platdeutsch* of the Königshof Vorort. 'You see I have not always had German names. I was born Irina Ivanova Zinkova but I married Georg Steinmetzin and after the war when the Russians behaved so badly, I could not find work with a Russian name so my husband and I quietly agreed it should be Ilse, and so it was. This may seem odd as the Germans had been terrible too but the *Platdeutsch* had been always the local language of this part and the German crimes, shocking as they were, were history whereas the Russian crimes were current frightfulness. So, I taught myself *Königshofer Rotwelsch*, took a German name and then I belonged. I was one of a crowd but you never entirely forget your roots and mine are in a Samovar and *zavanka*.'

She paused and they sipped their tea and nibbled the soft little tea cakes that came with it. 'But I don't think that you came here to see me to talk about Russian tea. What would you like to ask me, to talk about?'

'Before the World War, I believe that you worked for Frau Feldstein and her family at the *Dwor*. Well, you may have heard that we have bought the house, Herr and Frau Sensky have bought the cottage and we are sharing the estate grounds.'

The old lady nodded, 'I am so glad. It was terrible to see it empty – so gloomy and sad.'

Detty went on to tell the story of the discovery of the shaft and the underground chamber. She paused at that point, frightened of the shock that she feared that the description of the three little skeletons would give to the old lady.

'You knew the three children of the family?'

'Yes, very well. They were a happy family. I was only young but I used to look after the children when Herr and Frau Feldstein were out or away. There was another maid, Hilda, but the children liked me and I was really close to them. They were like my own – almost like younger brothers and sister. Rivka. the girl was the eldest then there were the two boys Reuben and Rafael. Frau Feldstein was Ruth and I thought that it was a bit funny that they all had the same initial but that was the way the Master and Mistress wanted it and it was really no business of mine. Frau Feldstein had another baby-another boy – after Rafael, but he died when he was a few days old – it was very sad.

'This is probably distressing for you but did you know what happened to them in the World War?' asked Detty.

'Partly but not really. You see my brother was shot as one of the hostages after the German soldier was killed. They said my brother was a partisan, he wasn't really but he had helped them. They didn't leave it at that though. My father was taken to a Concentration Camp and we never saw him again. My mother and I were arrested and we were sent to a Concentration Camp for women, Ravensbruck, it was called- you may have heard of it.'

Detty nodded. 'Well, it was pretty bad and we were treated worse than animals. My mother died in there. Amazingly though, I survived and before the end of the war I was let out and I came back here – walking and getting a lift when I could. I arrived back in the village just before the Russians arrived. I had nowhere to hide as I had been away and the Russian soldiers raped me several times. My own people who I grew to hate! Eventually an officer said he would look after me. I knew what that meant, but at least I was fed and sheltered and one officer was better than every passing soldier. When I was more settled, I tried to find out about 'my family' as I called the Feldsteins. Apparently, Jacob and Ruth had been rounded up in the night, with many of the other

Jews of the District just after I had been arrested. They were put in a train of cattle trucks which left for the south in the gloom of our long winter night. A few people witnessed the train leaving but could not see who was on it with the shut trucks, the crowds and the darkness. I asked about the children. Most of the locals thought that they had been put on the train with their parents but nobody was quite sure. A few people thought that they might have been taken on a train to England – some had been. However, that late in the day, it seemed unlikely and just wishful thinking. Most of us were resigned that they had been murdered with their parents in *Auschwitz* like all the others. We never knew.'

She paused and Detty took the plunge and explained their finding. When she had finished, Ilse stared silently ahead for a long time with a grief etched on her wrinkled face that she could not express. After a long interval she surprised Detty by saying:

'I think Frau Ruth was going to tell me where the children were hidden if she knew that she was going to be deported with Herr Jacob, but that was impossible. The parents were taken in the night and we, my mother and I, had already been arrested the day before. Poor, dear children. I wonder if they starved or ran out of air. Perhaps suffocating would have been kinder and, dreadful as it must have been, it was better than being gassed amongst terrified people. Thank you, Frau von Ritter, I am glad the puzzle is finally almost solved. You see I never understood but Frau Feldman spoke to me one day when we began to hear the dreadful stories. I think she said. 'Irina, (I was still Irina then) the children will be all right. You can save them. Before we are taken, I will tell you how.' 'At the time I thought that she was just rambling with fear. She never told me. Of course, when they were taken, I had already been arrested so I was never told how I could save them. Anyway, when I was freed, it would have been far too late – poor little darlings. They were such lovely, happy children.'

At last, she wept a great torrent of tears. Detty just waited in silence, struck dumb. Then she kissed Ilse and left with Kurt who had remained silent for the whole time. Just before Detty left, Ilse dried her tears and asked.

'Did you find the ring and the locket?'

'I'm sorry, I don't understand' said the puzzled Detty.

'You see one thing that I have just remembered. Rivka, the eldest, the little girl, had a gold ring and a locket, quite tiny, that she had been given by her grandmother on her ninth birthday the year before. She could not be parted from them. The ring was too big for her so she kept it in the locket which she wore round her neck night and day. I wondered what happened to them.'

'We never found them but she might have hidden them before she died. I will have good look.'

Detty thanked Kurt and dropped him off in the village. Then, instead of going back to Krenek, she wheeled round and headed for the *Dwór*. As it was technically still under investigation, there was a bored, cold policeman outside the barn. There was a light on in the caravan but it was empty and Jan's car wasn't there. He had probably gone to Bialovsk to see his girlfriend. The policeman recognised her and made no problem about letting her in. She didn't want to use the big work light which anyway wouldn't reach the vault. She realised that she had forgotten her torch and swore to herself in very un-convent English, but she thought that there was one in the back of the four by four. She rummaged amongst the children's clutter and eventually found it. Miracle beyond miracle, it actually worked. On the spur of the moment, she also took a screwdriver from the car's tool kit.

She went back to the barn, climbed down the borrowed ladder which was still in place and went along the narrow passage into the vault. She flashed her torch round. She looked carefully over the floor in case the locket had been dropped when the rags of clothes had been moved. Then she started to look thoroughly at the walls. In several places there were cracks in the stone and concrete. She investigated several cracks and probed them with her screwdriver but they were empty. Then she noticed one crack near the stone slab 'bed' which appeared to be full of straw. Now there was only a little straw on the floor of the vault but there had been plenty in the barn above. She pulled the straw out of the crack. She did not need the screwdriver. There was a glint of gold in the bottom. Her finger reached the fine gold chain and pulled the locket out. She didn't want to try and open it in the gloom in case the ring or anything else dropped out and was lost. She put the locket in her jeans pocket, climbed back up the ladder, out of the barn and put on the strong interior light of the four-by-four. The locket had only a simple clip. With trembling fingers, she opened it. There were only two things inside. The first was a plain gold ring. The second was a folded piece of yellowed paper. Detty opened it very carefully. She managed it, to her relief, without tearing the old paper. On it was written in pencil in a neat childish hand. She could read the writing, it said:

> *Der Stein wurde nicht bewegt.*
> *Vielleicht wird es nie sein.*
> *Wir haben wenig übrig zu essen.*
> *Heute höre ich auf zu essen*
> *Meine kleinen Brüder müssen haben, was noch übrig ist.*
> *Ich wünschte, ich könnte ihnen meine Luft geben.*[18]

She went back to Krenek and thought of the heart-rending message and the terrible interview with Ilse that she had just had. She also thought about the interview to come which might be even more terrible.

Marc was coming back that evening. She loved him deeply and she knew how gravely he took his nation's guilt. From the few times that it had been discussed between them, she knew that he steadfastly refused to use the excuses that were prevalent and often used publicly or privately by his compatriots. He never said, 'I wasn't born then' or 'my family had nothing to do with it'. As far as she knew, his only close relatives had been in the *Wehrmacht* and had died in the snows, ice and hell of Stalingrad. However, all he ever said was 'we were, are all responsible and our nation will remain guilty to the end of time. No

---

18. The stone has not been moved.
 Perhaps it never will be.
 We have little food left.
 To-day I am stopping eating.
 My little brothers must have what is left.
 I wish that I could give them my air.

other nation employed the machinery of a modern state to carry out such a monstrous crime.'

She had challenged him then 'Horrible as it was, it is just not true we, Germans, were not the only ones. Look at the Belgians in the Congo, the Americans at Wounded Knee, the Australians with the Aboriginals, the South Americans in several countries, the British in India, South Africa and my own native Ireland.'

She had deliberately said 'We Germans' to show her solidarity with her dear adopted country but it was no use. She had tried pointing out what Germany had done in the last seventy years to shore up humanity, peace and justice with much more persistence than many other countries. Germany had hardly put a foot wrong for over seventy years. But it was no use, he just shook his head and stayed silent. She knew that that evening was going to be very, very difficult. She knew that they must stay at Krenek and that she had to abandon her children to Gianna for another night. They needed to be alone to discuss this. Even the Oblovs would get in the way.

Marc came in after the long drive looking tired. She tried to put off the discussion. Without telling lies, she couldn't.

'How did it go with Frau Steinmetzian?' he asked. She told him the whole story. As she knew he would, he looked desperately troubled. He asked a few questions about details in a flat voice. If she knew the answers, she told him – unadorned facts – no subterfuge would help. He then looked utterly miserable as he wrestled inside himself. This was her resourceful hero. She had never seen him like this.

She knew that she had to ask him one important question. 'Knowing what you now know, *Schatz*, can you live in that house? Can it be our home?'

The pause lasted minutes but it seemed like hours. At last, he looked up, his still young face looking taut and grey. He spoke in English,

'I don't know, my love, I must have time.' Then after another long pause, 'I shall go to the mountains and lakes of England. That will be the nearest that I can get to a neutral place. It needs to be neutral – my Bavarian mountains are tainted and in Ireland I would think only of you. I have been before to the English lakes. There I shall walk and think. I will come back after a week or so and give you my thoughts and ask you for your answer. I can take leave. I have it owing. I shall make the arrangements and leave in two days.'

A very German scheme, thought Detty, to become a Wanderer to try and find an answer to an insoluble problem. She said nothing and just kissed him. They went to bed but neither slept. They returned to the Hansehaus the following day. He then made his arrangements but said very little. Finally, he kissed the children, said he would be back soon and left.

14
WINTERREISE

suche mir versteckte Sege
durch verschneite Felsenhöhn?[19]

WILHELM MÜLLER *WINTERREISE* 20
WEGWEISER

She heard nothing. It seemed the longest week of her life. She loved him so much and yet could do nothing to help. It was dreadful to think of him alone struggling with his daemon, in both senses, without being there to help him. She took her mind off her worries, to some extent, by going down to Ziatov armed with a bag of treats in order to visit and thank their four legged heroine. *Sieglinde* was lying with her brother outside the Inspektor's little office making the most of the spring sunshine. Detty stroked her on her neck and told her what a clever girl she was and that she had saved Niki. Detty was careful to divide the treats between the two evenly. After his share of treats, *Siegmund* soon lost interest, gave a snuffle and went to sleep. *Sieglinde* however cocked

---

19 And seek the hidden ways
   Over the rocky snowy heights

an ear comically at Detty. Turned over on her back and clearly wanted some more stroking.

A voice behind her said.

'She's a typical girl – can't get enough attention like most girls.' Then realising who he was talking to, added in a fluster. 'Oh, I'm so sorry, Frau Komturin, I didn't mean to offend you.'

'You haven't, *Inspektor*, not at all, you are quite right but could I just add that like many girls, she is intelligent, brave and resourceful.

'*Kühn ist sie und weise auch!*[20] Except that is the wrong character.'

Inspektor Kunz hadn't a clue as to what she was talking about and only said:

'Yes, I expect that you are right, Frau Komturin. Anyway, I am so glad that she found the little boy – how is he, by the way?'

'He's fine. Getting around on his walking splint and showing off as usual' and feeling wicked, she added 'like most men.'

The Inspector had the grace to blush. He knew that he had been bested in the exchange.

*

The 'phone rang often in the President's apartment and even more often when she was in her office at the opera house. She jumped each time but it was never him. Then at long last, it came, with a start she looked at the number +44 491................ It was the fixed line from their neglected little Henley house. What on earth was he doing there? And if it wasn't him, who was it? The Irish girl, Grace, who kept an eye on it when they weren't there, never rang her at Königshof, although she did have the number in case of any disaster. Detty answered the call.

'How are you, Darling? I reckon that I was a complete bastard leaving you as I did.' The fluent English was clipped, precise but unmistakeable.

The relief swept over her. 'It doesn't matter as long as you are OK but I have been worried- you were so low when you left.'

---

20 She is brave and wise as well
    Wagner: *Siegfried* Act3 Sc1

'I think that I shall be back to-morrow but might have to have a night in Berlin depending on flights. I didn't know when I was coming back so I didn't book. I'll do it now then I am going to the pub.'

'That sounds better. Have one for me,'

Then she got a message 'Sorry, it will have to take two days. I will stay in Berlin at the Mess. I didn't think that I would be able to find another beautiful Irish girl to walk with down the staircase at the Grand.'

This was Marc back to his old teasing self, referring to their first stay at the Grand Hotel in the *Friedrichstrasse*, after they had rescued Tamara. Smiling for the first time for a week, she sent a message back. 'You dare!'

The Marc who walked into the apartment at the Hansehaus two days later looked weather beaten and a bit tired but definitely a different Marc from the one who had left the week before. He hugged the children then took Detty in his arms and kissed her long and hard:

'What did I do to deserve a wife like you, *mein Schatz*,' he whispered in her ear. Then he dived into his bag on the floor and produced a bottle of Bushmill's Malt. 'This is the best that I could find at the Airport for some reason they seemed to have run out of Jameson. Is it any good?'

'It's very good and I will forgive you getting me Protestant stuff. It comes from the oldest distillery in the world. We had better wait until I have got the children in bed, then we will sit down and have one and please tell me all about it. The Oblovs are opening yet another Trade Fair with a dinner afterwards and I've sent Gianna off to do her Italian Institute thing, so we are by ourselves.'

Bed time done, she poured the whisky and said, 'Now tell me about it.'

'I stayed at a pub which I had been to years before in my early days in the *Heer* when we were on a NATO exercise with the British Paras. We used to go in the evening just for a drink but I knew they had rooms and I liked the atmosphere. First class food and shepherds gossiping in the bar, it seemed right for sorting myself out. I took my Wordsworth with me and just read his poems in the evening with no television and only the weather forecast on the radio. It rained very hard for three days, real storms with drenching rain and high winds. I just kept on reading

Wordsworth, but I was beginning to get frustrated. The fourth day it was still raining and the weather was still bad but it wasn't quite as stormy as it had been, so I set out really early, at first light, for Helvellyn. The weather still wasn't easy going with cold driving spring rain in my face and poor visibility. I suppose I had the German *Bergsteiger's* arrogance 'these little English pimples couldn't be difficult, could they?' I was wrong and probably should not have been out there in the bad weather. There was almost nobody else around. The Striding Edge and the last connection to the summit were challenging. Fit as I was, I made slow progress but at last I made it to the wide summit plateau.'

'Miraculously then, the weather suddenly cleared, the rain stopped and the clouds rolled away. There was no wind and the sun warmed up. I sat down upon a flat steaming rock. I got a wet rear from the rain but it didn't seem to matter and anyway it soon dried. I spent some time looking at the fantastic view, over the Lakes, to the sea and fancifully all the way to Scotland. My thinking suddenly became clearer. I realised that to leave the *Dwor* – was to run away from the double tragedy which had been forced on the couple and the children by my people, would be quite wrong. It would be doing what many others in Germany had done 'I don't want to know. I wasn't born then. My family had nothing to do with it. They always opposed Hitler.' Excuses and lies in equal measure. No, we had to stay. Let our children play where little Rivka, Reuben and Rafael had played. But how should we do it and how should we honour them and their parents? Facing this dilemma, I got out my Wordsworth again from its plastic bag. It was an old edition, cloth bound printed on thin Indian paper with the date of publication 1910 reprinted 1923. I had bought it for a couple of Deutschmarks many years ago from an English language second hand bookshop near the University in Munich, to try out and test my school English. I remember that I was on a visit to Munich from school with my parents. The book had a signature inside 'James Willoughby Symonds'. Obviously, I knew nothing about the signatory but I was fascinated. Was he one of the many expatriates who, before the World War lived in our capital city? Who knows? But, to my surprise, I then started to love the poems and I treasured and still treasure his book. It was the beginning of my enduring passion for

English romantic poetry. We have great poets but, at least in that period, the English were somehow different – fresher,

First, I read *The Intimations of Immortality* – perhaps with *Tintern Abbey* Wordsworth's greatest poems, but it wasn't what I was seeking on that mountain top. Almost unconsciously I turned to the fable *The Westmoreland Girl*, the little poem about the ten-year-old girl saving the lamb from drowning and her later history which Wordsworth wrote for his grandchildren only five years before his death. It is not one of his great poems and most people despise his late poems, but it struck a chord with me. It was not obviously relevant to the sins and guilt of my beloved, benighted country but it touched the right emotion, particularly the last two verses:

> *Watchful as the wheeling eagle,*
> *Constant as a soaring lark,*
> *Should the country need a heroine,*
> *She might prove our Maid of Arc*
>
> *Leave that thought; and here be uttered*
> *Praise that Grace divine may raise*
> *Her humane courageous spirit*
> *Up to heaven, thro' peaceful ways'*

'Somehow it spoke for Rivka, the selfless little Jewish saint, bearing our sins. With the aid of Wordsworth, I knew what I must ask you when I got back. The sun was still out as I started down. I looked out over the sea towards Ireland, your Ireland, and the westering sun was red and beautiful. I thought how much I loved you and the children. I came down the Swirral edge opposite the one that I had climbed that morning. Now I was able to think as I could see my way easily. The light was still OK although it was getting dark by the time that I got back to the pub.'

'I still had three days, so I thought that I would go to Henley and open up and air our house. The spring weather had turned really warm. I walked up to Temple Island, watching the swans, ducks, and the other water birds. I made the walk or run to Temple Island several times each day. The river always showed a different face. The Thames has a gentle dignity – I can see why the English call it 'Old Father Thames'. Then in the evening I would go to the pub. From the pub I could still watch the river, as we used to, I could still see the swans, ducks and moorhens. It was restful for my troubled soul. It continued the healing that had begun on Helvellyn. I thought that I might see Steve and Abbie but they didn't appear. I could have 'phoned them but really I was glad to be by myself.'

There was silence between them for a long while. 'You haven't told me what you have decided.'

'It is not for me to decide. It is for us, although I know that you were afraid that I could not cope with the awfulness of the story. However, I have a plan to put to you. We continue to restore the house. We fill in the vault. I don't think that we would want that to be under us. We ask the Chief Rabbi in Königshof if it would still be possible to arrange a proper Jewish funeral for the remains of the three children after all this time. I am not sure what is possible. I know that Jewish funerals normally take place very soon after death but I will ask. I hope that the remains can be buried in the Jewish part of the city cemetery. Lastly, I think that we should plant a memorial garden to the entire family outside the barn at the *Dwor*. I thought a simple marble slab with their names and perhaps an appropriate quotation, again we might ask the Rabbi, quite a small slab and surrounded by a small garden – not too big which we would look after. What do you think?'

Detty nodded. This time they both slept.

The Chief Rabbi was gentle and helpful. Marc had made an appointment with him, insisting that he went by himself. When he got there and had received a quiet *shalom*, he went straight to the point.

'I am sensitive and deeply touched that you are prepared to receive an officer in the German army.'

'You are not here as an officer in any army, *Mein Herr*, you are here as a compassionate human being. Now let us have a look together at the problem of honouring this family.'

For the next hour, Marc learnt more about Jewish funeral ritual guided by the gentle explanations of the Rabbi. He learnt about *the kaddish* or funeral prayer and the *shiva,* the seven days that followed the funeral. He learnt about many other aspects and what might be appropriate and what was not possible in the unusual situation. In conclusion the Rabbi said.

'I will arrange an appropriate Synagogue service allowing for the unusual circumstances. You mentioned being moved by a poem which reminded you of the sacrifice of Rivka. Would you be prepared to read it at the graveside in addition to the usual Eulogy which, for obvious reasons will be short, particularly for the boys?'

'I should be very proud, if I am acceptable.'

'These things are usually, of course, done by friends or relatives of the Jewish faith but I think it would be appropriate for you to do it at the graveside, particularly given your involvement and the strange circumstances.'

The Rabbi continued. 'I will get my staff contact the undertaker to make the other arrangements – coffins, internment plot etc. Then we will appoint pall bearers for the cemetery. There are of course, as far as we know, no living relatives, but I am sure members of our community will be pleased to serve. I think that that is all for now. Thank you for coming.'

'One thing more. Rabbi. My wife and I would like to meet all the funeral expenses.'

'Thank you. You are very generous, Herr Graf – my best wishes to the Frau Gräfin. I attended one of the liberation *Fidelios* and met her afterwards.' He smiled, 'I know that people of all faiths in this country owe a lot to your wife and yourself. We would not have been planning this memorial when we were still under Travsky.' That helped.

The simple triple grave in the Jewish section of the City Cemetery had a wide headstone crossing all three tombs. It was wide enough to accommodate the full prayer:

"*Tehe nishmato/nishmata tzerurah bizror hachayim*"[21]

---

21 May his/her soul be bound in the bond of life

*

Detty had warned Hanna on the plane to Stansted that she would be introduced to a new world. Detty had rung Grace asking the Irish girl to be kind enough to air a couple of beds. They went to Henley for the night and after some *Viennoiserie* which Detty managed to find in the freezer, they set off at the crack of dawn for Cheltenham.

After a certain amount of swearing, Detty got into the Owners and Trainers car park and they entered the Racecourse. Hanna had some idea that horse races were run over fields in the countryside. She was staggered by the size of the stands and the massing crowds of the opening day of the Festival. Detty's metal badge and guest badge opened a way for them to get to the Owners and Trainers enclosure. There they found the Firebrand party and Detty introduced Hanna to Christy and Deidre and to some of the rest of the Kildare group.

Like most aspiring singers, Hanna had good English, acquired as much for professional and business reasons as purely artistic ones. She was however taken aback to hear about fetlocks and withers. She was lost completely when she heard that somebody had bought a rig at the yearling sales without bothering to look (this caused gusts of laughter). Somebody else had apparently done better. She had had a pony on the rag in one Clonmel race, which had trotted up at double carpet. The conversation then went on to race tactics. Hanna heard, equally uncomprehendingly, that you needed to be covered up towards the front of mid division until the two-furlong pole, then you can let out a notch, but only really come off the bit at the distance unless pressed very hard. The opposition was probably better than last year but their mare was fit and well and they were hopeful. The racing jargon had gob-smacked Hanna but the panorama of the course framed by Cleeve Hill was breath taking. She muttered to Detty how beautiful it was. The latter just smiled and said:

'Yes, it's the finest jumps course in the world – for me, Irish though I am, the finest of all the courses in the world. Punchestown is pretty good but even that doesn't rival this. It must make a change for you to see so many hills.' Fortunately, they had a nice day – chilly but bright spring sunshine.

The earlier races on the card slowly went by. Detty persuaded Hanna to have a small bet on the Supreme Irish second favourite who obligingly won after a photo finish. She was happy to pass the time by explaining the difference between a Grade Race and a Handicap, the difference between a steeplechase and a hurdle race. She was not sure how much of it Hanna understood but it helped Detty control her anxiety. Hanna was quietly amused. She had never seen her laid back *Professorin* so tense, even before an important first night.

When it was time they went down to the paddock, Sam, her lass, was walking Firebrand, looking imperious, round the paddock. She appeared magnificent and was calm relaxed and professional. Even Hanna noticed the difference between the mare and her stressed owner. The bell rang and Jess mounted her. They paraded then cantered to the two mile plus start.

Then they were off to the Cheltenham roar. They went up the famous hill past the stands then on to the highest point on the course. Jess kept her in the classic position just behind the front group of four horses. They came down the hill with Jess sitting completely quiet. Over the second last he eased Firebrand forwards and passed two more until there were only two left in front. After rounding the bend, starting up the final hill approaching the last, she led and had a steadily widening lead. It looked as if it was all over. Then Rapid Recorder, who was known to be a young improving hurdler from a big Lambourne yard, shot through the pack, and caught Firebrand so they were in the air together over the last. There was a gasp of anxiety from the layers in the crowd. Jess pulled out the last notch and the mythical Firebrand sprint didn't let him down. For some seconds, the talented English gelding hung on but then quite suddenly his race was run and Firebrand had joined the small elite who had won three Champion Hurdles.

Detty turned to Hanna, Christy, Deidre, and the others,

'I don't know whether she is exhausted but I know I am. She had me scared for a moment.' When Jess dismounted in the Winners Enclosure, Detty just said a heartfelt but quiet:

'Well done' to him.

He laughed. 'When the English youngster caught up with us at the last, she just said, 'How dare you!' and then she started to race. I didn't have to do anything except encourage her a bit. Then he said very quietly. 'She is amazing. I shall never sit on her like again.'

'I wasn't really scared,' said the phlegmatic Christy, 'but I didn't know how good Malcolm's was. We didn't go for the Christmas Hurdle at Kempton but his one, Rapid Recorder, won it on the bit and looked good which was a bit worrying. It's a much easier race, mind. Anyhow everything was all right on the day.' After the Prize Giving, they left rapidly for their hotel, champagne and smoked salmon, an early night and Manchester.

'I could get hooked on that, Detti. Can I come next year?' said Hanna.

Detty smiled.

15
THE BALL

No sleep till morn, when Youth and
Pleasure meet.
To chase the glowing hours with
Flying feet

BYRON: *CHILDE HAROLD'S PILGRIMAGE*

She had done quite well, she thought. When she had formally accepted the Intendant's job, she hadn't known that in addition to her other tasks, she would be President of a State Ball. Once she had got the problem of the dance floor sorted it became easier. Mara had wanted to get rid of the tracks which had formerly held the panels of the tiered boxes. These were now left open for the opera and ballets. These panels had made the half partitions separating the boxes from each other in the first four tiers of the auditorium. The divided boxes certainly had not been used since the war and were a relic of a past aristocratic age when going to the opera was as much social as musical. Detty had demurred.

Detty had found Mara unusually depressed and from time to time downright bitchy over the last few weeks. She had never known her like that before. She thought that it might be the pregnancy but it was odd timing that it had come on so recently.

Today she was definitely waspish.

'It's pointless,' she had said with Ministerial decision, 'we shall never use them. It's just clutter. I am surprised at you Detty – having tiers of boxes obstructing the sight line is not very Wagnerian. The Bayreuth lot would have apoplexy'.

'I'm not so sure,' Detty had said 'It seems a shame. They are part of the theatre and its history. It is after all a National Theatre and may have to perform different functions that we haven't yet thought about in the future. We are just talking about the partition tracks and they don't really get in the way. Anyway, if they are taken out, the scars left will have to be made good. It is just more work.'

She had looked round the restoration committee seeking support. It wasn't forthcoming. Then she had asked.

'Does anybody know what happened to the original panels themselves which ran along the tracks?

Again, blank faces but Detty hadn't given up. She made more inquiries. She hardly thought the old panels would have been destroyed deliberately but they might have been destroyed in the war, sold or given away. She knew from pictures that they were covered on each side with a rather fine old gold velour nineteenth century wall covering – thick paper, she presumed. It was Olga, the high priestess of the Green Room, and who presided over the magnificent new coffee maker, who suggested a possible answer. Detty and Mara had come in for a meeting and a tour of the theatre with visiting Spanish diplomats. These had now gone off for lunch and the two of them were luxuriating with the reformed coffee.

'You know the scenery store two streets behind the *FreiSenderLivonia's* studio and headquarters, Frau Komturin? Where the sets of the old productions stored?'

'Sure, I know it, Olga. but they are not there, I have looked.'

'Did you look in the cellar?'

'No, I didn't know there was one – there is no entrance from the store above.'

'No, there isn't, you must go through the furniture warehouse on *Zwetschgenbaumstrasse* right round behind just before you get to the *FSL's* studios and offices. There are big sliding doors at the back of the furniture premises then a slope down. The store does belong to us – (Detty liked the 'us' – it was the sort of group spirit that she encouraged) – but is very hard to get in so the old stage staff only used it for things that they never expected to use.'

'Why then did they keep them at all then?' the expanding Mara said sharply. She had been on her feet too long, trying to be charming to the visitors on the first warm day of that year's spring and obviously was now feeling tired and footsore which added to her pervasive bad mood.

'I really couldn't say, *Frau Ministerin.*'

She didn't follow it with 'it's not my place' but Detty thought that the implication was there. Detty was however grateful to Olga, and as soon as she was free, she rang the furniture warehouse to get let in and arranged to go and explore the following morning alone. Mara's frequent bad moods distressed her and puzzled her. If she had a problem, why didn't she share it? Detty wondered if she had missed something. However, she concentrated on her present task. The cellar opening out of the back of the furniture warehouse was exactly as Olga had described. She went through the big sliding double doors and down the ramp. The contents looked halfway between a treasure house and a junk store. All the stuff, Detty thought, dated from before the Civil War, but it was a dry sheltered area and the props, although old fashioned were in a surprisingly good state. To her delight there, stacked at the back were tier upon tier of the partitions for the boxes, each panel covered, not in paper, but in superior quality velour fabric. They were, of course, also covered in cobwebs and filthy; however, surprisingly, there appeared, at least on first inspection, to be very little permanent damage. She counted the panels and made a note on the back of an envelope. She cursed herself for not bringing a tape measure but, remembering where she was, returned to the now deserted furniture warehouse and found a tape measure in an unattended drawer in the sales staff's desk. All the panels had the same dimensions which was helpful.

She noted the measurements and took some photographs where she could get enough access to the panels. She then spent a few minutes looking at a rich set of period flats and furniture which could have been for *Le Nozze di Figaro* or *Der Rosenkavalier*. She had never known these existed. They were clearly pre-war and she wondered if they could be made to fit the new stage. She wondered if there were any costumes, and if so what sort of condition they were in. There were several large trunks. They could contain costumes. She tried the lid of one. It was locked but the lock was simple and would provide no problem for a locksmith. She was excited by the idea that they might do a 'heritage' production, particularly if it was *Der Rosenkavalier*. Better start learning *Die Marshallin*. She pulled herself together and said to herself 'You are getting carried away, Bernadette, isn't the *Götterdämmerung Brünnhilde* enough to be going on with? She stuffed the envelope in her pocket and headed off to Daina for a late reward breakfast.

Restored by cappuccino and croissants, she thought, there is no time like the present and headed back to the front office of the firm whose warehouse she had invaded. She knew that they had an antique furniture department. She accosted a rather startled senior salesman who, fortunately, was in the office when she got back. He was a smart young man in his thirties, she thought, with wavy brown hair and an attractive smile. Her face was well known in the city and he obviously recognised her,

'Good morning, *meine Frau*, I mean, Frau Komturin', he said looking confused.

'I have come to return your tape measure. I stole it from the desk in your showroom on my last visit.'

'Would you like to keep it, Frau Komturin? I am sure KS Möbil would be pleased, honoured, if you accepted it with our compliments.'

'You are very generous. It is a good one and in my new job as *Intendantin* of the *National und Hof Opera* it might well come in especially useful. Thank you.'

There was a twitch of the attractive smile on the Sales Executive's mouth and he was joining in the fun.

'But I have a question. Do you have a firm doing cleaning and restoration of antique furniture, when it is needed, before you put it on sale?'

'We do indeed. In fact, we have two, Wilhelm Karsen is a fine craftsman. He has a workshop behind the old Harbour and is particularly good with delicate old fabrics – tapestries etc. Then there is Metropol Reinigung GmbH, they are a much bigger firm equipped to do large orders and do both fabrics and cabinet restoration work.'

Detty produced her measurements and photos and explained her problem.

'I think this is one for *Der Metropol*. Could you possibly be kind enough to see if you can get me an appointment?'

He rang the firm and they said that she could go round at once.

At the firm, she showed her photos again and explained,

'I think that there are roughly two hundred and fifty panels. They all need careful cleaning and proofing. Some may need the wood underneath repaired or even replaced. This is for the National Theatre and I can guarantee an acknowledgement will appear in the Silk Gala Ball Programme, I can also arrange free half page advertising for a year in the regular programmes if the price is strictly competitive. If I don't think the quote is reasonable, I will go to Germany for other quotes. One other thing, which is off the record, there is a degree of Government opposition to the restoration of the boxes and I may have to underwrite the cost personally, so that is another reason why the estimate must be extremely competitive.'

She didn't add that the Government opposition came from her dear friend the junior Minister for Arts, Culture and Sport who she was about to meet for lunch.

'*Verstehen, Frau Komturin.*'

Lunch at Golabki went well and the Junior Minister had appeared to have lost her fit of gloom. She seemed happier and more cooperative than she had been for some time. Detty thought it wise to refrain from saying that perhaps it was a bit cooler and Mara's shoes were more comfortable. She did dare to mention that she had found the panels and was finding out about cleaning them up.

'That's OK' said Mara 'there's still some money for this year in the capital fund. I am sure we can meet the cleaning bill. It certainly wouldn't be right for you to foot it.'

It was a completely different attitude from the one that she had met a few days before. Detty was emboldened to explain the hard bargain which she had proposed to the restoration company.

'You haven't lost your negotiating skills then, *meine Allerliebste*,' said Mara and she laughed.

'Hang on' said Detty 'it hasn't worked yet.'

'They would be stupid if it doesn't. A year's free advertising in the programmes of the most prestigious theatre in the country. They ought to bite your hand off and do the restoration for nothing.'

'Perhaps you would like to ring up *Metropole* and tell them that. You could also say that if they don't cooperate you will have the whole board arrested and sent to the galleys, Frau Ministerin.'

'The Hansa never used galley slaves.'

'I am surprised Travsky didn't think of it. As you and I both know, he thought of most other cruel and unusual punishments.'

'I am going to change the subject to something a bit more cheerful which is dreadful but has a happy ending. You remarked some time ago that my father, the greatly respected President of this country, was behaving like a schoolboy planning a first date. You weren't far wrong but there was a reason but it takes a bit of explaining. I now have Presidential permission to explain it to you.'

'Recently, one of the handful of people who got out of the Winterburg alive, asked to see my father. It was an odd request as he wouldn't give Petra a reason. Well anyway this man, Lev Solkov, had apparently been a messenger at the Winterburg, which was suspicious. However, Tanya's lot investigated thoroughly and could find no evidence that he was anything but a low-grade functionary. He wasn't NAS and there was no evidence that he was involved in War Crimes except very indirectly, taking messages, opening gates etc. He had been investigated by the Truth and Reconciliation Court who found him clean.'

'In spite of this, it was agreed that a person-to-person interview with the President, particularly for an undisclosed reason, was too risky. However, he went on insisting that he had information that my father would want and that it was 'for his eyes only – at least at first' – impasse! My father was intrigued though and wanted to know what Solkov had to confide. The resourceful Tanya devised a system to get round the problem. She used a scrambled confidential person-to-person line from different rooms in the Security Headquarters. Nothing would physically pass between them and Solkov would be strip searched very thoroughly before the 'meeting'. Solkov had to believe that the authorities would conduct their side of the bargain and that the interview would not be monitored. To the surprise and the relief of all concerned, he said that he had faith in the President and he would believe him, as he had given his word, and he agreed to the precautions. That in itself was testimony to Solkov's genuineness, unless of course, he had some undiscovered fiendish plot to assassinate my father. Tanya investigated long and hard again for any flaw or trap but could not find one and the plan went ahead. Well, to cut a long story short, Solkov said to my father that, as a messenger in the Winterburg, he had witnessed my mother being shot in the Winterburg courtyard during the third week after the coup, as he left the Gate Lodge to cross the compound on an errand. What is more he had, presumably at great risk, taken a photo of the execution on his phone which he showed on the screen in the interview room. It was a terrible photo but he agreed to leave the camera on the table in the interview room so that it could be examined safely by independent experts. In due course, these were able to confirm that my mother was among the prisoners who were shown being executed in the photo.'

'Under the strictest oath of secrecy, I was the only person told except my father and the security people involved. I was terribly distressed and kept waking at night from nightmares of seeing my beloved mother taken out and murdered by a firing squad. You may have noticed how tense and gloomy that I have been. I was told that I should not even talk to David about it but I am afraid I did and he helped me a lot. He didn't talk to anybody else and I knew that he wouldn't. In addition to the other horrors, I was afraid that my strange behaviour would damage our friendship and that would be dreadful.' She paused. 'I was beginning to think that I should go back to Munich and seek out the psychologist who had helped Masha, but just as I made that decision the awful hopeless black cloud began to lift. One night when you and the children were down at Krenek, I had a very long talk with my father. Gradually, he explained to me that his mourning and horrors had been earlier, when he had been under house arrest taunted by Konradin who told him that as well as murdering *Mutti*, I was to be forced into State Prostitution or murdered. He would have lost both of us. Then you and Marc appeared on the scene. You rescued me and had executed Frederick Kovacs, the psychopathic doctor and Gregor Tushkin, the sadistic armourer. My father still thinks that you are an incarnation of an avenging angel. Once the third of the devilish trio, Konradin, was firmly locked up in the island prison, in a strange sort of way, it also helped him to come to terms with the loss of my mother. He knew, well before I did, what must really have happened to her. He also thought that by a miracle he had been given me back. He began to think that he would be being ungrateful to you and God if he did not rejoice in my salvation, even though it couldn't bring his much-loved wife back. So, there it is.'

'It is the first time that I have been paired with the Deity particularly as I have contravened the Fifth Commandment several times,' said Detty smiling, 'I am not sure what my Jesuit confessor in Ireland would make of that. However, you have explained a lot.'

'There is more and it is a happier bit. For over two years now my father has virtually known that he was a widower but now, he was sure. He has grown very close to Petra Mikhailovna Nuraska.'

'His PA –she's great.'

'She is. Anyway, one morning a few days ago, *Vati* asked me to into his study with him in a conspiratorial sort of way. It sounded as if I was going to get a dressing down, except that he never does that and I had not done anything wrong that I knew about- not recently anyway. When he had sat me down, he asked whether I would object if he asked Petra to marry him. I am afraid I burst out laughing. It was such a bizarre situation. There he was, President of the Republic, asking his daughter whether she minded him asking a delightful widow to marry him. I don't know whether he was shocked at my reaction, but anyway when I had finished laughing, I told him how happy I would be, and he looked mightily relieved.'

'He then said that perhaps I would think that they were old enough to know better but they were both romantics and wanted to announce their engagement at your Ball. Anyway, that is the full measure of the Hansehaus inside gossip.'

'It sounds as if I am going to need another Lanoure model – I wonder what I can do to write this one off.'

'I would like one too but I am not sure what Petra is going to wear and I do not want to upstage her. Anyway, I am not sure my ministerial salary would stretch to Lanoure. Now there is another thing too. *Vati* is determined that Marc's and your entire family should be his guests at the ball. He wants your parents, Nuala, your aunt, Deidre, and Christy to form part of his party together with the whole Von Ritter clan, including Bill and his current girlfriend, and there will of course be Petra, David and me. He said that Petra too had insisted that they all come. So please arrange it.'

'*Jawohl,* Frau Minister – my father usually finds it difficult to take time away from his practice but I suspect a personal invitation from a Head of State might get him to make an exception. He admires your father enormously and I do not think it was to do with his status. What do you make of entertaining my brother-in-law by the way?'

'It is old history, Detti. I gather that the Viennese goddess has been replaced now by a ballerina from Budapest,' she laughed, 'and any way it gives me a chance to show him that I have now got a real man.'

'Wow!' was her friend's comment 'Fighting talk.'

*

It was a warm spring morning and Detty decided that she was a very lucky woman. In fact, she was triple blessed. She was walking down the *Rue St Honoré* on the arm of her handsome and adored husband. She was on her way to have lunch at Le Grand Vefour after having had a fitting of her dove grey ball gown at the fashion house of Lanoure. Life, she decided, doesn't get much better than this.

Königshof that late autumn morning was electric with expectation. The St Nicklaus Ball had caught the imagination of the press and TV, and even those who professed to care nothing about celebrities or politics were surreptitiously interested. But nowhere was more chaotic and dynamic that the Hansehaus itself. It was agreed that the entire Presidential party and a dozen or so Ministers and Service Chiefs would dine with the President the night before the Ball. To this end all the diplomatic bedrooms had been opened and the great banqueting table had been luxuriously laid for the fifty odd diners. Mara had been in command of all this activity, but had been assisted by the town's top caterers and Petra, as she was able to maintain her cover for the moment as the President's PA. Mara had arranged that Petra should attend the dinner, again ostensibly to recognise her help as Nicklaus's PA. She was sat between Marc and David, both of whom were in on the secret, to avoid her being asked any awkward questions. Neither Mara nor Detty need have worried about upstaging her. For the pre-Ball dinner she wore a delightful fuchsia Merino cocktail dress embroidered in gold and black with a black back bow which set off her shoulder length lustrous dark hair perfectly.

The following day, before the Ball, it was agreed that the party would meet for a glass of Sekt before the limousines arrived to take them all in the official motorcade to the opera house. It was a very short journey but clearly could not be taken on foot. Petra arrived from her room wearing a floor length burgundy ball gown with the skirt modelled on a Russian Sarafan. The gown bodice was off the shoulder in paler rose silk, embroidered in gold. It was stunning and Mara and Detty could only whisper 'Wow!' They had no idea where Petra had sourced the gown but, with no disrespect to Königshof, it didn't look local.

Detty just whispered to her when she had the chance. 'You look absolutely stunning!'

'Thank you' said Petra with a broad smile 'As I might be about to change my role, I thought that I ought to celebrate my last occasion as the President's personal assistant.'

'You certainly have but I am not sure that you will be changing your role – just adding to it. I should think.' said an admiring Detty and they both laughed.

The arrangements had been carefully thought out. The floor in the opera house reached back level over the stalls, the orchestra pit and the stage. The orchestra was on tiers at the back of the stage. Despite protests from the prima donna, she was expected to sing the National Anthem after the entry of the President's party. She therefore had to leave the Presidential party early. It was his particular request and she had to comply. There had been talk of a debutantes' parade as in Vienna but it was decided that this was outmoded. The National Ballet gave the first display on the floor then, as a compromise with those in favour of the debutantes' parade, it had been decided that a display of the youngsters in national costume would be appropriate. Detty remembered the one that had been organised at Krenek. She had drawn up the ground rules and then asked for volunteers between 17 and 25. The girls were to wear white blouses and dark figured skirts in the national tradition. They should also wear the pretty local *Karuna*, as a crown. This could be home made to circulated instructions or could be bought at the national costume department of a Königshof department store. The boys were to be dressed in long knee length black coats over tight trousers and thigh length boots in the local tradition. The response was overwhelming and eventually they had to draw lots for the 150 couples to take part. There were three rehearsals with coaching in the traditional dances from members of the ballet school under the control of a *Tanzmeisterin* who a staff member of the Dance Academy was also. The final dress rehearsal was on the day before the ball when the floor was in place. It went off very well. On the night itself, general dancing followed young peoples' dance display and the youngsters were then encouraged to go off to the rehearsal stages where there was a rock band and disco. The caterers had produced a spectacular buffet laid all round the salon over the front entrance. Temporary waiting staff served food and wine in the boxes. Before the supper interval, Detty, who functioned as Master of Ceremonies, resplendent with her green and white sash, called for silence and Nicklaus came to the front of the quadruple box occupied by the Presidential party.

'*Meine Damen und Herren,*

'I have chosen this prestigious occasion to make two announcements.

The first, which is, for the best of reasons, a poorly kept secret, is that I hope to become a grandfather this summer. My daughter, Tamara, has promised me a grandchild in August of this year.' (He waited for the applause to die down.)

'The other announcement may be more surprising to you. I also intend to become a bridegroom in the spring. I have asked Petra Mikhailovna to be my wife and she has done me the honour of accepting. I have also obtained my daughter's permission'. This caused a lot of laughter, before he went on.

'As we have already worked together for some years, Petra has had time to discover most of my bad habits. We have a lot in common. We were both widowed tragically under the previous regime here and we have both worked hard to try and secure the future prosperity of this country. Petra has told me that she would like to say something this evening so I will now pass the microphone to her.'

Petra came to the front of the box looking positively regal in her stunning Russian dress and spoke assuredly and calmly.

'Herr Präsident, *Meine Damen und Herren*,

You may realise how astounded and flattered I was by the President's proposal. However, I have loved and admired him ever since I started working for him shortly after the Civil War so it did not take me very long to say "yes". I do not need to tell you about his thoughtfulness, kindness and humanity as these are recognised by the entire country, but they are especially valued by those of us who, in one way or another, have had the great honour of being particularly close to him. I have one major anxiety – I am not sure that I shall easily get used to calling him Nicklaus rather than *Herr Präsident* but I will try to remember. We love each other and I will do my utmost to make him very happy both now and after his term as President ends.'

After more applause, Tamara stepped forward:

'*Meine Damen und Herren,*' she announced clearly 'I would like to propose a toast to my adored and adorable father and the fine and noble woman whom I heartily welcome to the family as my stepmother. My father, after many years of solitude, has found himself a wonderful wife – perhaps this is yet another example of his resourcefulness. In the past few years, I have tried to fulfil the unofficial role of First Lady of the Republik as well as I could. However, particularly as I have rather suddenly acquired the additional roles of wife and minister, and to these I hope soon to add another as mother, I am incredibly happy now to pass the title to Petra who will have earned it by right. When the dancing starts after the interval, I would like you temporarily to clear the floor and allow the first dance of the second part of the evening to be led by my father and his fiancée.'

'Mara, you didn't warn me of this – you know that dancing is not my strong point' Nicklaus protested. Mara switched off the mike. 'Don't worry, *Vati*, as usual, Petra will sort you out.' She switched the mike on again. 'May I ask you all to raise your glasses to *Petra* and *Nicklaus*.'

*

As spring advanced at last the house was ready. Marc got more leave. He kept asking about the heating and air conditioning installed in the *Dwor*. Detty was puzzled as she hardly regarded her tough soldier husband used to the rigours of a Franconian winter as a wimp wanting to protect himself from the cold.

Meanwhile the wimp had made clandestine visits to Bayreuth. He did not go up the *Grüne Hügel* and indeed took trouble to avoid the many people that he knew in the town, from his visits accompanying Detty. Reluctantly, he even avoided *Die Eule* in case it blew his secret. No, instead he turned off the *Maximilian Strasse* and consulted his piece of paper. He had been there before but he still needed to remind himself where to turn. The paper read:

Klaviermanufaktur Steingraeber & Söhne
Steingraeberpassage 1
95444 Bayreuth

Finally, he turned into the correct side street and parked the car. He entered the building and introduced himself at reception. He was greeted with a warm handshake. 'It's ready – come and have a look.'

They went through and there in all its splendour was the Chamber Concert Grand[22] that he had ordered and was to be part housewarming present part anniversary present, as they moved into the *Dwor*.

'May I play?' said Marc diffidently. 'Of course, *Mein Herr*, it's your instrument and I had it tuned this morning when I knew you were coming.'

'Have you contacted the Königshof tuner?'

'Yes, he will come when we have installed the instrument and set it up.'

'And your colleague will check the temperature and humidity?' 'Certainly'

Marc sat down and played several scales then Chopin's A flat major Ballade.

'You play well, Herr Graf, if I may say so.'

'Only an amateur and rather out of practice, I am afraid.'

---

22 The Chamber Concert Grand Piano

16
AFTER THE BALL

abend ist mein Ball
-von dem bin ich die Königen und dann...

Arabella- Hoffmanstall/Strauss Erster Aufzug [23]

A few days after the Ball, Detty was still having a torrent of phone calls. Most were from the media about the Ball and a few private ones thanking her for her part in the organisation. One however stood out, it read 'The President has asked to see you and Maestro Professor Helge at your convenience. I have asked Maestro Helge and he suggests 18.30 tomorrow at the Hansehaus. Can you make that?' It was signed, Detty noticed, by the recently appointed young assistant PA not by Petra.

She had texted back 'Fine, I'll be there'. She wondered what was going on. Presumably it was something to do with the Ball but everything, she thought, had been OK for that. The last time that they had had a mystery meeting with the President, she had been amongst the conspirators obtaining *die Ritterwürde* for Tamara. Now the shoe

---

23   This evening is my ball
     where I shall be Queen and then...

was on the other foot. He sat them down and came straight to the point.

'We are hoping to get married on the last Saturday before Lent. Fortunately, Easter is very late this year so that is March 10th. Petra asked me, wistfully, whether there would be an opera on which could be made part of our celebrations. You may not realise but she has been a faithful fan in the fourth circle for everything that you do. She even stood for *Tristan* at Bialovsk.'

'That made two of us' said Detty with a chuckle which got a smile from the others 'but I obeyed Nilsson's Law.'

Helge laughed. 'I am sorry, Herr Präsident, you may not be familiar with the story. When the great Birgit Nilsson was asked in New York, what was the secret of singing *Isolde*, she replied 'A comfortable pair of shoes.'

'Ah – I see now' said the President 'Petra said you were fantastic and she was terrified by your narration and curse. She said that she could understand why you scared the fascists. She was too shy to compliment you to your face when she saw you back here. Anyway, when we decided on our plan, she said to me,

'I suppose my new status will stop me going to the National Theatre in the gods.'

'Sadly, I am afraid it will. Quite apart from making it look as if the country is bankrupt, there is no space for security up there. I do however know her favourite opera and, I know it's a lot to ask but I wonder whether there is any chance of putting it on.'

Detty gave a sidelong look at Helge. She wondered what impossible task was going to be suggested. As calmly as possible she just asked:

'What is her favourite opera then?' This was the crunch,

'Well, her favourite is *Arabella,* you see she is a Strauss fanatic.

'It was Helge who broke in, 'After what you said about the Bialovsk *Tristan*, I thought for a dreadful moment that you were going to say *Parsifal* – not I hasten to add, before the Frau Intendantin assaults me, that I have anything against *Parsifal* but it's not the easiest show to put on with limited notice. But before we go on, Herr Präsident, may I ask Bernadette for her reaction?

'Right, well first off, the name part is a great part for the leading soprano and if I am going to be allowed to sing it, I would love to. I think that I can learn it in time. I know some of it already. The main problem I can foresee is set design and production. How do you feel about the orchestra, *Maestro?*'

'I will need to talk to Michael Storen and Luisa Stocken but I think that probably we can do it OK. It's quite a complicated score but they like a challenge. It used to be panned by the critics but it's come in from the cold recently. From my point of view, I would look forward to playing it. I agree with Petra. As Detty says, the main problem may be sets and production.'

'I think we might ask Anna Stolz to direct' said Detty 'She is good and a very safe pair of hands. She knows the ropes locally after *Tristan*. To put it bluntly, particularly as time is short, we don't want to get stuck with a hyper-artistic newcomer with an overblown ego who will make impossible demands. Leave it to us, Nicklaus, don't say anything to Petra yet and we will come back to you as soon as we have firmed things up.'

'Thank you so much. That sounds promising. I will await further signals. Now, a glass of wine for you both? I have an excellent source of dry *Silvaner Auslese* from a very reliable *Weingut* near Würzburg. I think that you may be familiar with it, Detty. I am wondering –we were wondering whether you could manage a charity Gala performance the day or two days before the Wedding?'

In a couple of days, they had the formidable support of Luisa and Michael and were able to go back to the President with a 'yes' and several tentative dates. These were agreed. Detty set about arranging a production team and casting. Here she hit the first snag. Anna Stolz had got a contract for a production of Weber's *Oberon* in San Francisco and wasn't available. Detty hit upon the idea of Gerry Flynn, the Irish director of her Bayreuth *Ring* but it was very short notice with only six months to go. She frantically found Flynn's New York agent and got on to them. Cagily they said that timetable wise it might be possible but they would come back to her when they had asked Dr Flynn. Detty urged speed and got on with the rest of the casting. This proved easier. She rang Walter Liebig immediately who said he could rearrange things a bit and do the dates. Miraculously, he also said he knew the key role of *Mandryka* and added with a laugh that he could even do a pretty good Croatian accent. Then she got on the telephone to Martina Schlerova, the excellent local lyric soprano, who was available and thrilled to be asked to do the second major soprano role of *Zdenka* in the President's nuptial Gala. A call to Hank established that he would be at Krenek teaching at the time and would be happy to do the relatively undemanding tenor role of *Elemer*. She had pencilled in Julia Kitze for *Adelaide* and Lev Forjela as *Matteo* and would contact them as soon as she could. She wondered whether Dieter Tinsel would take the bass part of *Waldner*. It would be a nice recompense for him in the latter part of his career after the debacle of *Sachs* in *Die Meistersinger*, but she thought the part might lie too low for him. It would have to be approached tactfully. Best to go and see him. They needed a coloratura for *Milli* but that and the other smaller parts could be auditioned.

She adjourned to Daina for a sandwich for lunch feeling pleased with herself. She had broken the back of the casting although they still needed a coloratura. Her *Handy* rang. She cursed it for interrupting her well-earned break but smiled immediately when she heard the speaker's accent in English,

'Thank you for thinking of me' said Gerry then immediately 'What about a designer?'

'Hold on. You're going to do it then?'

'Keep me away!'

'Right, I think that we need a simple but traditional design if you agree. Late 19th century Vienna – it's supposed to be 1860. Have you anyone in mind?'

'Helmut Lansdorf – I used to drink with him at Griechenbeisl when I was doing *Helena* for the *Staatsoper*. He insisted on going there despite the tourists because of its history. He is old Vienna to the core and doesn't get much work now because he hates modern *Regietheater* productions.'

'OK, can we meet up? The three of us with Helge von Grunstrand, the music director. Then assuming there are no hitches I will get our finance people to sort out contracts with your agents. When can we meet and can it be here so you can look at the theatre? You haven't seen it since the fire, have you?' 'No, but I have read about it. I gather it's posh.'

'We think so but come and have a look, so you know what you are letting yourselves in for.'

'You seem to go from strength to strength, Detty, dramatic soprano, *Intendantin* and *Rektorin* of the Conservatoire.'

'Yes, too much – Jill of all trades and mistress of none and it's all your fault – you started it at Bayreuth.'

'It was a joint effort with Dr Meisl to say nothing of poor Annaliese's misfortune but it worked, didn't it?'

'I'll say.'

Towards the end of February there was coughing in Christy's Curragh stable which disrupted his plans for Cheltenham. Rather reluctantly Detty had agreed to let Firebrand go for a fourth Champion Hurdle, but in truth neither owner nor trainer were too sorry when the decision was taken out of their hands. Christy was more upset at losing some of his other entries. Detty knew that right on top of the *Arabella* and the Presidential Wedding she could not have gone to Cheltenham anyway. She felt that Firebrand could not add much to her high reputation even if she won a fourth Champion Hurdle whereas to lose it would tarnish her spectacular career. There was a deeper reason, she had a superstitious feeling that Firebrand had done enough on the racecourse and although the situation was different, she was always haunted by the death of the great race mare, Dawn Run at Auteuil. Besides this she had plans with Christy for Firebrand as a brood mare.

The children, together with her duties at the theatre and the College in Livonia had meant that she was reluctant to take on many engagements away from Königshof. She had been invited to sing *Sieglinde* at Bayreuth and had accepted. Bayreuth was special and anyway she could stay with the children at Oberdorf. She also had had a rather attractive invitation to sing Strauss's *Ariadne* at Nuremburg. This also had the advantage that she could commute from Oberdorf, although, of course, it was further. She hadn't finally decided whether to accept or not but thought that she would make a short trip by road leaving the children with Gianna in Ziatov. Niki remained, for the time being, at his Königshof school. It was a bit awkward from Ziatov because he had to be driven in each day which meant an early start but Gianna managed it very well.

She enjoyed a superb dinner at Oberdorf with her father-in-law spoiling her with a mature Pomerol to go with the *gigot*. The following day, she set out for Nuremburg. She was enthusiastically received, liked what she saw. She agreed to do the five shows the following year and made a note to inform Julian, her London agent. She then went to Bayreuth to confirm a few details before returning to Oberdorf for a second night and beautiful local trout accompanied by Max's own *Wurzburger Trocken Silvaner*. In the morning she breakfasted and set out for home. She would stop to break the journey for the night south of Prague.

There was only a month to go until the *Arabella* performances but the cast all knew their parts. All that was now needed were the two *Sitzproben* then the technical week followed by the private and public *Hauptproben* just before the first Gala night. She went through the timetable as she drove along checking that nothing had been forgotten. As she crossed the Czech border, she felt tired. Not surprising, she said to herself; she had had a very busy couple of days and some long drives. By the time she arrived at the small hotel south of Prague, where they often broke their journey between Livonia and Bavaria, she had a sore throat and felt feverish. I am probably getting a cold, she said to herself, but she really knew it was worse than that-? flu – she thought and swore to herself a very un-convent girl oath.

She slept a bit but really fitfully. She took a couple of Paracetamol which she had with her but they didn't make much difference. When she woke, she realised that she was not fit to drive. She phoned down to the receptionist, apologised for speaking German and asked whether she could have some water and explained that she didn't think that she could leave that day. The hotel was run by a sympathetic married couple. The motherly wife bustled in with the water and suggested that they got the local doctor in. Detty said that might be a good idea but that she would like to contact her husband, who she thought might have arrived home. She rang. He was in Königshof having just arrived from Ingolstadt – a bit of luck, she thought. Could he get her? Of course. What about a second driver? He would try and see if either Mara or Petra could meet Niki from school and look after Liese. If so, he would fetch Gianna and they would drive down together to get her.

A pleasant Czech doctor arrived and examined her. She had a bad sore throat, she said, and some swollen glands in her neck probably due to the throat. Normally she would take a swab and get a blood test but as Detty was desperate to get home, there wasn't time for that. The doctor left her a prescription for antibiotics and suggested she took more Paracetamol when the time came. As the doctor was leaving, Marc rang on Detty's *Handy*. He was coming with Gianna. They would stay the night then they would leave early the following morning. The kindly Czech lady confirmed that there were two rooms available. It was all arranged.

Left alone, Detty slept a bit then examined herself thoroughly. She found more swollen glands and her throat was very sore. She cursed as she realised that she hadn't asked anybody to get the antibiotics. More than that, she was now terrified. Before her eyes, was the spectre of her friend, Sandy, the organ scholar at Oxford who had first introduced her to Haydn Roberts, who had become her singing teacher. At the following end of term, Sandy was just preparing for his Christmas duties and was working with Detty on a Bach Cantata solo. One morning she got a message that they couldn't rehearse that day, as he wasn't very well. That evening Sandy was admitted to the John Radcliffe Hospital and a month later he was dead. The diagnosis apparently was a very aggressive Non-Hodgkins Lymphoma. Later Detty had confirmed with her father that these were now usually treatable but not always. Sandy had been unlucky that the disease had taken a hold so rapidly. This didn't comfort Detty as her present fever, sore throat and swollen glands all over were identical to the way Sandy's illness had presented. She had catastrophic thoughts of Marc widowed and her children orphaned. She tried to tell herself that it was illogical but try as she might the nightmare was still there. The irony struck her that having survived her terrible dangers under the Travsky regime in Moltravia, she was now, young as she was, threatened by an illness.

In the evening Marc and Gianna arrived, Marc was clearly worried but was calm and capable as ever. Gianna showed her normal practical resilience. They were a good team and it comforted her to see them. The following morning, fighting off the well-intentioned protests of their

Czech hostess that Detty ought to stay, they bundled her into the car and headed for Livonia. They had only been in their Polish house a couple of months before Detty's Bavarian trip but it was clean, heated, provisioned and had everything that they immediately needed. On arrival Detty was ashen and trembling. Marc bundled her into bed then phoned the local doctor who, miraculously, answered the phone himself and said that he would come with his nurse in the morning and take the necessary tests. Did they mind if he was early before his consulting in the village started?

Marc assured him that they were only too pleased with his service and of course they didn't mind if they were early. Anyway, his patient was a doctor's daughter so she understood these things.

'Oh, I didn't know that' said the doctor 'the Frau Komturin is a multi-facetted person.'

Detty had, in fact, wondered whether to telephone her father. She had decided against it thinking that there wasn't much he could do at that distance and that it would only worry her mother.

It was a very tense wait. Detty remained feverish with her painful glands and throat and ate nothing. Her usually robust frame started to wilt. Marc got his leave extended on compassionate grounds and Gianna looked after Detty and the children tirelessly. The results came after four days. The pleasant doctor returned smiling, saying:

'You have got infectious mononucleosis, Frau von Ritter. The tests are conclusive. It is a severe attack but no more. In a couple of months, you should be as right as rain.' The relief was huge. Marc said he thought that was a disease that students got from kissing each other. They could laugh again but Detty was unable to respond physically. After ten days she felt better and immediately began to worry about the Gala Wedding performance and the other four *Arabellas* which were to follow. It had become obvious that she was in no fit state to sing a major role or indeed anything else. Mara had visited her straight away and knew the situation but she, of course, was not really involved with the artistic side. Detty struggled to ring Helge, Walter Liebig and, really as a courtesy more than anything else, Hank who was in New York singing *Siegfried* at the Metropolitan. He said how distressed he was but added that sadly, flexible as his voice was, he didn't think that he could sing Strauss's heroine. However, he added cryptically:

'You have given me an idea. Give me 48 hours and I will see if I can come up with something.'

So, saying he rang off and Detty really hadn't concentrated on his last mysterious remark. She swallowed two more Paracetamol and drifted off in an exhausted sleep. Nothing more happened that day but about midday the following day Detty at last felt a bit better. The better she felt the more worried she became about the Gala. Even when she had to escape from Moltravia to fulfil her contract at Bayreuth, she had never cancelled an engagement. She muttered to herself 'Perhaps I can do it' but she knew that she couldn't. Anyway, it was better to cancel than to perform badly and wreck the excellent vocal reputation that she had painstakingly built up. The problem was that normally a singer withdrawing, particularly with a cast iron reason, could fairly safely leave the abandoned management to sort out the problem. In this case, however, she was head of the said management so there was nobody else in charge to take hold and sort the problem. It was a real worry.

Just after her boiled egg for lunch, she dozed off again to be woken by her *Handy* going off on her bedside table. She wondered whether she could summon up the energy to be nice to anyone while they wished her well. She answered monosyllabically.

The responding voice said, '*Zuerst, wie gehst du?*' It had a very slight *Berlinerisch* accent which sounded familiar but which she could not immediately place. Whilst thinking, she answered that she was a bit better and thanked the caller for enquiring.

Then the voice said with a chuckle,

'I think that it might be pay-back time, if you agree, Bernadette.'

Then the penny suddenly dropped, the caller was Annaliese Seiling, her friend, role model and the leading contemporary dramatic soprano.

'I gather that, unfortunately, you might need somebody to cover your *Arabella*. That dreadful man, Hank Schliessen, knew from a casual remark that I was free next month and asked if I knew the part. He asked me if I could do it. Now it so happens that I sang it in Munich early last year and I know it (and love it). I've done it quite a few times.

If you tell me that I am too long in the tooth, I will scratch your eyes out and never speak to you again. What about it?'

'*Meine liebe Anna,* when I had the great good fortune to go on as your cover at Bayreuth, I had to pinch myself to believe it was real but even then, I didn't imagine you ever offering to be mine. If you really mean it, you are my guardian angel and of course I accept with profound gratitude. I have already studied your recordings when I was learning it. I am sorry not to be able to put what I have learnt into practice but what a treat our public have in store. I am sure by the way, the Präsident and the Frau Präsident *gewählt*[24] will be equally thrilled. Thank you so much. Please get your agent to contact the Finance Office. Can you make the *Sitzprobe* next Thursday?'

'I shall have ridden into the flames three times by then and be bored with it, so I ought to be able to make the *Sitzprobe.* I should be able to get a flight OK even if I must sit on Hank's lap and brush up with my score.'

Detty suddenly felt well enough to laugh. Annaliese had a commendably svelte figure for a dramatic soprano but she was a big woman and the idea of her travelling across the Atlantic on the huge *Heldentenor's* lap was comical.

'At least since the rebuild you will have a decent dressing room. I usually use my own office so there shouldn't be too much clutter but I will get them to tidy it up.'

On the following day Detty got another phone call. 'Detty, its Birgitte, Birgitte Frankland from Finance. I am so sorry to bother you when you are ill but I have a problem, albeit a nice one. Apparently, Frau Seiling's agent has been in touch with our Finance Department and the junior officer who took the call was a bit out of his depth, so they referred it to me. Usually, I don't deal with contracts and payment – we follow a standard scale. The problem is this. Apparently, Frau Seiling has said that she will take no fee for the Gala as it's for the *Conservatoire* charity and she wants €2,000 per night for the other four i.e., €8,000 for the entire run. Now I don't know but I guess that she gets more,

---

24 President's wife elect

probably a great deal more, than $8,000 per *night* at the Met and what she is asking us for will barely pay her flight across the Atlantic and her hotel. What should we do?'

Detty thought about it and phoned Birgitte back the following morning. 'I think this is what you must do, Birgitte. Go back to Frau Seiling's agent, say that you think the fee is very modest. If it is confirmed ask her to thank Kammersängerin Seiling for her generosity and leave it at that. Frau Seiling knows what she is doing and I am sure that the generosity was deliberate.'

17
THE RHEIN JOURNEY

The river nobly foams and flows-
The charm of this enchanted ground,
And all its thousand turns disclose.
Some fresher beauty's varying round:

BYRON: CHILDE HAROLD'S PILGRIMAGE

It was a very odd feeling. She was better but if she sat up too quickly the room spun. She felt extremely tired and only wanted to sleep all the time. The sun was pouring in through the long windows of the *Dwor*. It wasn't a warm sun; the year was still too early for real heat in the late Baltic spring. But for all that it was cheerful and welcome. The day after to-morrow was the Gala. It was to be televised nation-wide as was the wedding the day after. Whenever similar events had been held in the past she had been at the forefront, but not this time. She still felt exhausted and wondered, rather desperately, if she would ever get her high-octane energy back. She knew that exhausted as she was, she must make one important phone call. She summoned up her remaining energy and was relieved to get straight through,

'Martina, how are your Strauss songs?

'First, tell me how you are, Frau Detti?'

'I think that I am better but feel like a damp rag and that is why I am phoning you. Now about the Strauss songs?'

'I know some of them and did sing them in a recital at College.' Martina Schlerova replied.

'Well, I was supposed to be singing three of them at the President's Wedding. Petra is a Strauss fanatic and I was going to sing *Mein Auge, Winterweihe* and *Der Rosenband.* These seemed to be suitable and a present for Petra. As it is I don't think that I could sing Happy Birthday to You at a children's party. Could you do it – one of the men might do it but it's much better with a soprano?'

'Well, I know *Der Rosenband* and if I remember rightly *Winterweihe* is straightforward and *Mein Auge* is very short. Yes, I think I can do it. I might have to have a score hidden as a precaution. Who's accompanying?'

'Helge, on the piano.'

'I have just had a thought. I know *Vier Letzte Lieder* and I could do *Frühling* – it's the most cheerful one and I also know *Winterliebe* which is entirely suitable for a wedding and very short. Would you mind if I substituted those?

'Not at all, if you choose ones that are suitable and I know that you will. Quite a lot of his songs are quite sad. I will leave it to you. Ask Helge if you need any help. *Toi, toi, toi* for *Zdenka* and *Arabella.* I shall be watching if I can keep awake.'

'I'm terrified. Singing opposite Annaliese Seiling is intimidating but she is so friendly and relaxed you almost forget that she's taken the Met, La Scala, Vienna, Paris and Covent Garden by storm to say nothing of all the others.'

'I know what you mean. I sang *Brünnhilde* opposite Hank in Bayreuth at short notice. Imagine what I felt like as I had worshipped him since I was a schoolgirl. At my convent I was obsessed with classical music but I had never heard of him. Mind you he was only just starting. I found an article about him in *The Irish Times* then I listened to every broadcast and recording he made. This young American tenor was fast becoming one of the greats. It was a real schoolgirl passion then I found myself singing opposite him at Bayreuth of all places – it was surreal but it seems a long time ago – a lot has happened since then.' She sighed 'I must drop off again now. Thanks for helping.'

'Before you go, I must share one thing with you. When I met Kammersängerin Seiling when she arrived for the *Sitzprobe,* she just said, 'Hello, you must be Martina. I'm Anna, Bernadette's cover – would you believe it?'

Weak as she was Detty muttered to herself with a smile 'Cheeky bitch!'

She drifted off to sleep to be woken by Liese in tears grumbling that Niki ran over the grass, newly mown by Jan, too fast for her to keep up. Jan had acquired, on Marc's instruction, a very necessary sit-on mower which was his pride and joy and fascinated the children. It had cost an eye-watering amount of money. but it did the job. The children were enjoying the freedom of the freshly mowed sward which she hoped in time would turn into a decent lawn. Having settled the dispute, she dozed off again and only awoke towards evening. There was stream of voluble Italian coming from the kitchen. Gianna had asked whether a school friend of hers, Simona, *una compagna del banco* could come and help while she was waiting to go to university again in the autumn. Detty was delighted because even before her illness, her duties at the opera house and at the college at Krenek meant that she was quite stretched, particularly when it came to day-to-day fetching, carrying and looking after the children. Marc was a great resource when he was there but like most soldiers his availability was unpredictable. They had acquired through Kunz, the police inspector, a lovely local lady, Vilma, who kept the house clean and tidy. The girls in the kitchen seemed to be competing with each other to produce the most refined glories of Tuscan cooking. They all tried to talk English in the house as both girls were keen to learn as much of it as possible. It amused Detty that neither girl realised that, after some serious sessions with the Italian language coaches, both earlier in Siena and more recently at the Königshof opera, her Italian had improved markedly and she was able to follow most of what the girls were saying, at least until they joked with each other, as a party trick, in broad *toscanaccio.* She suspected that Gianna did realise that her boss's Italian was a lot better than she let on but the realisation only came to Simona when they watched together a DVD of *Gianni Schicchi* filmed in Munich with Detty as Lauretta. Simona remarked, with some surprise, after *'O mio babbino caro'* 'really Frau Detti I didn't realise that you spoke Italian so well.' Detty thought that it was a somewhat back-handed compliment but just laughed. The present discussion concerned the proper cooking time for a *ragu*. The dish for that evening was *Pici con acciughe, pomodori e pancetta*, which was a particular favourite with the children. The verdict from the cooks was that the *acciughe* were fine but the Livonian approximation to *pancetta* wasn't correct. However, the children pronounced it delicious and Detty complimented the cooks. She hadn't got her appetite back and sadly ate very little.

She was alone for the night. Marc was coming back from Ingolstadt to have a day at home before the gala and the wedding the following day. She had slept better and treated herself to her favourite form of relaxation – a steamy hot bath in their new bathroom. She did however take the precaution of asking Gianna to stand by through the door into the bedroom in case she had another dizzy attack.

She was delighted to see Marc when he arrived in the late morning having driven all night, as was his custom. It was agreed that he would join the President and Petra for the opera and the wedding and then drive back to Ziatov afterwards. He wanted to stay with Detty and watch the opera and the wedding on the TV but he had to attend the celebrations even though she couldn't. Anyway, he had been asked by Nicklaus to be joint witness at the wedding with David, which really had decided the matter. Mara and a friend of Petra's called Elfriede from the Civil Service were the matrons of honour. Even with no Detty, Marc really had to be there, particularly as the bridal couple were short of relatives on both sides. The cruelties of the Civil War had seen to that, albeit that it had made their marriage possible.

Detty awoke on the day of the gala feeling better for the first time. In full wife mode, she checked that Marc had got everything with him to make a black-tie change at the Hansehaus for the opera and his formal *Bundeswehr* uniform for the wedding. Secretly, he would like to have worn his uniform and decorations from the FWL as a compliment to the country and the bridegroom; but his semi-clandestine involvement in the Civil War was still a sensitive subject. Particularly as the media cameras of the world would be at the ceremony, he thought that he must play safe and attend in his substantive role as a *Bundeswehr Heer* major.

In the evening Detty had the TV set up in the main salon of the *Dwor* with a bottle of Von Ritter Sekt already in the ice bucket. The children were allowed to stay up to see Nicklaus, Petra, Mara, David and Papà arrive at the Opera House and hear the Fanfare from the Swans Band. Detty had invited the two Italian girls to join her for the gala and share the Sekt. Detty had a strange, through the looking glass feeling. It was very, very odd to be looking at a Ceremony on TV that she had chiefly arranged and in which she should have had a major part. She still had a tingle that it was her responsibility and she was desperately anxious that it went well.

The TV cameras focussed on the arrival of the President's party with Petra now by his side as his fiancée. The Swans Trumpeters played the presidential fanfare to the delight of the children who were gradually dispatched to bed by the firm but gentle persuasion of Gianna who arrived back after some time carrying the child alarm, so Detty was able to concentrate on the opera. She was excited and relieved as Annaliese's and Martina's voices blended splendidly in the first duet sequence of *Er ist der Richtige*. Hank and Anna clearly had great fun in the *Elemer* and *Arabella* brief scene. Detty wondered if they had ever, in their long association, sung that scene together before. She must ask them. The long scene between *Waldner* and *Mandryka* introduced Walter in great voice and Dieter Tinsel had got his self-confidence back after the disaster in *Die Meistersinger* rehearsals. Detty was pleased that she had gently persuaded him to take the part. Then she reflected on Walter's enthusiasm in taking his part. No way was he a Croatian but there was something about the rural squire's role which spoke to the heart of the mountain bred Bavarian. Not an easy scene but they got away with it. Then there was Annaliese, a secure honeyed line floating over Helge's surging strings and wind in *Mein Elemer!* bringing the act to a close.

She poured a glass of Sekt for them all and listened to the interval talk. The *FreiSenderLivonia's* interviewer talked to Helge about the score and how for years it had been disparaged but recently it had been recognised for the masterpiece that it was. There was a clip of Gerry Flynn, the Irish director, claiming that it was a work that almost produced itself if you had the courage to leave it alone. Then they were off again soon with *Und du wirst mein Gebieter sein.-* one of the most beautiful duets that even Strauss had ever written. She was never quite sure about *Milli's* coloratura yodelling but Regina Brecht, an import straight from the *Wiener Komische Oper*, did it very well and she supposed that dramatically you needed a let-down after the emotion of the duet. The complicated muddle of the pseudo betrayal was deftly handled by Gerry and brought the act to its end.

In the second interval the FSL announcer said that she had two unusual short interviews. The first one was with Annaliese Seiling who explained how delighted she was to sing the wonderful name part although it was very sad that Bernadette O'Neill's unfortunate illness had prevented her from singing it. She then explained, for any viewer who didn't know the story, of how Bernadette had replaced her at very short notice in the Bayreuth *Siegfried* after she had broken her ribs. So, there was a certain symmetry in her being able to help this time. The second interview was with Petra who explained that she was very nervous as this was her first public interview as the President's fiancée. Despite this she seemed calm and assured. She said that she was so touched that the National Opera had put on, at her request, her favourite opera, *Arabella*. Bernadette's illness was sad but how amazing it was to have her replaced by one of the most famous singers in the world. She then added with a blush that she had squeezed her fiancé's hand during the beautiful '*Und du wirst mein Geliebter sein,*' and added it was a wonderful moment. The interviewer then asked, 'Are you going to fetch a glass of clear spring water for him to-morrow?'

'I suppose I ought to' she replied smiling rather coyly. Clever girl thought Detty. She has won the hearts of the nation with that. She sighed and poured them all another glass of Sekt.

They sailed through to *Das war sehr gut Mandryka*. It was a treat of heartfelt singing from Annaliese and Walter, admirably supported by the others. After the first few curtain calls, Anna brought a smiling and applauding Helge from the wings and they all gathered for more curtain calls. Helge proudly acknowledged his orchestra with his hands then signalled for silence.

'Herr Präsident, Frau Nuraska, *Meine Damen und Herren*. I ask for your applause for somebody who isn't here. Please show your appreciation of Frau Komturin Bernadette O'Neill who works so hard for this theatre and works hard for this production. Get well soon, Detti, we are all thinking of you.'

As the warm applause started, Helge shot off the stage like a scalded cat and re-appeared with his orchestra, who were still applauding, back in the pit. Annaliese Seiling, looking very glamorous, still in her beautiful cerise ball gown, stepped forward to the footlights and again asked for silence with her hands.

'Bernadette has allowed me to deputise for her tonight in the performance and I would like her to allow me to deputise for her in another respect as well. I understand that it is traditional here to finish galas with the National Anthem, usually, of course, sung by its author. Tonight, I will be proud to be allowed to take her place. Maestro von Grunstrand please.'

The orchestra gave the prolonged drum roll of the *Freiheitslied*, the audience stood and Annaliese started the first verse. Detty at home could only mutter to the others 'I didn't expect that.' She was wet eyed and said to Gianna and Simona 'just as well that I haven't got any make-up on.'

At the wedding, the following day, Martina sang her three Strauss songs, miraculously with no obvious mistakes, and the cathedral bells rang out as a very happy Herr and Frau Oblov appeared on the steps below the great west arch under its supplication for the Mother of God to pray for us. The reception was held in the Great Hall of Schloss Krenek. Annaliese Seiling had been invited to the Wedding and Reception because she was staying to sing the other *Arabella* performances. At the Reception, she congratulated Martina on her performance of the Strauss Lieder in the cathedral but, somewhat to Martina's surprise didn't mention the gala performance the night before. She must have thought that I was terrible and was being tactful, disappointed, Martina said to herself. She tried to think no more about it. Later Annaliese hurried off to ask for her briefcase at the cloakroom.

Back in the Hall, she found Martina again and from her briefcase passed her a quarto reinforced envelope. Martina asked if she might open it then and was told 'Of course'. Inside was a silk gala programme for the performance of *Arabella* with a double inset of fine paper showing a finished print mounted on each side. The first was of the cast, chorus and orchestra of *Arabella* grouped, which she recognised as one that they had posed for the press after the *Hauptproben*. On the opposite side of the inset was another photo, this time of *Isolde* at Bayreuth. The second photo was inscribed:

'To a fabulous Zdenka, my friend and colleague, Martina Schlerova, with love and all best wishes for the future from Bernadette O'Neill's Stellvertreterin[25], Annaliese Seiling.

Arabella Königshof March 20--)

'I thought that you would like the inscription mainly in English so that you can show it off when you successfully audition for the Met and I am sure that will be soon.' smiled Annaliese.

Whenever Martina performed in the future, in Königshof or anywhere else, the photos were displayed proudly in her dressing room in a double silver frame. Martina saw that they were locked up carefully after each performance.

Detty wrote Annaliese a letter which she sent to her private apartment in Koblenz, thanking her for everything that she had done during her visit and in particular making one young singer very, very proud and happy. She got a card in reply later sent to the *Dwór* from Milan.

Detti,

I do hope that you are fully recovered. Do look after yourself. I loved my stay, your superb theatre and more than anything your great team. Hank did me a real favour when he twisted my arm and I was so pleased that I had a space.

May I come back? Love Anna xx

---

25 Understudy/cover

As soon as she was well enough, she took the card into the theatre and displayed it on the Green Room notice board.

Marc returned to the *Dwór* from Königshof after seeing the bride and bridegroom off for a very short honeymoon at Menton on the Côte d'Azur. He was privy to this, as he had arranged it and presented it as a Wedding Present from the von Ritter entourage. As he drove up to the house, he heard *Dove sono?* coming tunefully from the salon accompanied by piano. He drew two conclusions from this. First, that his beautiful *Steingräber* piano, recently arrived from Bayreuth, had been set up and tuned in his absence and second, that his wife was better. Both pleased him hugely and he had a broad grin as he tried to open the front door as noiselessly as possible and waited behind it for *Dove sono?* to finish.

Their hug lasted several minutes then.

'Please don't get ill again, darling, you frighten me rotten if you get ill. I was worried sick.'

'I don't know why. I was aware that my husband was at, not one but two high society functions in Königshof, and that, handsome as he is, I was sure that numbers of delightful young women, some known to me, were queuing up to flirt with him.'

'You have recovered your cheek, young lady, I see and I suppose that is a good sign. Anyway, I would point out that you can't always reckon to get the world's leading dramatic soprano to act as your cover. But she was marvellous, wasn't she? Nicklaus, Petra, Mara, David and I went round to her dressing room after the show and all she could do was ask about you, were you eating? Had you seen the right doctors? Was the new house warm enough? Were you going to get a reasonable rest to convalesce? It went on and on. When we at last got a chance to say how fantastic she had been. She just said 'Thank you. But it wasn't difficult, I was only part of a great cast.'

Detty reckoned that she had lost the argument and gave up. 'I have put some champagne in the fridge' she said.

*

She was luxuriating in her newly acquired director's chair with a reporter's notebook on the flap table beside her and a cup of rapidly cooling coffee in the cup recess. Sitting in the sun in front of the portico of the *Dwór,* she had kicked her shoes off, realising guiltily that she would have scolded the children if they had done the same. She had been in to Krenek the day before to settle details of her new project with Helge von Grunstrand, Michael Storen and Luisa Stocken. The plan was to form a group from the orchestra which could act as a small chamber ensemble but also split into various even smaller chamber groups as required. It had been agreed that the title should be '*Das Waldhüter Kammerorchester*. Michael and Luisa had been delegated the tricky task of forming a list of players to be invited which they would then submit to Helge and Detty for final support and approval. Detty was tackling one of her easier tasks. Later she would have to organise singers, when required, for the chamber group, and but for now she was engaging on sketching provisional programmes for starting of a series of Coffee Concerts. These were to be held in the reception hall of the Opera House which stretched from the first circle over the front portico. It had been created by stripping out a corridor, some redundant cloakrooms, two small bars and one larger one. It passed through the arch between the auditorium second circle and included the space over the portico. This provided a large public area which had already served for the reception after the gala opening night but, as the acoustics seemed good. Detty had had her eye on it for some time as a possible site for chamber music concerts. Next summer, if it all went well, she might get back to arranging her pet lakeside concerts at Krenek. The first concert at the opera house was already scheduled for a month's time then they planned one per fortnight until the summer break, four in all. She was going to plan programmes for these four recital/concerts then they would decide whether to carry them on during the autumn season.

She scribbled on her pad (1) Brahms Sextets prob. Op36 (2) Schubert Goethe songs (me) (3) Vivaldi Oboe Concerto R450 (ask Luisa), Mozart Symphony 36 (Linz) (4) Top Krenek Student Quartet (ask Helge or Head of Strings)? Haydn Op24 Nr4 plus Shostakovich 6 op101. That should do, she said to herself. Gianna should be back with Niki soon and noises from the upper windows suggested that Simona was romping with Liese.

She thought about her future planning. She still had a full diary. However, she had been relieved of the major organisation for that year's Nicklaus Fest as, fortunately, Martin Holman, the brilliant young Australian assistant conductor, who had joined them the year before straight from La Fenice in Venice, was a *bel canto* specialist. He enthusiastically had relished being given the lead role in organising that year's *Nicklaus Fest* with a *bel canto* theme. He had checked with Helge and Detty about his proposals for the festival. He had already been told that he had a reasonably free hand for the festival *bel canto* content to re-balance their repertory. He suggested *Rossini's La Cenerentola, Donizetti's Maria Stuarda* and the jewel in the crown *Norma* with a certain Maria Angela Spinelli singing her debut in the role. At the planning meeting the year before, Detty had quietly suggested that it would be good to have Signora Spinelli to sing *Norma*. The young Australian's eyes had popped out on stalks.

He had said. 'You must be joking Detty. You're right she has prepared the role but she will want to open La Scala with it or do it at the Met – in a smaller house like this we don't stand a chance of booking her – even if we could pay her fees.'

'Do you have the expression in Australia "it's not what you know, it's who you know? *La Totti* told me, when I mentioned it to her, that she would like to do it first in a smaller, less prominent house and that we would suit her well.'

'You must have incredible powers of persuasion, Detty,'

'If you permit me to interfere in your casting, I think that I can fix it. Have you ever conducted her?'

'Wow! Yes, I was given one *Traviata* at La Fenice when Carbonara was ill or had found something better to do. I was terrified but she was fine. She gave me a big hug afterwards and thanked me for being so helpful from the Pit.'

'That sounds like *la Totti,* I'll give her a ring – she likes to fix her agent herself – I'll tell her that the coffee is now up to Italian standard, that should convince her to come.'

'I didn't know that you were close friends' said the rather awestruck Australian.

*

That had all been fixed the previous year. She was now able to concentrate on the recitals and then get back to *Der Ring* for the following year. There had been a lot of discussion about whether they went for the full four night *Ring* in one go or do it bit by bit which was the usual practice in smaller and some bigger houses. In the event for several reasons, mainly to achieve the right casting. they had decided to go for broke and do the full cycle straight off.

18
DAS WISSENDE WEIB[26]

mich musste
der Reinste verraten,
dass wissend würde ein Weib!

GÖTTERDÄMMERUNG ACT 3 SCENE 3[27]

It was May and the weather was becoming hot. There were six weeks to go. They had handed over to the *Techniks* in the main theatre, allowing them much longer than the normal technical week because of the four linked shows. Every member of the cast and orchestra were still going through their difficult bits in every available space. Bars, cloak rooms, dressing rooms and stores had all been called back into service to add to the normally very adequate, rehearsal space of the re-built theatre. Every piano in Königshof that could be hired, begged, or borrowed was in the theatre. The theatre at Bialovsk and available rooms at *Schloss Krenek* were fully used to add to the rehearsal spaces. The staff

---
26 The wise woman
27 The purest must betray me
   To make a woman grow wise

repetiteurs, exhausted with bags under their eyes, had been augmented by appropriate members of the academic staff from Krenek. There was so much apparent chaos that Detty wondered what she had done unleashing this maelstrom. In her gloomier moments she thought that it would all end in an internationally publicised disaster.

Anna Stolz and Gerry Flynn, who got on together, had asked from the beginning that they should be joint directors. For *Das Rheingold* and *Siegfried,* Anna was officially *Direktorin* and Gerry *Dramaturg,* and for *Die Walküre* and *Götterdämmerung,* they were the other way round. In practice they co-operated together on all four productions. This was an unusual arrangement but to everyone's relief, it worked very well.

When Detty got depressed over the apparent chaos, Gerry reassured her,

'Bayreuth is just like this before a new *Ring* – well you've seen it for yourself. Just relax and concentrate on *Brünnhilde* – that would be enough for most people.'

She didn't believe him about Bayreuth – her recollections were that everybody, except her, was calm and professional. She agreed, however, that she should concentrate on *Brünnhilde* and tried to.

One morning, the previous summer, she had escaped from a hot Königshof and gone back to the *Dwór* for an hour or two's peace to work on the difficult Act Two Scene Four of *Götterdämmerung* which, although she now knew it well, still made her anxious. She was doing,

Betrug!Betrug!
Schänlichster Betrug!
Verrat! Verrat!-Wie noch nie gerächt!

for the umpteenth time. It had to be screamed in agony and yet remain musical and was therefore very difficult. Her *Handy* rang. She swore very loudly in her extremely non-convent way, then looked at the screen – David, that was different.

'David, have you news?'

'Yes, I have. Three o'clock this morning, Mara gave us a daughter. She was in labour from early last night but wasn't progressing and the consultant saw her and suggested that he did a Caesarean to which we readily agreed.'

'What size? And have you a name?'

'3.36 kilos'

'Wow' said Detty 'Poor Mara – that's a lot for my tiny friend.'

'Yes, I'm afraid she married the wrong husband and that my daughter takes after me not her mother.'

'Not a bit of it. Perhaps she is dramatic soprano material' laughed Detty.

'You could be right. She is to be called Gisela Bernadette – after her late grandmother and you.'

'That is very touching. Can I come round and see them? Perhaps to-morrow?'

'I think that's OK. She is a bit tired today but I'll check if they reckon tomorrow is possible.'

'Many congratulations, *Vati – bis bald!*'

She tried to get back to her betrayal but kept thinking about Mara and Gisela Bernadette. She admired Mara for remembering her loved and tragic mother at this important time in her life.

*

Now, nearly a year old, Gisela Bernadette was thriving and they were grappling with another birth, an artistic one of *Der Ring des Nibelungen*. With only twenty-one days to go the Technical Director announced, with some pride, that they were ready. The production team and the musicians could have their theatre back. This was a relief. Before the eight *Hauptproben,* Detty and Hank, as Co-Directors of the Conservatoire invited the entire cast, production team, front of house staff – in fact everybody involved to Krenek for a Reception. It had been decided not to add to the chaos in the theatre by holding the party there. A truck was organised from Würzburg to bring two pallets of *Sekt* and the Krenek kitchens produced a huge array of cold table. Several coaches were hired to bring everybody out and back from and to the city.

Even Detty, who had been at the centre of the organisation from the start, was still amazed when she entered the capacious hall at Krenek and saw just how many people were involved. Fortunately, the summer weather was warm and they were able to spill out onto the terraces. Professor Poliziano had booked for the first cycle. He had agreed to combine this with giving invited lectures to the Krenek students on *The Camerata de' Bardi and the Florentine Road to Opera in the 16th Century*. With his sardonic humour, on seeing the crush at the party, he quoted:

> *e dietro le venìa sì lunga tratta*
> *di gente, ch'i' non averei creduto*
> *che morte tanta n'avesse disfatta.*[28]

Detty, overhearing him, would have been the first to admit that her Dante was not strong, however she knew enough Italian to recognise the quotation as the one T.S. Eliot had used in *The Waste Land* and replied, 'Surely it's not as bad as that, *Professore?*'

He congratulated her on her understanding the quote. They had a good laugh and it started the party on a cheerful note. After drinks were served, Detty called for silence:

'This is not an evening for speeches but I would like to thank everybody for the colossal amount of work that they have put in and what you have all already achieved. In view of my shared past experience with Kammersängerin Seil*ing*, who visited us so successfully last year, I will not wish you all *Hals und Beinbruch*[29] which is too close to the bone (loud groans). She sends her greetings and thoughts to us all for the present enterprise. I just wish you all *Toi, toi, toi* for whatever task you have from tomorrow onwards.'

---

28 And behind there came so long a column
   Of people, that I ne'er would have believed
   That death had ever undone so many.
   Dante: *Inferno* Canto3 vv55-57
29 Break a leg and your neck

*

The Foyer was full of excitement. The opening night of any new *Ring* was always special, but this one was like the coming-of-age party of their still young democracy. At last, she got away from the well-intentioned, chattering crowds in the front of house and slipped into her normal seat in the centre box. She had the comforting presence of Marc on one side and Nicklaus and Petra on the other. The Oblovs were not exactly incognito but had arrived without any special ceremony. Mara was feeding the baby back at the Hansehaus and was coming to the second cycle. David, realising that this was an important moment but being far from a convinced Wagnerian, had tried to suggest that Gisela Bernadette provided an excuse for not attending. He was informed sharply by Mara that, clever as he was, he couldn't feed the baby. She would feed her in the President's withdrawing room behind the box during intervals and at other appropriate times. Their young help, Klara, would look after the baby during the actual acts. He had then protested,

'But Detty isn't even in the first one and, how long does it last?'

'The first one is two and a half hours without an interval, and you must go to it, to understand the other bits' answered his severe wife. He had been incredulous and further infuriated his wife by asking. 'Could I bring a pillow?'

Mara had the fervour of a convert. In truth she had known little about opera, apart from being introduced to '*Va pensiero*' – the Chorus of the Hebrew Slaves by her first love and had known nothing at all about Wagner before meeting Detty. It was, however, difficult to be long in Detty's company without her enthusiasm washing over you, which usually resulted in either conversion or hatred. In Mara's case it was definitely the former. Detty herself had a more mature view and realised that Wagner 'was not for all markets.'. She also thought that perhaps it was a bit unfair, as the three cycles had been sold out for weeks, and that a ticket was going to somebody who was definitely not one of the faithful. Wisdom suggested however that she didn't get involved in the Sensky's matrimonial tussles which reminded her of *Wotan* and *Fricka* in Act 2 of *Die Walküre*. The outcome was the same, *Wotan* (David) was vanquished by *Fricka* (Mara) and as a result he was coming to the second cycle of *Der Ring*, including *Das Rheingold* whether he liked it or not. Detty had witnessed most of this conversation and was killing herself with partially suppressed laughter.

She was still laughing silently to herself remembering this conversation as the lights went down. Then she felt tense, they had all put so much into this 'journey to the Rhein'. Helge rose up in the darkened pit almost like a spectre. He had adopted the method that he had seen elsewhere, to conduct the beginning of the *Vorspiel* with the pit dark and with a focussed pocket torch, which could be seen only by the players. It was the nearest way you could imitate the totally dark atmosphere, without the *Klagenbende* of Bayreuth. The whispering double basses emerged from blackness and silence. When the horn arpeggios entered over the continuing low basses, the desk lights gradually came up. Light was coming to the primeval world, then at bar 136 the bright voice of Eliza Connors, the *Woglinde* broke the E flat major chord. Detty momentarily felt jealous – this was her cue and she had to restrain herself from singing:

'*Weia! Waga! Woge du Welle,*

as she had done so often before. With an effort of self-discipline, she left it to the very capable Eliza. She thought about the strangeness of singing *Brünnhilde*. It was one of the longest and most demanding parts in the repertory but you didn't enter until the second act of the second show, so there was a long wait. And then what an entry! Fortunately, she had a good top and she knew that she could compass the high C sharps of the battle cry that made some of her colleagues struggle but none the less, it was the hell of a way to start a role, particularly if it was your first time. Well, she had practised long and hard. Tomorrow will show, relax and enjoy tonight.

*

She had been tempted to go into the wings to hear at least the end of the first act of *Die Walküre*. For some reason, she didn't. She knew that some regarded it as unprofessional but that didn't really bother her. She knew that she had two huge acts to come but that wasn't really the reason either. She thought it was because she felt that she should let her two protégés get on with it, although they wouldn't know she was there anyway, so that was absurd. In any case, she had heard Lev and Hanna in rehearsals and could see it again on the video. Act One ended with Lev's clarion,

so blühe denn Wälsungen blut

bringing down the curtain. Then the applause and cheers rocked the theatre. This meant, she was sure that they had brought the wonderful act off with distinction.

*

'*Frau O'Neill, funfzehn minuten bitte!*'[30]
How often had she heard that with the *Assistentinspitzientin's* German accent announcing her Irish name? She had always stuck to 'O'Neill' professionally although most of her roles had been in German speaking countries. She knew this would be followed shortly by:
'*Frau O'Neill, zur Bühne, bitte*'
She seized her spear. The costume was very simple with just the suggestion of a breastplate on her silk tabard and an unadorned silver cap as helmet. But she had a spear as did *Wotan*. The directors had taken the view that *Wotan* was unbalanced without a spear that was so central to his character. If he had one, why not *Brünnhilde*? So, she got her spear.

The battle cry triumphed. Gratefully she felt that her voice was OK. Later sitting at *Wotan's* feet, she wondered why they had ever worried about Walter. He sailed through his huge scenes with power, dignity and massive expression. Why had they ever doubted him? It was hard to believe this overwhelming singing actor was the same man who dangled her children on his knee with his moustache twitching merrily. She took her weapons and stood back as Lev poured out his love over Hanna.

---

30 Frau O'Neill fifteen minutes please

They came to the pivotal *Todesverkündigung* which she had sung with Lev before in concert. Then the fight and the death of *Siegmund*. There was sustained applause but the tragic end of the act made it more muted. She sat silent and deliberately alone for forty-five minutes in her office/dressing room regaining her breath and her focus. In no time she was off with her vigorous stage sisters. She still had time in the prophecy to admire again Hanna's

> *Oh hehrstes Wunder*
> *herrlichste Maid[31]!*

after she herself triumphantly sung the first *Siegfried* motive. It was on to the pleading to Wotan which she had tried to sing as a schoolgirl beside the River Barrow when, as she now realised, she had first had that eerie feeling that it might be her destiny. She regained her nobility joining Walter's heart-rending farewell and, at last as he kissed her chastely, the Fire Music arpeggios gently dimmed. The relief of the tumultuous applause and the curtain calls brought her down to earth. She was just so grateful to have been allowed to sing that amazing music. In a bemused state she signed programmes at the stage door until Marc arrived with a car and scooped her up to take her to the *Dwór* and a late-night Jameson in front of the darkening terrace. Tomorrow was a day off then *Siegfried*, the scene of her first triumph.

Because it was the most familiar, difficult as it is, she approached *Siegfried* calmly, she knew her single long scene well enough. She had conquered it before. The huge vocal line was almost familiar friendly territory and above everything else there was Hank, who had been her rock in Bayreuth and was still her rock now. After she finished on her triumphant final high C, he wrapped his arms round her as he had done before and, as before, the applause exploded. Another Jameson, another day's rest, then the biggest test of all. She had been enfolded in *Die Walküre,* at home in *Siegfried* but she was still frightened by *Götterdämmerung.* She knew the role, she had practised it endlessly, she

---

31 O highest wonder
    Most noble woman

had been through it bar by bar with Eileen but there was still a primitive terror in it and she didn't really know why.

*

It had been a gruelling evening but she had got through it OK. Her voice was still sound as she stepped forward to sing the immortal *Schlussgesang*,

> *Starke Scheite*
> *Schichtet mir dort*
> *am Rande des Rheins zu Hauf!*[32]

She did not even feel intimidated by the line of famous ghosts sitting on her shoulders. Solemnly she sang,

> *mich musste*
> *der Reinste verraten*
> *dass wissend würde ein Weib!*[33]

She promised the *Ring* back to the *Rheintöchter* then summoned the ravens and sent their message to *Wotan*. Buoyed up by her concentration and the excitement, her voice flowed dramatically on until she reached,

> *Siegfried!Siegfried!Sieh!*
> *Selig grüsst dich dein Weib!*[34]

At that moment there was a barely audible dull thud that did not appear to come from the orchestra pit. Detty gripped her thigh momentarily then resumed role and dashed off into the funeral pyre stage left. The orchestra, uninterrupted continued into the climax of

---

32 Pile on pile of mightiest logs
   High on the edge of the Ruein
33 The purest had to betray me
   That a woman might become wise
34 Siegfried, Siegfried look!
   Blissfully your wife greets you!

Valhalla burning and the river flooding. Finally, there was the tranquil closure of the *Rheintöchter* music, back where it all started, and the redemption theme.

Meanwhile there was pandemonium backstage, Detty's wound which had been barely evident until she dashed off was now pouring blood soaking her tights and shift. Two stand-by paramedics had rapidly stripped down her costume revealing a shallow wound, almost only a graze across her right thigh just missing the previous scar. The bullet had clearly grazed her thigh and passed out to be found later by the police backstage. Detty was claiming loudly that they must quench the flow and allow her to go on and take her curtain call. The more forceful of the paramedics told her not to be absurd and to stay where she was.

Gerry Flynn, the co-director, with admirable presence of mind, first ascertained that the gunman had been apprehended by the police in the fourth gallery. In fact, he had turned his revolver on himself and indeed, was in police hands, but dead. Gerry then went to the front of the stage and announced that unfortunately Frau O'Neill had been shot by a would-be assassin. Her injuries were fortunately very minor and the perpetrator was in the hands of the police. However, she would not be able to receive the audience appreciation for the wonderful performance that they had just witnessed.

Detty was checked at the hospital but released to Marc. She was allowed to go home with an appointment to have the wound checked the following day. The first thing she did in the morning was to ring Helge and assure him that she was quite fit to sing. Indeed, she said that she had sung the Immolation scene in the ambulance on the way to the hospital, to correct the errors that she had made on stage. It wasn't quite true, but the fact that she could joke about it did re-assure Helge, who was in the middle of working out how he could get an experienced *Brünnhilde* for two Ring cycles at zero notice. Unfortunately, Annaliese, who would willingly have done it, was in the middle of singing *Electra* at La Scala.

'No, really, Helge, I am fine and I will get you a medical certificate to prove it, if you don't believe me. If you don't let me sing, I will sue the theatre for breach of contract,'

That, for the moment seemed to settle the argument. Detty consumed a *Frittata* prepared by her Italian duo for lunch and told Marc that she would need champagne at the right hour. Early in the evening a couple of days later, there was a scrunch on the gravel and an appropriately disability-modified car drew up at the front door. The occupant seized her crutches and leapt out with remarkable speed, greeting Detty who was sitting, champagne glass in hand, enjoying the evening air.

'Hi, Tanya, this is a surprise'.

'It shouldn't be. My entire department has been going crazy sorting out who wanted to shoot Ms O'Neill on the stage of the National Theatre. We have come up with some answers. There's quite a lot of information.'

'Before you start, have a glass of champagne. My husband says it is a tonic.'

'He had better tell mine but I am not sure that even an *Oberst's* pay stretches to champagne.'

'I heard about your promotion. You have really shot up through the ranks. Congratulations – the youngest colonel in the army.'

'If you play any more stunts like this, I shall be old before my time. Well, I will spill the beans. Your assailant's real name was Kovacs although he used an assumed one to get here recently. Now Kovacs is a very common name particularly in the southeast of the country but this one was interesting. We tested his DNA and it agreed with a record that we had of the notorious medical man, your friend Frederick Kovacs. We were lucky that we still had the record, but for some reason the big wigs and the NAS top brass stored their records in a secret bunker by the old harbour so avoided the fire work display at the Winterburg. Anyway, it appears that Piotr Kovacs was the younger brother of Frederick. He had a history of psychosis and violence – he had strangled two girls who refused his advances and was in St Michaels, the top security hospital here, until the fall of Königshof when he escaped. He wasn't heard of for some time but apparently while he was away, he researched his brother's death and discovered that you had killed him. He appears to have become obsessed with the desire to avenge his brother on you. He got back into the country under an assumed name, we think with the help of the Russians, who are now very happy to discomfort us. He got a ticket for the opera from one of the touts. It was interesting that when I interrogated this unsavoury gentleman, he was terrified. He had reason to be – there was not a man in Königshof who wouldn't have hanged him from the nearest lamp post for his part in the outrage – you have a very big fan club, *meine Allerliebste*. Our tout said that the perp wanted to book a box but there were no boxes still available. The tout thought it strange as the man seemed to be by himself. Anyway, he didn't seem like the sort of bloke who would spend north of 20,000 thalers for four seats for a *Ring* cycle. As there were no boxes available, our tout sold him a ticket for the fourth gallery, which is all that he had available. It appears that our perp had a rifle. It wasn't a very good one but would have been quite enough from a box near the stage to dispatch you to Valhalla. When he couldn't get a box, he had to change his plans. There was no way that he could get out a rifle, which he was going to strap to his body to avoid detection at security and use it from a tight seat in the fourth gallery. So, he bought a revolver from another dodgy arms dealer, who we have also found and arrested. Well, as you would know, it is quite one thing using a rifle from a stage box and another to use a handgun from a high gallery. It was remarkable that he hit you at all because his neighbours said that he pulled it out and fired very quickly. However, as you know the bullet was spent and I gather the medics say that you are OK. He then turned the gun on himself and got that right.' she said grimly.

'Two things in summary' she went on.' The first is that you have been very, very lucky that he got several vital things wrong. The second is that we are sure that he was a lone criminal, working for himself for personal reasons. Therefore, with him dead, there is no further abnormal danger to you at the theatre or anywhere else. I gather that you have already told Maestro Helge von Grunstrand that you intend to sing the remaining two cycles but you can expect to find your theatre teeming with security men and plain clothes police, just as a precautionary measure.'

'Fair enough' said Detty 'I hope that they like Wagner but anyway thanks for your explanation. Now how is Eva Maria? Now we have this place you must bring her down for a romp.'

'I will if the visitors to this country stop using our *Prima Donna* for target practice, I might get a bit of time with my daughter.'

*

Before the second act of the second cycle *Die Walküre*, the curtain twitched back to the accompaniment of the standard groan from the audience. Fore curtain announcements usually indicated a substitution or an apology for a suffering performer. This time it was the music director, Professor Maestro Helge von Grunstrand who appeared, smiling,

'*Meine Damen und Herren,* I have had an argument with Frau O'Neill and for the first time in our long, fruitful not to say tumultuous relationship, I have won. Audience research suggested that after the incident during the last *Götterdämmerung*, you would greet Frau O'Neill's entry this evening with uncontrollable appreciation. Now I don't need to tell the experienced Wagnerians amongst you that such an interruption, understandable as it would be, would make it difficult for all the artists involved and contravene the Master's intentions. Therefore, we suggested the unusual step that Frau O'Neill would take a curtain call *before* the beginning of the Act to allow the music to continue unimpeded. *Meine Damen und Herren,* Frau O'Neill:

Detty walked onto the stage, in costume, to the anticipated roar from the capacity audience. Eventually it quietened,

'Herr Maestro, *Meine Damen und Herren,* as you can see after the little incident during the first *Götterdämmerung*, I'm fine. Thanks to the extraordinary speed of the authorities, we are all quite safe as my lone assailant is dead. If *Brünnhilde* has a slight limp you can attribute it to her struggle to retrieve her last dead hero. The spear might help as a prop. And now, uninterrupted please let us give you two great acts.'

She walked quickly off into the wings to re-enter after *Wotan's* summons, with a lusty *Hojotoho! Hojotoho!* some minutes later.

ACKNOWLEDGEMENTS

To Elizabeth and Malcom Ecclestone for their comforting and expert musical help and text editing, Janet and Dick Turpin for reading the texts and helpful suggestions, Lauren Bailey and Holly Porter of Troubador for putting up with me, Kirsti Neumueller for helpful Bayreuth advice.

Also encouragement and advice from: The late Jennifer France, Diana du Luart, Ted Edmondson, Peter Pearson, Jo Cummins, Steve Robson and many others.

ABOUT THE AUTHOR

Sixtus Beckmesser, a character from Wagner's *Die Meistersinger*, is the pen name of Richard France.

He was, formerly, a GP and cognitive psychotherapist in Hampshire, UK. Since retirement he has enjoyed travelling round Europe and going to music festivals at home and abroad. Out of the festival season he has lived in Hampshire and the Tuscan hills making wine, book binding and writing, whilst still finding time for music in Florence, Milan, Venice, Germany and London.

He has always been interested in how people manage to survive terrible circumstances and events. This has led him to write the five books of the *Livonia* series. This is number five.